ARCHIVE OF UNKNOWN UNIVERSES

Also by Ruben Reyes Jr.

There Is a Rio Grande in Heaven

ARCHIVE OF UNKNOWN UNIVERSES

a novel

Ruben Reyes Jr.

MARINER BOOKS

New York   Boston

This is a work of fiction. Names, characters, places, and incidents are products of the author's imagination or are used fictitiously and are not to be construed as real. Any resemblance to actual events, locales, organizations, or persons, living or dead, is entirely coincidental.

Silencing the Past by Michel-Rolph Trouillot copyright © 1995 by Michel-Rolph Trouillot. Reprinted with permission from Beacon Press, Boston, Massachusetts.

ARCHIVE OF UNKNOWN UNIVERSES. Copyright © 2025 by Ruben Reyes Jr. All rights reserved. Printed in the United States of America. No part of this book may be used or reproduced in any manner whatsoever without written permission except in the case of brief quotations embodied in critical articles and reviews. For information, address HarperCollins Publishers, 195 Broadway, New York, NY 10007.

The Mariner flag design is a registered trademark of HarperCollins Publishers LLC.

HarperCollins books may be purchased for educational, business, or sales promotional use. For information, please email the Special Markets Department at SPsales@harpercollins.com.

FIRST EDITION

Designed by Jackie Alvarado

Library of Congress Cataloging-in-Publication Data has been applied for.

ISBN 978-0-06-333631-5

25 26 27 28 29 LBC 5 4 3 2 1

In memory of all the lives cut short by war,
in El Salvador and across the globe

Any historical narrative is a particular bundle of silences.

—Michel Rolph-Trouillot, *Silencing the Past:
Power and the Production of History*

When we return to our ancient land
that we never knew
and we talk of all those things
that never happened

we will walk holding children by the hand
who have never existed

we'll listen to their voices and live
that life we spoke of so often
but have never lived

—Daisy Zamora, "When We Return"

R,

I woke up thinking about Cuba. Do you remember the things we did as shadows danced on our shoulders?

That was only a year ago and already it feels like a lifetime has passed. Our cause, which started as musings and theory and theology, seems more important every day. It terrifies me that a war is around the corner, but I see no way of avoiding it.

Amid it all, the intensity of our relationship still rattles me. Being with you, I know I mislabeled my feelings in the past. Love is what I have for you. And I'm sorry for the moments I've failed to express it. You said once that love is a spring that wells inside you until you want to scream about it, and that your only regret is that the world doesn't want to hear it from men like us.

You're right that the world begs for our silence, pushing us into the shadows. I've shared their desires, beliefs I still cling to some lonely mornings. I know that makes you unhappy, and I'm sorry. At least I'm able to appreciate things for what they are, even if I'm not ready to shout them to the world. That also must be a sign of maturity, of growth. We're still young now, but we're no longer kids.

I miss you. The idea that people were made for one another seems melodramatic to me, and logically, it seems impossible. There are so many people on Earth and the idea that there is a perfect pair among billions is ridiculous. But sometimes, when I am missing you, I let myself believe that we were fated to meet. Made for each other.

Don't mistake my softness for weakness. I hold strong in the weeks we spend apart, even though some nights the yearning resembles physical pain. Of course, I can't continue on like this forever, but there's an end in sight. That keeps me going. I think back to Havana, and I think onward to the next time I can run my fingers along your bare back, touching the notches of your spine.

Love,

N

2018

The cautionary tales were endless. Desperate people viewed the device as a cure for their disappointments, some to the point of madness. Seeing their other lives didn't give them what they desperately desired: leadership skills, business acumen, emotional maturity, religious clarity, clairvoyance of all sorts. Thinking oneself more powerful than the All-Knowing had never worked out for man, and the issue of alternate universes was simply the latest iteration of a long line of mortal mishaps.

Ana's mother, Felicia, had echoed this warning many times, so when Ana first used the Defractor, she swallowed her shame and told herself it was for the sake of her academic work. Now, as she stared at the blue neon light that shone through a quarter-size hole on the machine's side, a pit formed in her stomach. There was no denying it: Ana was here for personal guidance.

The light shone bright as the base of a flame. Two earbud-size patches hung from the machine, just above a touch pad. Before she could lose her nerve, Ana attached them to her temples and looked into the machine.

THE DEFRACTOR©, HEARBY REFERRED TO AS "THE TECHNOLOGY," IS THE EXCLUSIVE PROPIETARY INTELLECTUAL PROPERTY OF DÍAZ MANUFACTURING LICENSED TO HARVARD UNIVERSITY, 2018. USER AGREES TO USE THE TECHNOLOGY FOR: RESEARCH—HISTORICAL, SOCIOLOGICAL, AND/OR INTERDISCIPLINARY. PERSONAL USE IS SUBJECT TO PENALTIES, INCLUDING BUT NOT LIMITED TO: ACADEMIC SUSPENSION, LIFETIME BAN OF USAGE OF THE TECHNOLOGY, UP TO $1,000 FINE. ACCESS TO THE TECHNOLOGY IS LIMITED TO THREE USES PER ACADEMIC SEMESTER. REPEAT OFFENDERS MAY BE PLACED ON INVOLUNTARY LEAVE OF ABSENCE. DO YOU ACCEPT THESE TERMS?

> Yes.

ENTER LOGIN CREDENTIALS

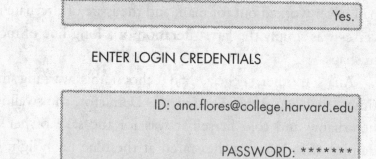

> ID: ana.flores@college.harvard.edu
>
> PASSWORD: *******

WELCOME, Ana Flores. LAST LOGIN, March 15, 2018. DURATION, 12 Minutes 34 Seconds. DESIGNATED INTERLOCUTOR, Canadian American singer and songwriter Alanis Morissette. HOW CAN I HELP YOU TODAY?

Archive of Unknown Universes

> I need to see all the alternate versions of my life.

> ISN'T IT IRONIC, Ana Flores, THAT CHILI IS TYPICALLY SERVED HOT, NOT CHILLY? PLEASE CONFIRM THAT THIS REQUEST IS NOT FOR PERSONAL USE.

> Yes, this request is for my academic research.

> OKAY. WOULD YOU LIKE YOUR ALTERNATE TIMELINES RENDERED VISUALLY OR TEXTUALLY?

> Visually.

> PLEASE PROVIDE A GUIDING QUESTION.

> Who is the Nicaraguan man on the ID my mother was hiding in her passport?

> YOU OUGHTA KNOW, THIS WILL TAKE A MINUTE. PLEASE WAIT.

A series of videos appeared, each one sequestered into its own geometric shard on the screen. On each slice of the kaleidoscope, Ana lived out possibilities she hadn't accessed in her timeline. They were, in essence, short films of what could have been.

Only one showed Ana and her mother in their Echo Park apartment. Felicia's fingers snaked through the waves of Ana's long black hair. It was a rare, but not unusual, way Felicia showed loved. More often, her affection manifested in cautious words: drive safe, apply sunscreen, call me when you get there. If the caress was a sign to spend the summer at home, Ana didn't want to see it.

A dozen other clips starred Ana and Luis, each with minor but distinct deviations from the life they knew. In one, they walked down the Charles River, taking a regular study break, an excuse to hold hands away from their friends. But Luis was beach blond, with a thick but close-cut black beard. He'd gone through a rebellious phase her Luis had not.

The shot would be easy to dismiss as fiction or forgery were it not for the way they held hands. Their pinkies were hooked together, Luis's loosely tethered to hers, a lazy way of holding hands all their own. Ana assumed no one else shared it, this quirk they loved and laughed about often. But there they were: blond-Luis and other-Ana, acting like it was their own little invention.

Ana pulled away, overwhelmed. Her phone chimed. Luis was walking to the library now. In her rush to power the Defractor down, she scrolled over a shard in the upper right-hand corner of the kaleidoscope. Her lips were locked on a stranger's. She clicked, and let surprise settle over her.

At the start of the clip, they sat next to each other at her usual table in Leverett Library, both typing furiously. They paused, their timing seemingly choreographed. The unnamed boy extended his slim fingers toward her cheek, turned her face toward his, and leaned in for a kiss. It was brief, but Ana watched her own face break into a smile: natural, contained, but full of joy, the way she imagined she'd look after kissing someone she fiercely cared about. At some point, she and Luis had moved just as easily, earnest in their affection. They'd sat at the same table, tucked in the western corner of the library. Watching herself do the choreography with another man, the motions felt distant, pulled from happier times.

Though he looked a bit like her boyfriend, with the same oblong face and deep-set eyes, the unnamed boy was not Luis. She was really, truly, deeply in love with a man she hadn't met in this life.

Taking the stairs two at a time, Ana rushed to rid herself of the Defractor. A librarian accepted the machine, and Ana put on her best poker face. A second later, Luis walked through the glass doors and swiped into the library. He smiled at her, and she forced herself to smile back.

"I forgot which dryer was busted and had to run my comforter twice," Luis said. "I hope your morning was more productive."

"Yes," Ana lied. "I made progress. Almost ready for Havana."

"I can't wait to be there," Luis said.

Luis kissed her. His lips were slippery, slathered in a layer of unscented Carmex. An excessive amount. Ana resisted the urge to wipe it off her lips.

"Can you believe Alanis Morissette was our age when she wrote *Jagged Little Pill*?" she said instead.

They were pumped full of adrenaline, the mix of nerves and possibility that makes a traveler's high so addictive. The air outside the airport smelled of car exhaust, and though the parking lot was filled with mid-century Fords painted in bright greens and oranges, they slipped into a dinky gray four-door sedan. When the driver asked where they were from, Ana said they were both from California, which prompted him to ask if they were siblings. Before Luis had a chance to answer, Ana told the driver they'd met in school. Luis stared out the window, fascinated by a tree with wide glossy leaves and hot-pink flowers shaped like pom-poms. Buildings were painted with the Cuban government's slogans: *Unidad, compromiso y victoria. Hasta la victoria siempre.* Luis whispered them to himself. Ana grabbed his hand, squeezed it. He returned the gesture before the landscape outside the window distracted him again.

The car passed by the Universidad de la Habana, cruised on the highway beside the Malecón for just a minute, and looped through a labyrinth of one-way streets ending at their apartment. Luis offered to carry Ana's backpack to the third-floor walk-up.

"I'm helping because I love you," he said, smiling. "Not because I don't think you can manage."

"Feminism thanks you."

Once their bags were unpacked, reality set in. They were in a country they'd never been in before, one they'd never imagined visiting. Simply too many obstacles stood in their way: the cost, the embargo, the mountain of bureaucracy required to get a passport, then a visa. Somehow, they'd done it, crossing into a new frontier together. Sunlight flowed in through a set of French windows, warming them up, making their faces glow, another gentle reminder that what they'd built between them was worthwhile.

"I should get to the university," Ana said.

"You have the whole summer," said Luis.

"Do you want to come with me?"

"It'd be weird."

"It'll be fine."

"I'll wait here."

"Alright," she said, heading out the door without a kiss.

The relationship had developed quickly, their reliance on one another growing fast and tight, like the strands of ivy on the redbrick buildings that towered all over campus. They constructed their schedules around each other. Luis was only ever a text away. Intimate secrets, shared as pillow talk, glued them together: neither had a relationship with their biological fathers, a civil war loomed in the background of their families' arrival in the United States, they both felt un-equipped and out of place at an institution that valorized wealth. Love formed in opposition to the ugliness and injus-tice of their lives. It felt freeing, like an act of resistance. But would tethering oneself to a cause, instead of a soul, tempt the thread to snap?

A year passed, and they were still together—mostly happy, mostly stable. You're my first love, they admitted to each other, and reaffirmed their growing belief that existence was a task best done in a pair. The heat in Luis's chest felt like love, and though he sometimes worried he could be misjudging his feelings, he chose to trust their relationship, lacking another to compare it to. Ana wouldn't have invited him to Cuba if she didn't want him there, which brought a sense of peace that carried them through finals and move-out.

His mother, Elena, had grown accustomed to who'd he become in college—sporadic, ever-changing—but she still asked him whether he was chasing his girlfriend to Cuba. Her voice was light and joking, but the question carried genuine curiosity.

"No," Luis said. "I got a grant to do thesis research. And who wouldn't want to see Cuba?"

"I'd love to," Elena said. Luis regretted his choice of words. They both understood she couldn't fly wherever she pleased, even if she had the money.

"I've been thinking about Neto," Luis admitted slowly, desperate to change the subject, but also prying open a conversation he'd been stewing over for weeks. The trip had unlocked an old memory. He was young, around seven or eight, which made the memory unreliable, though it felt true. His mother was at work, and his grandmother Esperanza was frying plantains in the kitchen. Esperanza could still talk back then, years from the disease that would devour her brain from the inside, but she wasn't paying Luis any attention, which was probably why he ended up snooping through her closet. His stringy elbows knocked a box over, and a handful of envelopes fell out. As he bent over to pick it up, he noticed his great-uncle's name scrawled on the lid: *Neto*. Luis pulled out one of the letters, the first line still clear in his mind: *I woke up thinking about Cuba.*

The memory blurred here, overrun by the shame of being caught. Esperanza yanked the brittle envelopes from his hands and told him never to touch them again. Luis didn't know why she'd reacted so hotheadedly, so unlike the gentle caretaker he knew. Now, given how the Alzheimer's had progressed, he'd never be able to ask. All he had was the memory of her, eyes ablaze, clutching the paper close to her chest.

"Abuela used to have a box of his things," Luis said.

"Your grandmother has a bunch of junk," Elena said. "Anyway, she never talked about Neto. Better to leave it all alone."

Somewhere between booking the flight and boarding the plane, Luis rewired the story he told himself. His great-uncle had referenced Cuba, a fact that felt preordained. If Neto had known the world, Luis should too. Ana wasn't drawing him to Cuba, though it'd be nice to spend the summer with her. It was Neto, calling out from the afterlife, asking that his nephew follow in his path, walk the streets he had, smelling the exhaust and ocean breeze. Luis wanted to see what Neto had seen.

Perhaps his uncle was not actually a factor at all, and the allure of Cuba was completely unrelated to the letters that'd popped into his head, but Luis chose the story he wanted to hear. Neto pulled him here, to Havana. Luis repeated that to himself until it felt real.

The university halls resembled Harvard's: marble tiles, walls clad with wood from floor to ceiling. Ana was meeting with a professor. One of his graduate students was gossiping with him when Ana arrived. The office was underwhelming, windowless and filled with messy stacks of books, but the professor spoke optimistically about Ana's project, a reassuring show of faith.

Ana's research goals were simple: to prove that the diaspora existed before 1980, that Salvadorans shaped the world before the war, before their global displacement. Growing up, only people who'd migrated from El Salvador, like her mother, knew where it was. The country felt unimportant, too small to matter. Of cultural irrelevance. Her research was going to disprove what she'd spent a lifetime believing.

At least that's what she'd written in a thank-you letter to the donor who'd be funding her travel that summer. The truth was a bit trickier. It was an unnamed Nicaraguan hiding in her home, not a Salvadoran, who'd set her on this path.

Ana had been searching for her own passport when she opened her mother's out of idle curiosity. Among the back pages, there was a card the size and thickness of a driver's license. A bearded man's portrait sat on the left-hand side. Felicia rushed into the room, feigning casualness, though her eyes immediately darted to Ana's hands, the passport in one and the ID in another.

Felicia was not one to share a story, of any kind, without a good reason, even with her daughter, the center of her life, but Ana asked anyway.

"Mami. Who is Antonio?"

"He was a stranger who came to my rescue once," Felicia finally said. "He forgot his ID when he left. I don't think that was even his real name. All I know is that he was Nicaraguan, and that he told me to stare at the ocean from Havana. It was one of the most beautiful places he'd been."

"You've kept it all these years."

"I was grateful for his help."

"What did he save you from?"

"Asking too many questions will get you in trouble, Ana."

Ana disagreed, but the few sentences her mother uttered were more than she'd ever shared about her life in El Salva-

Archive of Unknown Universes

dor, so she simply pressed the ID card, precious enough for her mother to store, into Felicia's palm.

When it was time to start narrowing her research topic, Ana thought back to the unnamed man. She imagined all the places the man had gone: San Salvador, Havana, Managua, Mars, the moon. If she could find a trace of him—perhaps his real name—she'd be able to write the kind of thesis that'd propel her into the upper echelons of the ivory tower: a PhD at Yale or Stanford. A stable job would free her. When she could support them both, Ana could shed the guilt that kept her under her mother's thumb. With the distance, and clearer boundaries, her mother might speak openly. Cuba was closer than the moon, so she proposed a research trip rooted in nothing more than a hunch, a conversation she'd had with her mother in passing, and the loose hope that the Nicaraguan would unspool the horrors that kept Ana and Felicia tied together so tightly.

"Does the university have a Defractor?" Ana asked the professor now.

"Alejandra can show you where it is," the professor said. The graduate student nodded, and packed up her bag. Ana thanked the professor, and promised to work hard all summer. He smiled, his teeth tiny as Chiclets. Alejandra opened the door for her, then gestured to the right.

"It's good you came," Alejandra said. "Too many people write about Cuba without ever visiting."

"I'm glad I'm here." Ana confessed that she almost hadn't made it. Predictably, her mother hadn't wanted Ana to travel internationally. Whenever they got close to anything prickly—her first husband, her immigration to the United States, Ana's father—her mother retreated into general platitudes about how scary and cruel the world was, as if Ana didn't see or feel its weight every day. Whether in small ways, as being talked over in lecture, or large, as the migrants being tear-gassed at the border, the world tried crushing her daily.

"Everyone is very excited about this machine," Alejandra said. "The university got it just last year."

"Have you used it?"

"No," Alejandra said. Unlike the overeager American tech sector, Alejandra was skeptical of the technology's abilities. Their aspirations, she thought, weren't convincing: Take the guesswork out of life's difficult choices! Never ask "what if" again! With money to be made, advocates wanted to make it a hot consumer product, regulation-free. A Defractor in every home! A Defractor for any problem! Who needs therapy with so much knowledge at your fingertips? Those who could afford the silver bullet would buy one, but skeptics pointed out how much the technology left open to interpretation. At best, it'd be a waste of time and money. At worst, society would suffer, seeking salvation in another distraction from the Anthropocene's failures.

"Plus, I have addictive tendencies," Alejandra said. "Don't want to tempt fate."

The Defractor sat on a desk in a small office, next to a scanner. Alejandra waved Ana goodbye. Grateful for the privacy, she pressed her eye against the machine. She asked the question gnawing at the back of her skull: *Was coming to Cuba with Luis a mistake?*

Archive of Unknown Universes

Universes materialized. She scrolled past images of herself and Luis studying at coffee shops or holding hands in art museums, searching for the unnamed man she'd kissed. There were a couple of images of her and her mother, but most were calm, domestic tableaus that didn't reveal much. When she found the sector where she was interacting with the mystery man instead of Luis, her heart jolted.

Research was all about hypotheses, which was why universities were allowed to use the technology, but some even questioned its use by academics. When Ana had shyly admitted that she'd used it to finish a term paper, Luis asked her why she couldn't come up with her own ideas. She was smarter than a machine that generated arbitrary simulations. What would he say if he knew she was using it now, to spy on a man who wasn't him, a man she was statistically unlikely to ever meet? Ana zoomed in.

Sitting in a familiar dining hall, they picked at a hodgepodge of foods: spinach, tofu, calamari, a veggie burger. Ana watched his mouth for a minute, before pausing and zooming in on different parts of his face. A well-trimmed beard covered his jawline. He cared about his appearance. His left earlobe had a small birthmark that looked like a piercing, and his nose protruded from his face. He was handsome. At least alternative-universe-Ana also had good taste.

Then she saw it: on his neck, a gold chain identical to the one Luis wore every day. It was thin, so she zoomed in until she could see the individual links. She followed the gleaming trail down until it disappeared behind the fabric of the man's T-shirt. The scrubber at the bottom of the screen indicated that there were only thirty seconds left in the clip.

As if responding to Ana's desperate need to know what was at its end, the man fiddled with his chain. It was nothing but a nervous tick, but one that would change the direction of Ana's life. The man pulled out the pendant, rubbed it, then stuck it between his teeth. The etched portrait of a man with brow-line eyeglasses was only in view for a few seconds, but it was unmistakable. Ana had seen his visage many times before: on Luis's pendant, hanging in her mother's living room, at the church down the street from her childhood home. But here, he was much older. His cheeks sagged; the edges of his eyes wrinkled. His aging was graceful, a blessing the martyr never experienced. The mystery man, the love of Ana's other life, carried an older version of Monseñor Romero's portrait as protection around his neck. The smallest detail of proof that, somewhere, the archbishop had survived his assassination.

Ana returned to the apartment, but she didn't confess to herself how quickly, and completely, she'd surrendered to her alternate life. She was uncharacteristically certain that the mystery man, her other boyfriend, held some sort of answer. About how to wrangle her mother's anxieties, about the life Antonio lived, about where her relationship with Luis was headed. The conviction was illogical, but true: the closest thing to faith she'd felt in months. It was soothing, this belief that the universe was organized by some logic larger than herself.

"How did the meeting go?" Luis asked.

"Good," Ana said. "Really good, actually."

When he suggested they go out for a drink, Ana told him she was too tired. She lay on their bed and remembered how upset her mother had been when Ana called to explain her plans for the summer.

"Am I your mother or your friend?" Felicia asked, her voice trembling on the other side of the line. "A friend you can see once a year, for just a few days. Your mother deserves more than that."

It's not about you, Ana wanted to scream.

"I promise I'll be safe," she said. "I'll take taxis everywhere, and only go out during the day."

"Ana," Felicia said, sweetness reentering her voice. "Everyone thinks they're untouchable until something bad happens."

There it was again, Felicia's favorite refrain. Ana had no idea why her mother was overly cautious, had been all her life. Not knowing bothered her, but it also didn't change anything. Felicia's overprotectiveness was an offshoot of her love. Whatever she'd gone through, whatever she'd lost, had created a force field between her and the world, one Ana couldn't escape.

"Listen," Felicia said, cutting the silence. "I know this is important to you. And I've told you what I think. You couldn't have picked a more dangerous place to go, but I'd feel better if someone was with you in Cuba," she continued. "For your own safety."

"A man, you mean?"

"Yes, Ana. A man. Ask Luis to go with you. It's not ideal, of course, but I don't want you to go alone."

Only then did Ana invite Luis, telling herself there was no real reason she hadn't before. She kept her conversation with her mother to herself. Unspoken, the secret festered like the core of a volcano, red hot and churning, threatening to burst.

Elsewhere, the machine continues to whir. With the lights off, the blue glow creeps up the walls, and though there's no one attached to its copper tendrils, it continues its work, sifting through infinite possibilities for the next time someone bursts into the room, searching for answers to the latest question on their tongue. If Ana had asked a different question, or pursued the truth longer, here's what the machine might have said:

> THE BODY FOLDS INTO ITSELF WHEN THE BULLETS PENETRATE OR WHEN THE MACHETE CRASHES DOWN OR WHEN A FIST CRACKS OR WHEN AN ANKLE SINKS INTO THE LOAM OF THE BLOOD-SOAKED, RAIN-SOAKED FOREST. A BODY TUMBLES, CRASHES, ACCORDIONS ON THE GROUND. ON THE OTHER SIDE THERE IS ANOTHER BODY, A PERSON STILL LIVING, WHOSE LIMBS ARE PULLED BY THE FISTS OF TWO GOVERNMENTS, THE NEARBY SALVADORAN AND THE FARAWAY AMERICAN. NO MATTER HOW THE BODIES SHUDDER, HOW THE EVENTS OF THE WAR DO OR DO NOT PAN OUT, NO MATTER WHAT: PEOPLE DIE. BODIES ARE PEOPLE WHO ARE DYING AND DEAD, LOST TO HISTORY.
>
> THERE IS WAR AND THERE IS REVOLUTION. WAR IS CADAVERS, AMERICAN DOLLARS, RONALD REAGAN, HELICOPTERS, CRATER-SIZE FISSIONS, DEAD PEOPLE, DEAD PEOPLE,

DEAD PEOPLE. REVOLUTION IS MAKESHIFT UNIFORMS, BOMBED BRIDGES, INFIGHTING, MURDERED POETS, SCAPEGOATS, HUNGER, TRIUMPH, POLITICAL SPACE, DEAD BODIES, DEAD BODIES, DEAD BODIES. THE FUTURE SPLITS INTO POSTWAR OR POST-REVOLUTION, DIFFERENT DEAD IN EACH HALF BUT LOST LIVES LINING EACH EDGE ANYWAY.

BUT IN THE YEARS BEFORE THE BODY CRUMBLES UNDER THE FORCE OF A NATION AT WAR WITH ITSELF, BEFORE ENTIRE GENEALOGIES UNRAVEL ON EITHER SIDE OF HISTORY, NETO LIVES. HE MOVES IN THE SHADOW OF THOSE BODIES, WHOSE SOFT SKIN HITS THE EARTH, WHICH LINE THE HIGHWAYS, BUT HE BREATHES THE AIR FREELY. HE TRAVELS TO CUBA—IN PREPARATION FOR WAR, WITH HOPES OF REVOLUTION— WHERE THE BREEZE IS BRISK, AND WHERE HE PRESSES HIS BODY AGAINST THE WARM FLESH OF ANOTHER MAN WHO LIVES OR DIES. THE OUTCOME DOES NOT MATTER TO EVERYTHING THAT COMES BEFORE.

1978

Neto and Rafael sit on the Malecón, listening to the waves meld with a guitarist's croon. They're not holding hands or kissing. They fight the aching urge, but their bodies still touch. Neto's pinky finger grazes the top of Rafael's fist, and Rafael subtly moves his hand toward him, to feel more of his finger against his flesh. The soft mist of the ocean reaches them when larger waves scale the concrete barrier separating them from the sea. Coupled with the strumming of guitar strings, the atmosphere is painfully romantic.

Neto stares at the man in front of him, and though he hasn't stopped admiring the topography of his lover's face since they arrived in Havana, he recommits Rafael's features to memory. His face is slender, divided by a sharp nose that Neto loves burrowed in his neck. Like Neto, Rafael has a beard, though his is longer and fuller. Well-groomed, it falls an inch from his jaw. Rafael's facial hair is thick and dark, and he always keeps it around that length, as is popular among counterrevolutionaries across the hemisphere. Neto dares slip his fingers into Rafael's and squeezes, for just a second, trying to transfer the depth of his love in a single gesture.

And then the distance. Truth is housed in the body, so

when Neto's hands drift farther and farther from his lover's, it's a signal of a burrowed sentiment he often avoids. The catalyst is a broad-shouldered stranger who wanders down the Malecón, not toward them but shuffling past slowly. He's preoccupied, staring out at the Caribbean, but that's more than enough to prevent Neto's skin from lingering on Rafael's. Their bodies play this game often, revealing the truth in the situation despite the intellectual loops Neto constructs to live with himself.

It's their second time in Cuba together, only the third time they've been close enough to see the craters in each other's complexion. But the distance and time and depth they've traversed over the last three years intensifies the moment. The ocean's spray sprinkles over them, so that by the time they stand and walk away, their clothes are spotted and damp.

Neto and Rafael retrace the path they took down to the water, searching for the restaurant where they've agreed to meet their comrades. Dusty, Spanish-style buildings rise above them. Through open balconies, they can peek into the lives of their inhabitants. From one, a woman tosses out a basket tied to a string. A boy, no older than eight, grabs a coin from it and places a plastic bag inside. As the lovers walk by, the woman pulleys the package just above their heads. They look up, briefly. Neto wonders if the woman knows their secret.

What Neto wants on this walk, and what he's sure Rafael wanted back on the cement border that separates earth and sea, is more than the freedom to hold another's fingers in his. He desires lips and a hand wandering downward to hold his waist. The simple calm of arms around him, disturbed only by the soft breathing that makes a chest vacillate. Neto wants to feel small, but not fragile. He wants no distance.

They're in Cuba for a master class in falsification. The Cubans have been at it longer, and they've agreed to teach Neto, Rafael, and six others how to best mimic official documents. All the revolutionaries are in agreement: a win anywhere in the hemisphere is a win for all. Earlier, they'd listened to a man, only a couple years older, explain the centerpieces of a successful forgery: consistent kerning, paper layered in the right order, gloss that shines evenly. Rafael and Neto were separated by half a dozen bodies. They focused on the speaker, and only dropped glances at each other by chance. When the session ended, and the other attendees figured out where they might grab a bite to eat, the two men said they'd meet up with them later. They wanted to see more of the city, away from the piercing gaze of the others.

After a few minutes of wandering—some intentional, others lost—Neto and Rafael find the restaurant. Smells waft up from a basement. Through slim rectangular windows, there's a visible oscillation of party lights. They descend a narrow, spiraling set of stairs into a dining room. Neto and Rafael make their way toward the back, where their comrades nurse beers against a prismatic flurry reflecting off the disco ball spinning aimlessly above the bar.

Here, they make an intentional choice. There are three open seats. Two are beside each other, between where the Salvadorans and Nicaraguans have congregated, across from their Cuban hosts. The third is comfortably among the Nicaraguans. Rafael walks without hesitation toward that chair.

No one would have said anything if he and Neto had sat next to each other, but both men know any lack of restraint could send their cautiously constructed barrier tumbling down.

As the men get louder in the restaurant, arguing about how the Salvadorans should proceed in a country ripe for revolution, Neto focuses intently on Rafael's knuckles. They're curled on the wooden table like a crouched animal, fearful and ready to defend itself. The conversation around them is not all theoretical, since the men are convinced their little slice of the Americas will soon be at full-fledged war. Despite being on the receiving end of the gunfire, the men speak of the triumph that will surely come, and do so laughing, grins cracked straight across their faces. Through it all, Neto watches his lover's hands: tactile, tender, the length of the horizon and nearly as beautiful.

When Neto and Rafael first met, their relationship remained uncomplicated for only a brief minute. Neto had traveled to Nicaragua with Alejandro and Anabel to garner support for the cause. In a nondescript apartment with the slimmest of furnishings, Anabel gave an impassioned speech, one they'd worked on as a group for weeks. It included the same talking points they'd used in letters to socialist groups all throughout Europe: The United States is trying to make El Salvador into another Puerto Rico. The Salvadoran government no longer works for us. They speak of those who dare organize as puppets controlled by the Soviets, but don't look at the fish-wire strings moving their own limbs. It was compelling and would prove more than enough to secure the Sandinistas' support.

But if there was a true shift for Neto, it was the small trembles that came after the formalities were done and the men had left the table to meander in the kitchen.

"I'm Antonio," Rafael said, his mouth upturned slightly. He was young, even for a group of revolutionaries whose youth powered their cause. He was about the same height as Neto, though his shoulders were bulkier and his arms more muscular. Neto noticed the five o'clock shadow on his jawline and wondered why it was its current length. Perhaps this man, like Neto, struggled to grow a full beard. Or maybe it was the opposite: his beard grew quick and thick, so he'd shaved clean just a day prior.

"Domingo," Neto said. They talked for a while, pressed close to a wall away from the apartment's central buzz. They weren't hiding from the others, not exactly, but still stayed in their own bubble, inches from each other. About an hour later, the visitors divided themselves and headed to where they'd spend the night. Their hosts had offered up spare couches and floor space scattered throughout Managua, so Neto and Rafael—still Domingo and Antonio to each other—left together.

Neto spent weeks mentally reframing the night's buildup as natural and predestined. And yet, he knew he'd followed sinful and primal impulses. His recklessness was seared in his memory. Their limbs hooked into each other's. Neto's slick pecs pressed up against the prickle of Rafael's chest hair. Real names confessed between moans. Hands wandering down, holding each other to their eventual end. And then the unexpected but welcome night's sleep. A hand laid gentle on a collarbone, as if Rafael's limbs were made of porcelain. Fingertips lazily tracing a knuckle until both young men were lulled asleep. Guilt, confusion, and the eventual promise to continue seeing each other came later. That night, there was no restraint, just the freedom they'd been chasing ever since.

Dinner comes to a close and the group of revolutionaries, bellies full and spirits lifted, ascend from the restaurant. Their chatter breaks through humid evening air as they decide where to empty a bottle of Havana Club rum.

"The best in the world," one man says, "made even better by nationalization." A couple of men splinter away, saying they're calling it a night, and Neto walks away with them. Rafael follows, and the four make their way back toward the ocean.

Their lodgings are just a few blocks from the Malecón, even closer than the University of Havana is. From the street, they turn, then stand outside a doorway as their host fumbles with his keys. A dark, wooden door peeks through the iron rods of the outer gate. The men step through and climb the narrow and winding staircase up to the third-floor apartment. Rafael is the last to enter, and as Neto walks up the white-tiled stairs, he feels Rafael's hand brush against his hip, then his ass, then his hamstrings. It could be accidental—the touches were so light. But Neto knows they weren't. He wishes, as he has for days, that they were alone.

The apartment has high ceilings, at least fifteen feet tall, and from where Neto lies on the couch, he spies the intricate Baroque trim where wall meets ceiling. The hallway to the bedrooms is narrow. Paneled doors open up to a balcony that offers a clear view of bustling pedestrians on the street. The space seems too opulent for a country in revolution. An entire second apartment could be squeezed into the expanse above them. A family could live there. But Neto isn't surprised. The revolution rewards its champions.

The Cubans bid Rafael and Neto good night and head into their bedrooms. They're alone, but not fully. Almost never fully alone, they've made do. Rafael opens the doors and steps out onto the balcony, leaving one slightly ajar. There's just enough room for Neto to slip in, sideways, and he does. The door doesn't move or clatter.

"Look," Rafael says, "I have something for you." He's brought out his bag, though from where Neto had been lying, he hadn't noticed it hanging against his lover's hips. He pulls out a stack of paper held tight by a thin piece of twine.

"Mi amor—" Neto begins to say. Rafael walks close to him, placing a finger on his lips. Neto has an urge to take it in his mouth, but he fights it.

"Every day that I'm home, I sit close enough to the door to hear the shuffle of footsteps just outside it. I sit there, reading or layering ink on a form, and wait. Most times, it's just the sound of a vendor or a neighbor walking down the street. But sometimes, it's what I was hoping for. A letter from you."

They've exchanged letters every few weeks since they first met about three years ago. Some have been lost in the mail, their confessions unsaid. But the correspondences have intensified, each one driving their affection deeper. Without the proper scaffolding, Michelangelo would have never painted the muscular arms of an angel on the chapel ceiling. Rafael and Neto's missives are just as important, elevating their affections, making them sturdier. The letters are architectural in the revolutionaries' love.

"I got you these," Rafael continues. "For you to write me more letters. You can think of me, and of these few days, as you write to me from Santa Tecla. When you put it in the mail, it'll already have a piece of each of us."

The stack of papers he hands Neto are blank. In the lower right-hand corner, there's an embossed insignia. It's small, but precise. An *A* and a *D* are connected by an ornate ampersand, and irregular curved lines fence them. The lines approximate a crest, though the shape lacks symmetry. Neto stares at the insignia, so precise and intentionally designed, and realizes why the lines feel familiar. They're coastlines: the place where El Salvador meets the Pacific, where Nicaragua curves around the Gulf of Fonseca, and the northern coast of Cuba, where they now sit. The symbol is coded. Their false names, the places they've been.

The packet of paper falls onto the small table in the center of the balcony. It's not dropped in anger or dismissal. It's simply that the sheets are the issue of least urgency. Neto grabs Rafael by the face, his hand along his jaw, and kisses him. The sun has set and the light from the apartment barely bleeds through the shuttered door. Shadows dance on their faces. There's no risk of them being seen or recognized from below, but that doesn't matter. They could be in the full shine of the sun at noon, and Neto would still be pushing Rafael against the balcony's concrete railing, his tongue against his lover's.

Rafael grips Neto's lower back, and slowly moves until he has a hold on his left hip. His hand wanders to his waistline and then into his cotton underwear. Neto licks Rafael's ear and lets out a moan when he feels a hand around him. He pauses, pulling Rafael's hand off his cock, and presses his lips against Rafael's palm. The kiss is soft, and lasts only a second, before Neto begins to lick the salty skin. He snakes his tongue in between Rafael's thumb and forefinger, spits in his own palm for good measure, and leads his hand back underneath his waistband. Their bodies press against one another; mouth on skin, slick skin sliding against slick skin. The balcony is hard and cold when a palm or bit of lower back presses against the rough concrete. They continue like this, mostly clothed, until both finish in their pants.

Rafael sinks to the ground, and Neto joins him, curling up against his chest. An ocean breeze passes them, bringing the salty smell of brine to their nostrils. They should stand up and go inside, each to the individual couches they'll be sleeping on that night. One of their hosts could wake up to use the bathroom, wonder where they've gone, and open the door to discover them like this: tender and panting. Risk abounds, but still they sit, listening to the sound of cars driving a few streets away, watching the stars stare down upon them.

The stack of paper that will become a stack of letters sits on the table. The edges flutter in the wind, waving over them like a white flag.

1979

Rafael drives his knife into the paper, making an incision straight down the page. His hands do not waver. The knife does not puncture the card stock any further than he desires.

Careful not to leave a fingerprint, he picks up the portrait and slips it into its rightful place. The identification card is complete, and once laminated, it will glimmer in the light.

It's the sort of document he's made many times before. Any time an international comrade arrives in Managua—to aid the revolution or learn from it—Rafael splices together the card which serves as proof that its holder is an ally, not a man underneath Somoza's spells. No one but Rafael knows how to make them exactly right, so even though it's nothing but a piece of paper, it is to be trusted.

Today's card is special. Precious, even. The man whose visage graces it is no stranger. The name on the card is false, but the man is real. Rafael has held him in his arms, in his palms, somewhere deep inside his heart.

Soon, Rafael will be heading to El Salvador to see Neto, on the pretense of business, though the truth is much more complicated than that. Rafael has promised to bring Neto a new document proving he's a friend of the Sandinistas, since Neto wrote saying his other had been lost. In the laundry, on the street, somewhere. And Rafael desperately wants him to be able to return to Managua, so he's hunched over the desk, finishing up his work.

He pulls out his own identification card from his wallet, holding it up to his new creation. They're identical, save for the pictures and information, which means he's done his job well. He places both inside his wallet. A number of extra portraits of Neto—unsmiling, so unlike the face he knows—are fanned out on the desk, and Rafael pops those into his pocket. Even though an entire country sits between them, the action makes it feel as if they're closer together.

Rafael goes to the mailbox, but there's no letter from Neto. He isn't exactly expecting one, since the last came only two days prior, but his hope is often illogical. Despite the million logistics to figure out on the eve of a successful revolution, Rafael stills longs for the sound of an envelope being ripped open. There is a government to build, a movement to cement, but still so much of his mind is on the next letter: when it will arrive, what it'll say. Underneath it all, popping out occasionally, burrows the fear that the next letter will be the last. Neto has admitted the possibility himself. Rafael pushes the thought away and walks back inside.

A half-packed bag sits on his bed. The desk is awry with his materials. He'll clean later. The clothes to be folded and stacked can wait. He sits and rereads the last few letters that have come from Santa Tecla. In the first, Neto asks whether Rafael thinks the conflict in El Salvador will escalate to the point of guerrilla warfare in the mountains, among the drooping limbs of vines and branches. Neto does not think he's the sort of man who'd make it out in the wilderness with a gun in his hands, but Rafael is the only revolutionary he can admit that shameful fact to. Another letter suggests Neto will finally introduce Rafael to his sister, Esperanza, though it seems farfetched. She doesn't know about them yet. Neto loses his nerve every time he approaches the topic.

Lying in bed, beside the duffle bag, Rafael reads the latest letter.

No one has any way of knowing if our liberation movement will succeed. But knowing we'll have to fight further to live the way we deserve, even if it does, that weighs heavily on me. The worst part, though, is that I worry there's no nation on Earth where we can be happy. But I desperately want to find one. If the search is fruitless, then perhaps we'll build our own country—inside or outside these borders. You'll be the president, and I'll be the president. You'll be the people, and I'll be the people. We'll rule over each other, until the empire falls.

It's Neto at his best, at his most caring and honest. Any relationship worth anything carries the slim shadow of fear, Rafael tells himself. He folds the letter in two. When he sees Neto, in just a few days, and finally gets the chance to hold him close again, he'll tell him what he thinks: a home is more than the nation one resides in. We can build a home, Rafael will whisper, anywhere we please.

1980

The men come in like a swarm of crows. Their dark uniforms meld together as they push through the wooden door of the small but tidy home in Santa Tecla. Once inside, the men scatter, a noxious fog fills every corner, including the one where the crying girl huddles into herself.

They shout and shush her before they begin ransacking the place. The men topple the pile of plátanos and mangos at the center of the dining room table, scrounge through medicine cabinets, and dig under beds and between seat cushions. Their frantic search is interrupted only by the soft cries of the young girl, a ghost in her own home. Nine years old, Elena whimpers as the men keep searching, though she's unsure what the soldiers so desperately seek.

A man shouts at her, quelling the whimpering, and continues the hunt. He sticks his head in the rusty oven in the kitchen, finding nothing but abandoned pots and pans. Another searches the refrigerator, and a third pokes at the ceiling with a broom.

They search and shout, shout and search, storming through every room though it's obvious that the person they've come after isn't home. Only the girl witnesses the soldiers' raid. Eventually the men prepare to leave, still pumping with the adrenaline of their task. From their upturned grins, Elena knows they're leaving with treasures in hand.

"Tell Ernesto we were here. We're not going to stop until we find him and bring him in," one man says. After a slight pause, he finishes the thought. "For questioning. Bring him in for questioning."

The swarm heads for the door. The last solider to leave holds a couple of books and pamphlets in his hands. He turns to the girl and motions with the collection in his grasp. Elena, who is old enough to be inquisitive but too young to truly understand who these men are, makes a mental note of the books they've taken: an old magazine with a faded orange cover falling apart at the spine, a pamphlet advertising a church gathering with the archbishop the following week, a slim collection of poetry, and a small stack of heavy sheets of card stock.

"These are evidence. Ernesto isn't supposed to have these, niña linda. Tell him for us, won't you?"

Archive of Unknown Universes

The men leave, cutting through the countryside in an unmarked van en route to rape or kill or kidnap; to seed fear in another woman, man, or child, a kernel that will sprout cruel roots that dig deep, making the heart so tender that anyone who gazes upon the swarm cannot speak of their fear. This is what they do: silencing, disappearing, and acting in a manner that will outlive them and their children.

The war rages on or it's cut short. Elena stays in Santa Tecla or leaves, but either way the horror sits deep inside her so that when she has a child, whom she names Luis, she cannot speak of what she's gone through. The tentacles hold her tongue close to the roof of her mouth, and when her mother finds her, she can only cry: terrified noises that replace what she wants to say but will struggle to for decades to come, which is that she doesn't know how she'll ever move past the sound of pounding fists on the front door and heavy boots on laminate and men shushing her as the world crumbles at her feet.

2018

Their unhappiness wasn't bitter or disruptive. It was unspoken, a misplaced piece of furniture they kept bumping into but refused to move.

In their bedroom, two weeks after arriving, Ana used a penny to scratch free the code on a Wi-Fi card. Thirty minutes of internet cost two dollars, but it was the only option for tourists under the nationalized system. Felicia asked to video call. The connection isn't strong enough, Ana wrote back. It wasn't a full lie, but she had no desire to try. If she spoke to her mother, Ana might blame Felicia for landing her in such a suffocating situation.

Another couple was staying in the adjacent bedroom, which forced Ana and Luis together, but only so closely. Most nights, Luis would stay out on the balcony, reading or drinking or both, until Ana had fallen asleep. On the days he lay next to her, he didn't grab for her waist. He whispered good night and turned over. She didn't reach for him either, despite their proximity. She'd almost never been the one to initiate, but she could have. She did very much enjoy the sex. Still, something was shattering, even though they kept silent as the cracks formed.

Archive of Unknown Universes

Was their discontent new, or had it always been there? When Luis had said I love you for the first time, outside the basement coffee shop painted sunflower yellow, unhappiness could've been hiding behind a snowbank. Or when a film camera's flash went off, catching Ana and Luis curled into each other at a party, impervious to their friends, sloshing red cups in their hands, a joint between Luis's lips. Ana had laughed, the image making her look more rebellious than she felt. Luis had freaked out, imagining a scandal decades later, even though he had no desire to run for public office. Had they ignored the shadows growing in the corner?

In all these moments there was empty space, a gap where their incompatibilities and insecurities could grow and mold and eat away at what they'd built. Luis hadn't looked in that direction, which didn't surprise Ana. His lack of attentiveness grated, though now she wondered if avoidance was a decent survival strategy. If they looked away from the rot, they might be able to salvage the relationship.

That's what we want, Ana told herself. Even in Cuba, where we're sharing a bed but not much more.

Fighting the urge to reveal too much, Ana sent her mother a message asking if she'd reconsidered her invitation to join her in San Salvador. The research in Havana was going well, and she'd collected kernels she might someday bake into an argument. Did she know, Ana had texted, that the Cuban government had printed updates about El Salvador in its state-funded magazines? A university student was detained in 1964 for distributing invitations to a rally. To justify the arrest, the police general, Arnoldo Rodenzo, distributed inaccurate, and borderline offensive, publications attributed to the Salvadoran Communist Party. Wasn't that fascinating? Didn't Ana need to dig deeper?

The professor had connected her to a museum in San Salvador, and she'd set up a time to look through their archive. All she needed was her mother's blessing, and hopefully her companionship. She couldn't bear asking Luis to join her there too.

I don't know, Ana, her mother wrote back almost immediately. It's impossible to get around there. And it can be dangerous, you know.

"You let your mom know you've alive?" Luis asked, walking into the room. He did this often: asking a question he knew the answer to. It annoyed her. She nodded anyway.

"Did you message your mom?" she asked.

"She doesn't worry as much," he said.

"All mothers worry."

"Not like yours."

It was a fair point. Early on in their relationship, right after they had sex for the first time, Ana admitted that she felt badly for keeping secrets from her mother. My mother keeps secrets too, Luis had said. Elena never wanted to talk about why she came to the United States or why his grandmother kept boxes of old junk hidden inside her closet. Back then, it had been a point of connection, but with distance, Ana realized Luis would never understand her relationship with her mother. Elena and Luis had a truce, both choosing to keep the thorny parts of their lives from each other. He didn't feel the weight of one-way secrecy. Felicia could have secrets, but Ana couldn't. Maybe it was an early sign of their incompatibility, these two fundamentally different ideas of what we owe our loved ones.

Archive of Unknown Universes

"I have to get to the university," Ana said quickly, hoping her voice didn't betray her. It wasn't fair to resent Luis for her mother's hang-ups, though there might be other reasons to. His subtle indifference toward her research, eyes going glassy when she explained what she'd done that afternoon. Or his inability—or unwillingness—to acknowledge the silence that'd come between them. Were these Luis's faults, or were they the inevitable result of his upbringing? There wasn't enough time to decide whether it made a difference, so Ana slipped out the front door.

Right outside the apartment building, Ana bought guavas from a fruit cart, as she had almost every morning since arriving. The streets were more familiar now, though she was still amazed at how narrow they were, only wide enough for one car. More than once, though, she'd watched two drivers pass by each other in a coordinated dance. One would pull close to a building, the other would slip by, and though it seemed physically impossible, the cars never collided. It's a sort of magic, she thought, to come so close without causing damage.

Luis's miscalculations churned inside him. All his research leads had dried up, and though he'd insisted otherwise, the thesis had always been an excuse to chase Ana to Cuba. He quieted the roiling in his stomach with the buzz of the city.

If he woke up before Ana had left for the university, he pretended to be asleep so they wouldn't have to fumble through a drowsy conversation in the kitchen. Once she was gone, he explored Havana as he was: an American tourist with too much time on his hands.

Alone, he sipped margaritas in the open courtyard of the Hotel Nacional, watching the sunset. Below, he could hear cars rushing down the highway that ran oceanside for miles. He took taxi rides in sparkling American-made mid-century cars and talked to drivers who tried convincing him to visit the beaches farther down the coast, promising unmatched beauty in exchange for a bit of cash. Luis meandered through the halls of the Museo de la Revolución, agreeing with some of the museum's claims and raising his eyebrows at others. He stood at the base of a massive stone memorial to José Martí that felt pulled out of a *Star Wars* film. He ate, drank, walked, sunbathed, shopped, listened, photographed, chatted, wandered, explored. Luis did everything but think about how his silence—how underplaying the state of his relationship—might be hurting Ana.

Whenever ugly feelings rose up his throat, Luis swallowed them. Ana insisted it was an unhealthy habit, so he tried divulging anxieties and fears, though he could only ever utter minor inconveniences. How annoying a classmate was, or how stressed out a social interaction left him. Even shallow complaints brought them together, as if they were the only two people in the world who struggled with social anxiety and ego-laden Ivy League try-hards.

What could he do now, when Ana was the source of the unhappiness clogging his throat? Other people called their mothers, Luis thought. Since arriving in Cuba, he'd only called Elena once, and though guilt was the logical end point, he only felt its faint echo. He knew he should feel worse—his mother and grandmother were the only family he had, and they were on good terms. At no other time in human history had it been easier to contact someone, and he still didn't pick up the phone. Ana called her mother every day, sometimes twice a day.

Luis scratched free the code on a Wi-Fi card.

"How's Ana?" Elena asked.

"Busy. Working on her research pretty much every day," he said.

"Are you fighting?"

"What?"

"It's what people do on vacation. They fight. You remember that trip to Yosemite? Guau, your abuela and I spent the whole time arguing."

"No," Luis said. "We're not fighting." Technically true. To fight, they'd have to be open about their discomfort. "How is Abuela?"

"Oh, you know her. The viejita is still kicking. She gave me such a scare."

"What?"

"Oh, it was nothing. Really, just a little thing. Nothing to worry about."

"Mami," Luis said.

"She spent a few days in the hospital."

"When?"

"Last week."

"Last week? Mami. Really—"

"Her blood pressure dropped, and she passed out. The doctor wanted to keep her overnight for observation. Just a precaution. It's fine. Honestly. I knew you were busy and didn't want to bother you with this. I have it under control. Okay, mijo?"

Grandmothers hold a family's stories. That's what Elena told Luis growing up, and it felt truest when Esperanza sat on the edge of his bed and told him tales she'd carried with her to California. A horse-faced woman seduced and killed men, but only those who deserved it. Another story described an intertwined pair of wolves, and there was the one about a tiny duende with a straw hat. When Abuela's mind went, so did her voice. The stories were lost, along with everything else. She'd been the person who made time for him: cheered him on at middle school trivia bowl, tried to learn how to play *Super Smash Bros.*, watched action movies. Only after she needed full-time care did he realize how often and easily Esperanza played peacemaker in their apartment.

Now, as he fiddled with his phone, the call cutting in and out, he felt a longing he hadn't in years. He wanted Esperanza to tell him a story. He imagined a life where it could happen, one where her telomeres had grown a little bit longer, keeping her lucid a few years more. Instead of a legend or a folktale, he'd insist on a story pulled from real life, not just from her memory but her body.

Tell me about your brother, Abuela, he'd beg. Tell me about Cuba, about El Salvador, about all the places in between.

Inside the university, where it was only slightly cooler than outside, Ana beelined for the Defractor again. Her research was at a dead end. She could hide under academic jargon and impenetrable theory for a few pages, but she was after dignity for a tiny country, a forgotten country, a country conveniently erased from the map. For that, she needed at least a sliver of evidence: a letter, postcard, diary, photograph, flyer—anything that'd prove the place her mother came from mattered. She wanted to do it the right way, but old-school techniques weren't cutting it.

> WELCOME, Ana Flores. YOUR DESIGNATED INTERLOCUTOR IS Canadian singer-songwriter Avril Lavigne. WOULD YOU LIKE YOUR ALTERNATE TIMELINES RENDERED VISUALLY OR TEXTUALLY?

> Visually.

> PLEASE PROVIDE A GUIDING QUESTION.

> How am I ever going to write a thesis based on what I have so far (which is basically nothing, if we're being honest, because I've been a little bit distracted, which isn't just an excuse, it's just the truth)?

> PLEASE WAIT A FEW MINUTES WHILE I RENDER. THIS PROCESS CAN BE A LITTLE BIT "COMPLICATED."

In a handful of clips, she sat in the same building with slight discrepancies: Ana had brought a different bag, someone was in the room using the scanner, books were splayed on the desk next to the Defractor. Zooming in, she spotted a couple of titles she'd never encountered, strands to push her inquiry forward. Already, the Defractor was proving helpful.

In most images, Ana wasn't at the university. She had taken the day off from research and was elsewhere: the apartment, sitting on the concrete barrier of the Malecón, on a beach outside Havana. She searched for the mystery man—her boyfriend in another universe—but he didn't appear anywhere. Ana swiped through all the universes again, quickly, not really paying attention.

She stopped swiping, stalling on a universe with Luis in it. They stood in front of a shop with doors that opened to a traffic-heavy, pedestrian street. Though she felt childish doing so, she zoomed in to better read the pair's body language. They were close together, but not close enough to rule out a purely platonic friendship. Their fingers weren't interlocked. Luis's hands were in his pockets. Neither fact revealed whether they were still dating in this other universe, so Ana scanned the screen, desperate for a clue that would set their relationship back on track. She zoomed in on her own face until it filled the screen.

> Avril, why do I look so happy there?

> HUMAN EMOTION IS DIFFICULT FOR ME TO UNDERSTAND AND/OR ANALYZE. I CAN COME UP WITH SOME THEORIES, IF YOU'D LIKE.

> I'm happy there. More than happy, really. Look at me! I'm smiling so wide. Is it because Luis doesn't hate me or isn't icing me out? Maybe I told him about how badly my research is going, and he

> actually paid attention instead of just saying what he thought I wanted to hear. Or maybe I made a breakthrough. I accomplished something I haven't been able to in this life. I found out who the Nicaraguan man is. That makes me sad to think about. Why have I failed here?

> I'M SORRY YOU'RE FEELING THIS WAY. CAN I OFFER YOU AN AVRIL LAVIGNE FACT TO MAKE YOU FEEL BETTER?

> Sure.

> KELLY CLARKSON'S HIT SONG "BREAKAWAY" WAS ACTUALLY WRITTEN FOR AVRIL LAVIGNE, BUT HER TEAM WORRIED IT DIDN'T FIT HER SOUND. THE MORE YOU KNOW.

Ana zoomed in on the grin spread across her face, some combination of satisfaction and elation. It had nothing to do with Luis or the mystery man, she realized. The book. It had to do with the book between her palms. Ana hurried out of the room and back to the library where Alejandra poured over an old newspaper.

"Can the Defractor print?" Ana asked.

"In very poor quality. Only black-and-white. But yes, it prints."

Ana returned with a warm sheet of paper, dropping it on Alejandra's desk.

"Where is this?" Ana asked.

"It looks like Old Havana. There's a couple of bookshops there, but they're mostly for tourists."

"I think I need to find this bookstore."

"Sure. I can take you later this week, if you want," Alejandra said. She pulled the paper close to her face. "Is that your *friend*?"

"Luis," Ana responded.

"Invite him. We can all go."

Ana lingered in the doorway, her eyes scanning the crown molding. When Luis set down his phone, she cautiously crossed to the other side of the room. Her side, Luis thought.

"I have to tell you something," Ana said, sitting on her half of the bed. Luis cleared his throat. "I've been using a Defractor."

"Again?" Luis said.

"And not just for my research."

Her honesty hit him first, salty as a splash of ocean water. In as much detail as she could remember, Ana described the mystery man to Luis—long face, close-cut beard, unattached earlobes, dark eyes brimming with warmth. Her voice was level, unwavering, a put-on flatness that could've hidden a deeper excitement. Luis pushed the thought away. He wasn't the jealous type, especially not over a man Ana had never met.

His true issue was with the Defractor. He didn't oppose the technology on ideological grounds. He simply thought himself—and Ana—above its false promises. For those with access to it, illicit use of the technology carried as much stigma as cocaine did. Among Harvard's social climbers and nepotists, it was no big deal. No one was going to snitch on

Archive of Unknown Universes

you for taking a bump or a glimpse, even if it was technically forbidden and definitely addictive. There were stories of people who saw the technology as a one-stop solution for all their personal problems. Many had capsized their lives for a shot at the enlightenment they suspected could be found in their alternate lives.

Luis was a pragmatist and didn't think asking "what if" would help him untangle the net of his life. Being present was what mattered most. Even when he failed to live up to this ideal—forgetting anniversaries, zoning out mid-conversation—Luis believed it. He'd ribbed Ana when she admitted to using the device for her research. Their classmates were fans of easy answers and shortcuts to prizes they felt they'd earned. Their relationship worked because life didn't bend to their will.

"I needed some guidance," Ana said.

"That's a cop-out," he said. "You can't live your life trying to change what already happened."

"The Defractor doesn't show you the past. It shows you what could have happened."

"Big difference."

"Asking for help is not weakness."

"It is so clear where this all ends," Luis said. "The Defractor seems fine now, but wait until it's available everywhere. People will claim to understand the technology and its messages better than anyone else. It'll be Jonestown, ten times over."

"Does someone pay you to be so cynical?"

"Profit didn't motivate anyone to make the internet better for users."

"Not everyone was born with all the right answers."

"That's not what I meant."

"I used it a couple of times. That's it."

"You're an adult, you can make your own choices. I'm just telling you what I think."

Ana looked at him, straight on. He hadn't meant to hurt her, or coax her into silence, but he feared he'd overstepped, the way his grandmother had once described flattening a gecko as a child. By accident, she'd crushed its brittle bones underneath her Mary Janes.

Hearing Ana justify herself, Luis wondered if he'd over-estimated their capability to balance each other out. Her, over-thinking, always with one eye on the big picture, fearlessly following her impulses. Him, soothing his anxieties with the details, eyes locked on whatever puzzle sat immediately in front of him. That's why the trip was proving so difficult. He told himself he'd come for Neto, but that was a lie. He'd followed Ana, and then resented her for kick-starting a summer with actual purpose, while he contemplated the best place to fling himself into the sea. For all his talk of personal agency, he was showing very little of it.

"Come to Old Havana," Ana spoke into the silence. "Will you, please?"

There it was. The familiar magic he'd been missing, catching him by surprise. Even now, on unsturdy ground, her invitation felt genuine. Ana was thinking of him, working him into her schedule, not treating him as a burdensome add-on or a convenient tagalong, but as the planet she orbited around. She wanted him by her side, and had even swapped a secret to entice him. Luis had already wandered the Spanish-style plazas with other vagabonds, so many from Europe, speaking

Archive of Unknown Universes

languages he couldn't pinpoint, but he would go again, if only to be with Ana.

If we're soulmates, we'll figure it out, Luis told himself. He pushed away the thought that followed: Fate is a balm for other people.

Luis and Ana walked out the front door and, without a word, turned left. It'd be easier to hail a taxi from the main street, a trick they'd learned independently but now shared. Alejandra was waiting for them on the corner, and after a quick hello, they slipped into a car.

The trio wandered through cobblestoned streets and sun-soaked alleyways. Outside a restaurant blaring music, a man with glimmering earrings directed them toward an open plaza. Tired-eyed tourists sat underneath umbrellas, nursing cocktails. Ana had never been to Europe, but as she stared up at the ornate, robin's-egg buildings that rose around her like the walls of a fort, she figured walking through Madrid or Barcelona must feel a bit like this. The Spanish influence was most visible in Old Havana's buildings: ornate, and maintained for tourists' glittering eyes.

At the first store they tried, a few shabby tomes sat alongside mass-produced knickknacks, but the book wasn't there. They moved on to another, again without luck.

The printout burned a hole in Ana's back pocket, where she kept it hidden, worried it'd force her to admit why she'd invited Luis. When she confessed what she'd been doing, it was out of superstition, not desire. If Luis didn't go to Old Havana, she couldn't re-create the conditions from her other life. The search was bound to fail. The logic was shoddy, but she clung to it. Asking for guidance isn't a crime, she thought. Even if it comes from a Defractor.

Luis leaned toward Alejandra, listening to her explain what it meant to have grown up relatively stable in Cuba, though secretly critical of the vast inequality around her.

"You can't say a government is all good or all bad," Alejandra said. "Revolutionary or not. We have health care and pretty widespread literacy programs. But some people go hungry here, no matter what the government wants you to believe. I like playing host to visitors who come study at the university. But they don't see everything. They see what they're meant to. The pretty stuff. The fun stuff."

"People go hungry in the States too," Luis offered. Ana and Luis only ever spoke to each other in English, so his Spanish caught her by surprise. It was accented, like hers, but was otherwise a dialect all his own. Messy, staccato, uncertain.

"Corruption doesn't have a political party," Ana said. The line sounded good but said very little.

"I'm not going to shame people for making a living," said Alejandra. "I just hate that the system relies on all these tourists who come by, see none of the neighborhoods where people actually live, and then fly home to tell their friends how beautiful Cuba is."

They looped back over the same streets a couple times. Sweat dried on Ana's forehead. Luis's cheeks were flushed. Ana couldn't concentrate on the conversation.

"How about we turn down this street?" Luis eventually offered. Ana was grateful for the suggestion, and for a brief moment, she was certain she could have it all. If Harvard had taught her anything, it was to desire more and more and more, shamelessly. The line between self-worth and entitlement was thin, but Ana wanted to tightrope across it. This outing, in the beating heart of the city, would bring her and Luis back together. Two explorers hiking over the mountains and into the Wilderlands. A pair of astronauts tethered to each other, reaching for the edges of the universe. They'd be together because of what she'd glimpsed in the Defractor, not despite it. Ana could have it all—her erratic belief in roads not taken, and a boyfriend unable to see the path between the trees.

The bookshop smelled of mildew, and most of the books looked as if they'd fall apart in her hands. In the center of the room, a sturdy table was covered with piles of paperbacks and magazines. Mismatched bookshelves lined the walls, a cave of infinite volumes. Two older men were engaged in conversation, their words quick and constant. They raised their voices, nearly arguing, before breaking into laughter together, as if they were alone.

Ana started with the closest pile. She set aside copies of Che Guevara's *Motorcycle Diaries*, academic books about Cuban racial politics, and a Spanish translation of *A Tale of Two Cities*. She moved on to a couple of magazines, their pages brittle but still holding together. One had the name *Bohemia* printed in orange and yellow lettering on the cover. It was from June 1962.

"Could this be it?" Alejandra asked. The book she held was too thin. A few minutes later Luis approached.

"This one?" It was closer in thickness, but the spine was far too intact. This went on for a while, until Ana noticed that the men were quietly watching them search.

49

"Are you looking for something specific?" one of the men asked Ana. What a ridiculous question. In the disorganized piles, not even an employee could possibly know what the catalog was composed of. And if they did, locating a particular book would be impossible. The messiness was part of the charm, and Ana would have reveled in it were she not searching for a clue her alternate self had already found.

"A book that looks like this," Ana said, showing the picture to the man. She avoided Luis's gaze, hoping he wouldn't spot himself in the printout. The man grabbed his glasses from the lanyard around his neck and put them on.

"It looks like a Bible," he said, squinting at the paper. "I've seen it around here before."

He walked over to a bookcase near where he and his friend had been talking and shifted some books around.

"What does it say on the cover?" the man asked.

"I can't make it out. It's too blurry," Ana said.

"Is it this?" Alejandra held up a book. The volume was a deep maroon, fraying at the spine, and about the right thickness. On the front, in small letters, some of which had faded, the book identified itself: La Biblia de Jerusalén.

Ana took it from her and held it with both hands. She touched the cover gently and opened to the front matter, scanning it for a date. The edition was updated in 1973, though the book itself was printed a couple of years later. She flipped it open, landing somewhere in the Book of John.

In Harvard's main library, there was always a Gutenberg Bible on display, one of only forty-nine remaining in the world. Ana visited it often, in awe of how it had survived, and eventually uncomfortable at what it meant that such a priceless object sat in a space she could swipe into whenever she liked. The Bible she held now was closer to the ones her mother had in their Los Angeles apartment. A Spanish-language translation, one of many of the same edition, worn out from use. It was not a particularly rare book, or a particularly old one either, but it still felt sacred in her hands. She stared at the pages, not reading them, but admiring the miniscule letters on the skin-thin pages. It was not a holy experience exactly, but holding the book made Ana feel as if she were living out a plan larger than herself. Though she prayed her face wouldn't betray her, she knew the discovery of the Bible was not going to be a wholly good revelation.

"How much for it?" Ana asked, passing the Bible reluctantly into Luis's hands.

"I'll give it to you for twenty-five," the man said. The price seemed high, but she wasn't going to let twenty-five dollars keep her from a chance at real guidance. If other-Ana had valued it, she should too.

"How about a drink to celebrate?" Alejandra asked once they'd stepped outside.

Luis's chin bobbed down briefly. Anyone else would have missed the tiny movement, the smallest of nods, a gesture Luis used sparingly but lovingly. When Ana ran off at a party, worried about abandoning him, he reassured her with a nod. Before he shut her door, headed back to his room for the night, the gesture meant he'd walk safely, keeping one eye out for danger. More than a simple yes, the nod was a promise that everything would be alright. It was a signal meant just for her.

For a split second, on an ultimately miniscule decision, they agreed in the silent, secret language of two lovers.

• • •

It was simple, really: Ana and Luis had had a good day. After weeks of disconnect, they'd accomplished something, together. She had included him in her life, in a way that felt real and substantial. Even if the couple of hours were an anomaly, the experience would smooth the resentments forming like calluses within them. Luis nodded, convinced that all relationships functioned this way. Enough happiness would outweigh any incompatibilities. It was as simple as balancing an elementary school math equation.

The cocktails warmed their bellies, reddened their faces, loosened their lips. Alejandra kissed them both goodbye. For the first time in days, Luis and Ana talked about unimportant things—Lorde's new album (miraculously better than her first), the weather (couldn't the human body invent a less disgusting way of self-regulating than sweat?). There were so many ways to maintain a relationship. Surely some were built on nothing but easy conversations like these.

Stepping through the apartment's front door, Luis relaxed. Even if the other couple was lounging in the living room, cornering him into awkward small talk, he'd manage. Ana would help out. She was great at speaking about nothing with warmth, convincing strangers at parties and concerts that they'd traversed deeper than they had.

No one was in the living room. The sound of a muffled movie came through the couple's bedroom door. Unhurried, Luis crossed through the kitchen, searching the fridge for a beer. As he cradled the cold glass against his cheek, he realized he hadn't been afraid of running into the couple. It'd been Ana who'd had him on edge. How silly, to be nervous around the person who knew him best, who heard the patter of his heart clearer than he could. True, they were both woefully avoidant, but that wasn't a death sentence.

Ana needed to charge her phone, so Luis followed her into the bedroom, sipping his beer.

"The Bible must be special," Luis said, his tongue fast and loose.

"I think so. You know how research is. A lot of throwing spaghetti on the wall, seeing what sticks."

Ana paused, then bent over to plug in her phone charger. The conversation could have stopped there, but she continued, the opening too precious to give up.

"I saw the Bible in the Defractor. You and I, we found it together."

"You've been following its lead," Luis said. Heat rose in his cheeks, kindled by booze, surprise, or a blend of both.

"I don't want to fight, Luis," Ana said. "I just . . . needed to feel that there's a larger plan. Destiny. The book was supposed to end up in my hands. That's what I saw, and boom. It did."

"You made a choice. You went looking."

"For basically my entire life, I put my faith in God. Si Dios quiere. My mom's favorite phrase. God worked in mysterious ways, and we had to roll with it, trusting in the larger plan."

"I understand what that's like," Luis said. He'd grown up Catholic too, though less stringently than Ana.

"I'm not sure you do." Then, to soften her words: "And that's okay."

"Have a little faith in yourself."

"I just need you to withhold judgment, for just a bit. I want to believe in a larger plan. Sure, maybe that belief is a crutch, but how else are we supposed to keep living?"

There it was. Honesty, plain and sweet. In the past, Luis and Ana had swapped secrets as easily as they'd swapped spit. Now, the truth gave him a sugar rush. As the question dropped from her lips, Luis believed her—fully, earnestly—which is why he leaned in, pressing his lips against hers. They were soft, as he remembered, though the sensation was only slightly stronger than a memory. Her body was stiff, so he pressed his lips harder against hers, pulling back only to slip his tongue inside her mouth, caressing the tip of her tongue with his. He snuck his fingers into her waistband, which finally made her lean into him, but as soon as he brought his other hand up to her breasts, kissing her neck all the while, Ana whispered.

"They'll hear," she said, gesturing to where the co-renters were, on the other side of the wall.

"I'll be quiet," he promised, pushing her down onto the mattress where he'd spent so many nights making excuses to stay away. He fucked her, hard. She bit his neck, harder than she ever had before. Could it be a sign to slow down, ease up, stop? He tried to remember how her body signaled pleasure, how her face shifted when she was enjoying herself, but it'd been weeks since they'd found themselves like this. Even if he did remember, it wouldn't be helpful. Her face was turned away from him, buried in the bedsheets. Luis pulled out and finished on the duvet, inches from her body.

Afterward, Ana said nothing. In the quiet, the rattle of the pipes was audible.

Archive of Unknown Universes

"I need to use the bathroom," Ana said. Luis said he'd get them water, following her into the hallway. She closed the door without making eye contact. The kitchen tap gurgled. Luis took a sip and placed the other glass on the small kitchen island.

Two guavas were nestled together, inches from the edge of the sink. He chomped one out of existence in five bites, ravenous. As he bit into the second, the bathroom door opened. Ana's bare feet on the floorboards clapped like thunder. She grabbed her glass but stopped mid-sip. Her eyes locked on his fingers, then darted to the sink.

"The guavas?" Ana asked quietly.

"I ate them."

"Both?"

"I didn't realize you wanted one. I'm sorry," Luis said.

"It's fine," she said, excusing herself.

The degree to which they were not fine was increasing, and they strayed farther and farther from "fine" every day. The weight of their unhappiness would not be counterbalanced, no matter how many good days they had. He could picture their relationship unraveling further over the next few weeks, saw themselves becoming colder to each other, hurting one another even more often with what they didn't say. Drunk, timid words would get them nowhere. A real conversation was all they needed. One sentence could break the silence open, splinter a love already cracking.

Still, Luis couldn't imagine doing it. The words would be thick in his mouth, uncomfortable to force out as if they were bile. As he fell asleep in bed, doing his best to stay on his side, he pictured them a few months ago, when they'd been happy and infatuated. Certain that the world only made sense when they were with each other. Their former selves, though, were ghosts who couldn't speak, who didn't even rattle around, opting instead for noiselessness as they remained tethered to a place and time they'd rather run from. Images of dead, haunted things lulled Luis into an unsteady sleep.

He awoke, gasping for air. It was three in the morning. Ana was fast asleep next to him. Scrolling Instagram for a few minutes might lull him back to sleep. Luis tapped in a Wi-Fi code. As soon as the connection went through, so did the messages from his mother. One after another, they crowded his screen. He'd missed a dozen calls too.

Communication with his family had always been sporadic, only deployed when he needed something from his mother, or vice versa, and even then, it was all business. Get to the point, don't linger or say anything you couldn't resolve in a couple of text messages. And now, in the dead of night, the pattern was shattered, which scared him. He opened the messages.

Archive of Unknown Universes

The machine is still whirring, waiting for someone to return. Will they? Who's to say, but that doesn't mean the work can stop. A machine does what a machine does. It mines, imagines, renders, constructs. It works and works and works. Let's imagine a boy wakes up in the middle of the night and walks through the solitary side streets of Havana, past the steps and the statue and into the building, until he finds the machine glowing blue. He leans in, tells it a secret, and the machine is ready. It can tell him, with confidence, what he wants to know:

A NATION IS A FICTION, AND LIKE ANY NARRATIVE, IT MUST HAVE A BEGINNING AND AN END. ITS SEAMS ARE IMAGINARY, INVISIBLE LINES OF STITCHES THAT HOLD IT TOGETHER, US VERSUS THEM, A COUNTRY AGAINST ITS ENEMIES. A BROTHER PICKS UP A GUN AGAINST HIS BROTHER, AND THE SEAM SPLITS. THE FICTION ENDS. A COUNTRY IS A FICTION THAT ENDS IN BLOODSHED, RUBBLE, A MOUND OF DIRT MARKED ONLY WITH FLOWERS. OTHER MEN WANT TO WRITE A DIFFERENT STORY, BUILD ANOTHER LIE. A KINDER ONE, LESS BLOODY BUT STILL STURDY AROUND THE EDGES. A COUNTRY NEEDS A BORDER TO PROVE IT IS REAL. NETO PRESSES ITS EDGES BETWEEN HIS FINGERS, SEEING WHAT WILL GIVE. WILL HE SEE HOW FLIMSY IT IS, HOW CONVENIENT A STORY HE'S COME TO BELIEVE? HERE IS WHAT HIS NATION

SOUNDS LIKE: A GIRL IS TERRIFIED, BUT SHE KEEPS LIVING. HER STORY DOES NOT END AT THE BARREL OF A GUN, AND THOUGH HER COUNTRY IS A LIE, SHE BELIEVES IT BECAUSE IT ALLOWED HER TO BREATHE LONG ENOUGH FOR HER MOTHER TO STORM IN. TO HOLD HER, TO ASSURE HER THAT NOTHING IS TORN, THAT LIFE WILL CONTINUE IF WE CLOSE OUR EYES AND PRETEND WE DO NOT SEE THE GASH DOWN ITS CENTER.

1980

Neto had taken precautions. At every public appearance he'd made for the Liberation Front, he made sure to cover his face. He wore a bandanna, which shrouded most of his features, and added a pair of sunglasses for good measure. A couple of times he'd even applied a bit of makeup to lighten his skin and downplay his thick black eyebrows. And yet, somehow, the government matched his face to his legal name and placed him on one of those lists; the hit lists of suspected terrorists that no one's seen, but most definitely exist. People disappear too frequently for them to be pure speculation.

"I shouldn't have left Elena alone," Esperanza tells her brother. The men had taken his more radical books and a couple pamphlets shipped from abroad, though no one had found the Bible stuffed under his mattress. When Neto saw his niece, the evening of the raid, he could have sworn he saw a slight shake in her thin but sturdy shoulders, as if the terror had burrowed itself deep inside her, emitting small aftershocks. Since then, it's all Neto and Esperanza have talked about.

They sit on a bench in Parque Daniel Hernández, a bag of groceries at their feet. The park is in the middle of town, its edges delineated by four roads that corral the open, Spanish Colonial–style plaza. Palm trees' shadows stretch across the park's centerpiece: an ornate concrete gazebo topped with a crown of pigeons. A short distance away from Neto and his sister, a group of men are laughing loudly, drinking illicitly out of brown paper bags, the cheap liquor barely hidden. Their drunkenness is far too joyous and carefree for his mood, but Neto still wishes for a swig or two.

"I wasn't gone long," Esperanza says. "I told her I'd be back soon. I was only getting bread from the corner bakery and then some vegetables from the market." She'd gone to the open-air market down the street from where they sit. It buzzes with the sound of haggling vendors.

Neto hugs Esperanza, biting his tongue.

"It's not your fault," he finally ventures.

"No, it's not. It's yours," she says. Her stare is cold, clear-eyed.

Neto wishes she'd yell, or scratch at him, or slam her palm against his face—anything but the truth delivered like an icicle to the chest. It is his fault. He's the one involved with the guerrillas, and he's the one who has refused to move out despite knowing it's dangerous to stay in the same place too long. His sister's home—their parents' home, really, which they'd shared ever since their parents' deaths nearly a decade ago—was ransacked because of Neto.

"So what now?" Esperanza asks. "You expect me to leave the home I've built her and take Elena . . . where?"

"I think . . ." Neto stumbles on his words. When he reluctantly signed up to carry the revolutionary banner in El

Salvador, he didn't realize it'd require these kinds of sacrifices. But he's in too deep.

"Where will she be safe?" Esperanza asks. She's harbored suspicions of Neto's activities for years, but now that it's impossible to deny the danger he's put them in, the slow burn in the back of her throat jumps to her tongue.

"I can try arranging something," Neto says. "We have allies in other countries, people who'd open their homes to you and Elena."

He isn't sure he'll be able to set up such a situation, but it doesn't fall outside the realm of possibility. As a last resort, he can always ask Rafael for help, despite the cruel things Esperanza has said about their love. A middle-aged woman walks past, her gait slow but strong, shouting that she has tamales for sale. Her voice sends a cloud of pigeons into a gray-and-white flurry.

"Even the women at church say things are getting bad. You've gone and made everything worse. Elena's just a girl, and she's been put through this. Just stay out of trouble, and maybe we can stay. Neto, won't you do that for me?"

Neto looks past Esperanza toward a uniformed policeman a few yards away. He eats a tamale he's bought from the vendor, but Neto can only focus on the gun strapped to his back. The park is bustling, the intoxicated men in the concrete kiosk marking its epicenter. Buses drive by, honking, and the vendors add a layer of syrupy voices to the uproar. Neto stays silent, fighting the urge to lower his head into his hands. He hasn't made eye contact with Esperanza during most of the conversation.

"I'll think about it," he says, though what he thinks, with a deep sense of desperation, is that it's already too late. The government has an idea of what he's done, and his whole family will be punished.

After Esperanza leaves to pick up Elena from school, Neto boards a microbus headed toward San Salvador. Even with its frequent stops, the ride isn't too long. In twenty minutes, he's approaching a building painted a muted, pastel pink. A floor-to-ceiling gate separates the front door from the street. This is the guerrillas' latest meeting house, the fourth address they've had in three years. Fishing a key from his pocket, he opens the gate and steps inside.

The rooms are badly lit, since the few small windows are covered by thick curtains that follow the guerrilleros from lease to lease. Neto cuts through the dust floating in the living room and sits at the dining table. He picks up a folder he left there that morning.

His fingers scan the inventory form, softly bending the paper toward him. Every sheet is marked with the name of a company that sells construction equipment. Neto scans the minute details, focusing less on content and more on style: the width of the lines, the fonts used in the letterhead and subheadings, the hues of the ink. Admiring his handiwork, he goes into the kitchen to brew a cup of coffee. A few minutes after he's drunk his mug, the front door opens.

"You're late," Neto says. A man and a woman stand in the doorway. To Neto, they are Alejandro and Anabel. In their formal correspondences with people abroad, they introduce themselves as Daniel and Cassandra.

"We got caught up with something. Sorry, bicho," Anabel says, slapping Neto on the back. Her curly hair, pulled into a tight bun, makes him think of Esperanza. Their faces are similar shapes, round like cantaloupe with close-set eyes that are almost all pupil. Neto and his sister share few features. His face is long, and his nose is angular, while Esperanza's is button-shaped. But they share the same eyes: dark, evasive, and surprisingly warm, like sunlight at a storm's end.

"You had something to tell us," Anabel says.

Neto recounts what his sister said, curating details about her disposition when she'd told the story. He isn't trying to garner their sympathy or instill guilt. He just hopes they'll understand the gravity of the situation.

"They're building a case against you," Alejandro says. "This is what they do. I'm glad you weren't there. Who knows when—or if—we would have seen you again."

He grimaces.

"They disappear people with a lot less evidence than what they have on you," Anabel says. From a drawer, she pulls out an Amnesty Report she's shown Neto before. "Just in the first half of February, they've taken ninety-three campesinos and three clergymen. Leaving the country, at least for a little while, is a good move."

She hands the report to Alejandro, who is waiting with an open palm. Neto's brain has gone foggy, and he wishes he'd grabbed another cup of coffee before it went cold.

"They found a woman with child, Isabel Linares, and macheted her into pieces," Alejandro reads from the report.

Neto thinks of all those months Esperanza spent pregnant, but quickly forces himself to think of anything else, as if by simply remembering those days, he'll cause a curse to befall his sister. Stories like these are not foreign to Neto. The deaths of innocent people, friends and strangers, motivate him to remain in the revolution, one he's uncertain about. But he hates hearing the names and details. The report won't change anything. It'll simply capture what he's been forced to accept: that the human capacity for evil is expansive, nearly limitless.

"I'll leave after I finish the forms," Neto says. His faith in the revolution has wavered in the past, so he wants to assure Alejandro and Anabel that he'll finish the job at hand before he flees.

"Get them done by the weekend. The Nicaraguans are waiting," Anabel says. There's a plan to smuggle guns and ammunition into the country, from Nicaragua to El Salvador, in hollowed-out bulldozers and excavators. Contacts in Managua will fill the machines with weaponry. With Neto's forged shipping and inventory forms, trucks will cross through Honduras and into the country.

"I'll have them ready by Friday," Neto says. Anabel nods, and Alejandro reminds her that they've set up a dinner in San Benito starting soon. They say goodbye to Neto with a kiss on each of his cheeks and remind him to lock up before leaving.

He rubs his temple for a second, before wandering back into the kitchen to brew a fresh pot of coffee. As he waits, he formulates a solution. Rafael is in Managua. They'll all go to him. Even if Esperanza refuses to accept the relationship, as she has since she's known about it, Rafael will welcome her and Elena. That's the sort of man he is: selfless, generous, coolheaded, with an eye for justice. He'll send Esperanza and Elena first, and follow soon after. It's not perfect, but it's a plan.

He walks back to the dining table, sits down, and stares at his incomplete work. It's one of the easier jobs he's done all year, but Neto can't remove himself from his chair. The war is swelling outside, growing louder and louder each day, and though his contributions are small—and oftentimes completed with a great deal of anxiety—they've felt worthwhile in recent months. Now, though, he faces the truth. It's as clear as the sounds of gunfire blocks away and as harrowing as the desecrated bodies that line the highway. A revolution requires blood sacrifices, and now it whispers his name, asking for his family's.

The thought makes his head cloudy. As if sleepwalking, he steps back into the kitchen. The coffee has finally brewed. Neto pours himself a cup, hoping the bitter burn will abate his fear. He's waited too long. The coffee has cooled again.

Whenever a comrade refers to Neto's work, they call it "forgery." The word carries such an ugly tenor to it, as if the act of shaping a commonplace trinket into a close imitation of a prettier cousin is inherently evil. Neto has always thought his work beautiful, a matter of praise and reverence rather than cheap trickery.

It'd all started six years ago, at La Nacional, where he studied literature and art history. When he began his course of study, he worried that it was frivolous, that perhaps he should be studying medicine or law. In the aftermath of his parents' deaths, Neto and Esperanza's only guarantee of stability was the deed to their home. But stability and joy are not synonymous, so in a prototypical display of angst, Neto searched for the little thrills that made life worth living.

On the edge of eighteen, he started university and found magic in Borges's short stories and between the strokes of Van Gogh's irises. Aesthetic pleasures romanced him and worries about the future fell away whenever he stepped into a classroom. Neto had no intentions of becoming a revolutionary, since he didn't intend to become anything at all.

Soon, though, his classmates' fervor became unavoidable. Friends invited him to meetings they held in empty classrooms after hours, sometimes led by professors who brought lessons from thinkers from around the world: Marx, Freire, Engels, Foucault.

"It's simple," an older organizer told Neto. "We want more political space in this country. We want to be able to vote for candidates who actually represent the masses. We're asking for basic promises a government should offer its people: a political voice, less repression, literacy, health care. That's the basis of it, but a revolution looks like the only way to achieve those goals."

Neto never fully agreed with his classmates, but still read the pamphlets from Guevara and Allende, allowing himself to get carried along. His occasional bouts of timidity and fluctuating strings of anxieties would have kept him out of the movement entirely, were it not for the gift he soon discovered.

At some point, university administrators got a sense of what was brewing and viewed the meetings as potential liabilities. They'd run any unsanctioned assemblies out of classrooms, claiming they didn't have official approval to be there. One of the lead organizers, two years older than Neto, offhandedly

Archive of Unknown Universes

asked him if he was any good at forging signatures, and though he'd never forged one in his life, he said he'd give it a try. With a bit of help, Neto re-created the administrative form used for room reservations. After a couple throwaway practice signatures on a piece of scratch paper, Neto mimicked a dean's elegant scrawl on the form, nailing the gentle rise and fall of the script. They turned it in to the registrar's office, the university remained unaware it had a falsification, and their meetings continued. Shoddy paperwork ensured revolutionary possibilities.

Neto was drawn to art for its precision: the gentle but successful crafting of a sentence, the way words collaborated with a reader's imagination to evoke entire images, the way a painting transformed in front of your eye depending how far you stood from it. When he began making forgeries, he tried to bring the same precision to his own work. His portfolio flowered: national identification cards, death certificates, university degrees, business documents, visas, passports, deeds, leases, receipts, invoices. Driver's licenses, checks, letters. On the work desk he furnished over the years, Neto developed a small army of tools: a high-end typewriter, an inkwell, scalpels of various lengths, pens, pencils, different grains of paper, light glues, dull paints, luminous pigments. He spent hours hunched over the bright light of his desk lamp, studying original documents and carefully mimicking them, altering only a name or a photograph.

Passports—some of the most difficult documents to falsify for their many layers, their many places to make mistakes—fascinate Neto more than anything else. If he makes an incorrect incision, or pastes pieces together sloppily, or has a photograph of the wrong size or quality, he'll be found out. Any misstep would give away the document as false, even to an untrained eye. But whenever he gets it right, after half a dozen Frankenstein copies of a passport from whatever new country he's attempting, it's almost magic. A great fake passport has no signs of where the identification picture had been sliced into the page. The page with the holder's information reflects in the light, glimmering in precisely the right spots; a spectacle announcing its authenticity and power. And it does harbor a sort of occultism. A perfect, artful forgery lets people travel and function under different aliases. As their new selves, they aide revolutions, journey to otherwise restricted cities, evade death, start over, make more of themselves than their real passports allow, and really, doesn't that make Neto's concoctions almost as stunning as any Van Gogh?

After years of experience, the shipping forms should be an easy job. Neto reassures himself as he goes to his office and opens the folder with his half-completed work. On his desk—an antique from the 1930s, rumored to have belonged to someone on Maximiliano Hernández Martínez's staff—lamplight bathes the paperwork. Without the bulb, the dull lighting in the room makes work impossible, day or night. Neto pulls a blank piece of paper toward him, scours his desk for a ruler, and picks up his thinnest pen. Without more than a pause, he begins re-creating the form, an incarnation at his will.

The lines build on each other, and the form begins taking shape, each stroke of his pen strengthening the whole, like wooden beams in a house or bricks in a fireplace. He works in silence for a while. If he goes too fast, he'll make mistakes, but without urgency, he won't finish in time. His wrist moves, carefully, tenderly, along the page.

"Have you heard?" Anabel says, startling Neto. He hadn't heard the door open but continues working. The motions are natural enough for him to multitask.

"They killed some folks at the university chapel, in broad daylight. Monseñor Romero's already condemned it in a sermon."

"Awful," Neto says.

"This is a case they can't turn against us," Anabel says. "They call us terrorists, but murder people at their place of worship."

"The world hasn't listened to our suffering," he says.

"We have to capitalize on this," she says. "It's a matter of justice, Neto. We have to show the country—the world— what this government is doing to us all."

Words are caught in Neto's throat. Making someone a martyr hollows them out. The politicians and security officers are quick to take someone's image and rearrange it to fit into their ideologies. The revolutionaries do it as well, but Neto wishes he could tell Anabel that he hates the way they use innocent people's deaths to build sympathy.

"Give the families the space to grieve," Neto manages.

"Of course," Anabel says. "Always."

Once she leaves the room, Neto's mistake registers. He misaligned his ruler at some point and has ended up with two unequally spaced columns on the left side of the form. The mistake is only off by a quarter of an inch, but Neto can't help but notice it. There's a chance the Honduran authorities will also notice it, especially alongside the other forms he's made error-free. He'll have to redo the form, more than an hour of work down the drain.

His priority, though, has shifted. Neto pictures a tiny corpse laid out on a pew, and it has Elena's face. He won't get the forms done that evening.

Instead, he calls a contact in Managua. Not Rafael, because he wants to be able to tell Esperanza that someone else will be escorting her and Elena, though ultimately they are headed to be with him. He leaves the safe house as dusk falls, and finds his way to his sister's home, where he tries his best to convince her that she must take her daughter and leave.

"The trip is short," he says. "Two, three days max."

"You could leave the Liberation Front. We could stay," she says.

"They killed children at the church."

"I heard," Esperanza whispers.

"I'm going to follow soon," he promises. "I just need a few days to wrap up loose ends here."

They talk further, circling the horror stories they've both overheard, but soon they both know the truth. A lack of affiliation is no guarantee of salvation. A Sandinista will meet Esperanza and Elena in Santa Clarita, a small town close to the Honduran border. He'll escort them through to Managua. Esperanza and Elena will leave in the morning. Neto will join them in a week.

Neto still hasn't completed the forms. He's tried, but he's made more mistakes. Instead of attempting and failing, he sees Esperanza and Elena off as the sun rises.

"There'll be a couple days in Honduras," Esperanza says, rattling off the route. "A day outside of Managua, and then to the final house . . ."

Neto knows it calms her nerves, so he nods quietly. They're standing in the doorway of their parents' home. From there, Neto can see into the kitchen. Elena is hunched over a bowl of cornflakes, bringing milky scoops up to her lips. She looks strangely fine, as if what's happened to her isn't as drastic, as life-altering, as Neto and Esperanza both know it is.

"We'll be back soon. We'll return to a better home, a better El Salvador."

Neto pushes the words out through his teeth, not because he believes them, but because he must convince his sister—and himself—that the cause is worth leaving the only home they've ever known.

"Goodbye, Neto," Esperanza says.

"I'll see you soon," Neto promises, which is as close to an "I love you" as either he or his sister will offer. He turns to leave, but as he's stepping away from the house for the final time, Elena catches his eye. Cornflakes are stuck to the edges of her mouth, and there's a milky mustache on her upper lip. She waves to him and laughs. It sounds like hope—her joy a fragile, fluttering thing.

Neto returns to the safe house later that morning. The botched inventory form waits on his desk. Instead of starting over, he writes Rafael a letter. The first version, whenever he writes a letter like this, is in plain Spanish. *My sister and my niece have left* . . . he begins, in a hurried scrawl. It doesn't matter how messy this version is, since he'll have to encode it afterward. In the envelopes he mails out, there are pages filled to the edges with numbers and colons, a cryptograph only Rafael has the key to. Neto writes a couple more lines, but soon accepts that he's avoiding his real task. He puts the sheet of paper into the desk drawer. Still, he can't seem to restart, so he wanders out to the kitchen, where Alejandro is hunched over a paperback.

"Here. Take this," Neto says. He folds the botched form in half, twice, and slips it between the open pages of Alejandro's book. "A souvenir."

Neto needs a refresher before giving the falsification another shot, so he heads out past the gate that opens to the street. The sun has drifted from its position directly above the Earth, but it still illuminates every bit of ground that isn't covered in the shadow of a building. Neto doesn't have his watch on him, but it must be around three o'clock. He has a good two more hours of work left before dinner. Hopefully the corner store will have Coca-Cola, just the thing to hold him over.

As he approaches the gated storefront, Doña Solis greets him in her soft but cheerful voice. The radio is playing. Neto sees her grandchildren running around the living room, visible through the gate. Doña Solis exudes warmth despite the fact that they met only a few weeks ago, and that she's yet to ask for his name.

"Do you have any Coca-Cola left?" Neto asks.

"Just one?"

Neto nods.

Doña Solis tips the glass bottle into a small plastic baggie, sticks a pink straw into it, and puts it down on the counter.

Archive of Unknown Universes

Tying the ends of the baggie shut, she hands it over to Neto. He hands her the coins she's due and turns to walk back toward the safe house.

He's taken three sips when an unassuming, beat-up black sedan pulls up next to him. Neto doesn't notice it, lost in thoughts about Esperanza and his niece.

A man wearing simple clothes—khakis, a white button-down, and sunglasses—jumps out of the back seat, grabs Neto by his biceps, and pins his arms behind his back. Neto screams but is met with a fist to the upper jaw. Another man materializes and presses a rag to Neto's face. The fabric reeks, and the fumes work their way into Neto's system as the men manhandle him into the back seat of the car. The car speeds off down the street. By the time Doña Solis runs out to investigate the screams, the vehicle is a speck in the distance.

On the sidewalk, Coca-Cola runs over the edge of the curb. When it dries, it becomes an ugly stain. Doña Solis walks by and wonders if it's a soft drink or a thin layer of blood, unsuccessfully scrubbed from the concrete. In a few days, once the guerrillas realize that Neto has been kidnapped, the stain will be bleached by the sun. The last trace of Neto, disappeared.

A NATION RISES AND FLOWS, EBBS AND SHIFTS, ITS EDGES TRANSFORMING INTO NEW SHAPES. IT WIDENS AND FORMS AN ESCAPE VALVE TO ALLOW ITS INHABITANTS TO FLEE NORTH WHEN THE RED-HOT CENTER BECOMES TOO SUFFOCATING TO BEAR. MIGRATION IS NOT SALVATION, BUT THEY TRY. THEY TRY TO FORGET WHAT THEY LEFT BEHIND. THEY TRY TO REMEMBER WHAT THE NATION SMELLED LIKE BEFORE THE CHARRED AROMA OF WAR DESCENDED. THEY TRY AND TRY AND TRY.

PICTURE THOSE WHO REMAINED, WHO KNOW THE NATION'S EDGES ARE MALLEABLE AND ARE DETERMINED TO SHAPE IT INTO SOFTER EDGES. TRY AND IMAGINE THEIR SHOCK WHEN A COMRADE GOES MISSING, KIDNAPPED, DISAPPEARED. IF THEY DON'T SEARCH, THE NATION WINS, SO THEY DO. TOGETHER, THEY RUMMAGE THROUGH BINDERS FULL OF CADAVERS, MOLARS, FEMURS, UNMARKED GRAVES, DNA SAMPLES, LETTERS, COURT RECORDS, TRIALS, INTERVIEWS. THEY SEARCH AND SEARCH FOR ANYTHING NETO HAS LEFT BEHIND. THE NATION GROWS. ITS EDGES HARDEN, ITS VEINS WIDEN AFTER RAINFALL, AND ANABEL AND ALEJANDRO SEARCH AND SEARCH.

IF THEY FIND HIM ALIVE, IT'S JOYOUS. (THERE ARE INFINITE PATHS THAT LEAD

Archive of Unknown Universes

NOWHERE, LEAVING THE BODY DUMPED IN THE BRUSH.) IN THE ADOLESCENCE OF A NATION DEFINING ITSELF, EVEN JOY HAS A LIMIT, AND NETO—WHO IS GRATEFUL TO BE ALIVE, EVEN IF SCARRED—REACHES IT. THE NATION OUTGROWS HIM, OR HE OUTGROWS THE NATION. IT SPITS NETO OUT OR NETO PRESSES IT UNDER HIS TEETH. THERE IS A WOMAN, UNTIL THERE ISN'T. A CHILD IS BORN, A BOY NETO NAMES DOMINGO. THE BOY ONLY KNOWS THE NATION BRIEFLY, BEFORE HIS FATHER TAKES THEM TO THE UNITED STATES. FAST-FORWARD SOME YEARS AND COME IN CLOSE. THE BOY HAS GROWN UP, UNAWARE THAT THE NATION WHO MADE HIS FATHER A REVOLUTIONARY SQUEEZED HIM OUT THROUGH ITS JAGGED MAW. STEP IN CLOSE, AND WATCH DOMINGO LEARN.

2018

The Barker Center always had the heat turned up high, especially in mid-February's frost, so like his classmates, Domingo shed his coat and sweater as soon as he sat down, stuffing them under his chair, where they lay like old snakeskins.

"Americans weren't dying by the thousands like they had during the Vietnam War, but that doesn't mean people weren't dying," Professor Vargas said from his seat. "We think of it as a 'cold' war because the deaths were happening in the so-called third world."

His small, oval glasses made his face look rounder than it was, squeezed tight by the blue turtleneck that hugged the edges of his gray beard. As he spoke, he gesticulated with his hands, which reminded Domingo of the photographs his father had of comrades he'd left in El Salvador, a gaggle of men who'd traded an academic education for lessons forged in the fire of revolution.

"Now, on to the article by Dr. Torres. We all read, right? Eh? To recap, even though we all read: Dr. Torres meditates on what the trajectory of her country of birth would have been if the Reagan administration had decided to pursue an interventionist, anticommunist policy in El Salvador. She essentially asks us to consider if the Salvadoran Revolution, or the FMLN Revolution, as she calls it, would have been successful if the United States had intervened."

The FMLN Revolution. Just the mention brought Domingo back into the conversation, sharpened his focus. His father had lived the cold war, so he'd grown up hearing stories about the beautiful triumph against Yankee greed and home-bred oligarchy. Those histories were family lore, an origin story. And yet, though he felt guilt at the notion, Domingo knew that his father had spoon-fed him convenient and incomplete stories. Like any myth, they transformed his complicated motherland into nothing more than a thin line. There had been mistakes: in-fighting, murders of the innocent, lives unnecessarily discarded. Even though the seminar would only be discussing Central America briefly, condensing the isthmus's sprawling past into a week, Domingo had signed up as soon as he could. He raised his hand.

"Domingo."

"There were similar conditions elsewhere at the time, right? And those organizing efforts failed. The FMLN can't have been particularly savvy. Not enough to beat a government that wanted to crush them."

"She says as much early on in the article."

It felt like a gentle reprimand. The next time you speak, Professor Vargas seemed to say, contribute an original thought. Domingo sunk into his seat.

"Historians tend to group El Salvador with Nicaragua," Vargas continued. "The parallels make a lot of sense, and it does look like the strategies used by the Sandinistas in seventy-nine worked for the FMLN in eighty-five. But Torres argues that the conditions in El Salvador in the late seventies and early eighties more closely resembled those in Guatemala. If Reagan had funneled millions of dollars in guns, ammunition, and military training into El Salvador too, its citizens would have experienced the same prolonged violence and displacement that Guatemalans did."

The last twenty minutes of the seminar were usually unbearable, but today was different. Domingo wasn't distracted by the thin flutter of snowfall outside the window. The discussion was genuinely stimulating, a rare case among the many dull, half-baked classes he'd sat through that semester, and he jumped in to speak every couple of minutes. The margins of his printout filled with notes and questions, hastily scrawled. And even though he wouldn't be able to decipher them later, when the class was over and everyone was bundled up again, the day's discussion felt more worthwhile than his entire last semester.

Stepping out into the cold, frigid air on his cheeks, Domingo's brain buzzed. Who would he be if he'd been birthed in the ash and gun smoke of war?

"I can't stop thinking about that question. Why wasn't El Salvador another Guatemala?"

Domingo and Ana sat in a restaurant, by a window that looked out onto Harvard Square. Passersby made for good people-watching, but even when a pair of turkeys walked by, they didn't break eye contact.

"I wouldn't have been born in the States," Ana said. "My mother always says she was exiled by the revolution."

Archive of Unknown Universes

"My father claims he fought to stay in El Salvador, but we ended up here anyway."

"Depends on who you ask, I guess," Ana said. "It's tricky."

"The past tends to be."

"If the history major says so, then so it must be," Ana said, which made him smile. This tendency to take himself too seriously must have been the inevitable result of living in the shadow of a figure like his father. He appreciated Ana's ability to cut through his anxiety, to remind him that the here and now mattered. He paused, admiring the way a sip of sparkling water tickled his tongue.

"I've been looking at flights to San Salvador, if you still want me to join for that leg of your trip," Domingo said.

"Obviously." She laughed. "Of course I want you there."

Domingo smiled and promised to finally text his cousin to ask if they could stay at his aunt's house while Ana did her thesis research. He kept forgetting, despite the notes he inked in his notebook and on his palms. It'd be his first trip back in years.

"There's this museum with an archive all about the war," Ana said. "It's run by a former guerrilla soldier, who is supposedly the only woman who—"

The waiter brought the check, and Domingo handed over his debit card without a second thought. As they left their table, he gave Ana a quick kiss on the lips before heading outside.

"You know," Ana said as they stood just beyond the restaurant's front door, "I heard the library just got a new Defractor. It has a longer playback, something like twelve minutes. It renders thirty-three universes. Maybe that's where you take your questions about the war."

Domingo flipped the switch, sparking a soft hum, quiet enough that it went unnoticed in the silent library. A blue glow shone through the eyehole. He pulled on the thin, gold pendant hanging on his neck and placed the flat metal between his teeth, biting down gently. It was a nervous tic. His father yelled at him whenever he did it, saying it was disrespectful to the man pressed in gold, Monseñor Romero, who'd fought for justice throughout Latin America until his death in 2000. Meekly, with the pendant still suspended in his mouth, Domingo lowered an eye to the machine.

ENTER LOGIN CREDENTIALS

ID: domingo.guzman@college.harvard.edu

PASSWORD: ******

WELCOME, Domingo Guzmán. LAST LOGIN, May 7, 2018. DURATION, 40 Minutes 18 Seconds. DESIGNATED INTERLOCUTOR, civil rights leader Larry Itliong. HOW CAN I HELP YOU TODAY?

From a geopolitical standpoint, is there a reason the Salvadoran Revolution succeeded while so many other antiauthoritarian efforts failed?

Archive of Unknown Universes

> WOULD YOU LIKE YOUR RESULTS RENDERED VISUALLY OR TEXTUALLY?

> Visually, please.

> A LITTLE PIECE OF ADVICE. NO ONE IS GOING TO HAND YOU WHAT YOU'RE OWED, EVEN IF YOU ASK NICELY. BE A MEAN SON OF A BITCH AND DEMAND WHAT IS RIGHTFULLY YOURS. ONE SECOND WHILE I RENDER.

Scrolling past a dozen shots of himself sitting in the library, Domingo watched the truth play out, his stomach turning with each scene. There he was, more muscular than he'd ever been, shoveling dirt in front of a beige stucco home. His biceps flexed, lit up by the sun, as he tossed down blocks of sod. Another universe landed him in a classroom where insulation and wiring poked through a loose ceiling panel. One slide over, and he was helping a woman find pants in her size at a small boutique store in the mall, his smile dropping the second he walked into the back room.

The ordinariness of his other lives gutted him. When he'd fantasized about growing up devoid of the privileges his father had granted him, he still cast himself as a hero. The scorned immigrant who used his humble upbringing for a greater good, striving to make something out of nothing. He'd organize in his neighborhood, against deportations or for labor rights, and shout into a megaphone, wearing a graphic tee that read: *The true revolutionary is guided by great feelings of love.*

But no, the Defractor confirmed a fear that'd been growing like mold. He was simply the result of his circumstances: a father who'd worked in the ranks of the Salvadoran government, a middle-class migration, SAT prep and music lessons on the weekends. Without a revolution, without a leg up, he wasn't particularly interesting or special. None of the brilliance or passion or success people attributed to him was earned. He was just lucky his life hadn't been derailed by a never-ending war, years before he was born.

He mindlessly ground the pendant between his teeth, the taste of metal filling his mouth. Guilty, he let it fall back down to his chest. As soon as he decided it was time to return the Defractor to the circulation desk, he spotted a corner he'd missed. Domingo and Neto were sitting in their living room, on the gray sectional. The flatscreen was mounted in the same spot above the mantel. A man Domingo had never seen walked into the frame. He appeared to be around his father's age, though the man was a few inches shorter and sported less of a beer belly.

When the man kissed Neto on the lips, alternate-Domingo didn't react. It was normal, ordinary. One of the small gestures of love between family members.

Domingo, who watched from the carrel in Lamont Library, pulled away from the machine quickly, his breath stuck in his throat. His father was a man of secrets, who only talked of the past when it was convenient, whose omissions bubbled under the surface of all their conversations about the country they'd left. Domingo hadn't come looking to understand his father's decisions, and the path he'd put them on all those years ago. But there he was: a relic from Neto's past, kissing him as if there was no other possibility in the world.

Archive of Unknown Universes

You are now Facebook friends with Rafael Martinez. Say hello!

Rafael: Hola. I saw Elena a few days ago, and she mentioned that you were on Facebook. That is new for you, right? Social media. I looked you up. Thought I would say hello.

Ernesto: Hola. Long time no talk. I'm shocked, actually, that you found me. Social media has always felt too public. So much information, so many pictures, so much available to strangers. But my niece told me it's an easy way to keep in contact. It's been less expensive than phone calls for years, she said.

Rafael: Elena looked well. And your nephew. He's gotten huge as well.

Ernesto: He was a kid when we left. But Elena posts pictures of him on her page. Another perk of the social media world, I guess.

Rafael: Definitely. You look good. From your photo. Healthy.

Ernesto: Nothing like I used to look. But yes, luckily, I'm still in good health.

Rafael: When are you coming back to visit? How long has it been? More than a decade, surely.

Ernesto: Almost fifteen years. Other than Elena, I don't have many reasons to go back.

Rafael: Your sister, she hasn't passed, has she?

Ernesto: She's alive. They say she's doing badly, though.

Rafael: Even more reason to visit.

Ernesto: Perhaps.

Rafael: It's strange. We used to do this often. Write to each other.

Ernesto: Those correspondences were much longer. It took a lot to write them, both time and courage. This hardly counts.

Rafael: Fair enough. If you come to San Salvador, let me know. We can go for coffee. It's overdue. I do miss you.

The bloated heads on the television screen spoke over one another. The government official with a receding hairline and blond buzz cut rolled his eyes at the woman sharing the screen. Her neat bob swayed slightly as she tried making her point, only to be interrupted. The host did nothing, opting to let them spar. In a smaller square between them, silent footage showed Guatemalan children in Texas, sitting behind a chain-link fence. The chyron read: "MIGRANT CRISIS" AT THE SOUTHERN BORDER.

"We're overwhelmed," the blond man said. "Parents put their children at risk by sending them here alone. If we don't make a strong statement about the sanctity of our borders, nothing will change."

Domingo was back in his childhood home, pressed against the springy cushion of a West Elm sectional. For years, his entire life, really, network television droned behind the bustle of his life. Political consciousness starts with awareness, his father had once said.

"Under US law, you must apply for asylum on US soil," the woman rebutted. "They're following protocol, and your agency is throwing them into makeshift jails."

Neto walked in and sat on the other end of the couch, squinting at his phone. His glasses were down low on his nose, belly pressing against the fabric of the brown polo he'd tucked into his jeans. He typed slowly, using only one finger.

"It's sad," Neto said when he was done. "All those kids."

"I'm working on a fundraiser with the immigrant rights organization on campus," Domingo said.

Neto grunted, acknowledging the information. Domingo thought his father would be impressed, or at least grateful that his son had identified an injustice and was acting to address it. The neutrality unsettled him.

"Your cousin, Elena, tried making it to the United States when she was a girl, probably around the age of those kids," Neto said.

Domingo's interactions with his older cousin were all blips: her interrupting the occasional call with Luis, a photo she posted on Facebook. From his only trip back to El Salvador, years ago, he didn't have a sense of her personality. She was washed out by nostalgic but unhelpful images: yellow-orange mangoes, the sizzling of plantains, and verdant green plants hanging down from the side of the highway. Still, he'd never pictured her as a child, let alone one in as dire a position as the Guatemalan children.

"You see," Neto said, after listening to the news for a few minutes, "the revolution helped lots of people. You don't hear about many children fleeing El Salvador."

"Some of the children are Salvadoran," Domingo said defensively, despite knowing that Salvadorans were fast-tracked in the asylum process.

"Let's hope a solution comes together soon," Neto said before segueing into a familiar pitch. A history degree from Harvard was respectable, but after graduation Domingo should go to law school, then run for public office. "Make a real change with your education."

"Politicians aren't doing shit to help these kids," Domingo said. "I don't even know if you can actually impact the world with electoral politics."

Archive of Unknown Universes

"You'll do much more for immigrants in politics than you will running tiny fundraisers. Work your way into the government. Make a difference."

Domingo's face went warm. The news transitioned from the children at the border to a discussion of the Speaker of the House's suit. A new pair of faces appeared—one to argue that it was a powerful symbol of the nation's shortcomings and another to say her interpretation was vapid, liberal nonsense. The argument became a buzz in Domingo's ear. A few minutes before he'd resented how alone he felt, but now he wanted nothing more than for his father to leave.

"You have to understand, mijo," Neto said. "What we did in El Salvador, it was nothing short of a miracle. Those with the guns control the country. That's what they used to say. Until we took over and established a government that worked for the people. From the dirt, we molded a social structure that people said was impossible."

As he spoke of the revolution, his crow's feet pulled so tight they almost disappeared. Swirls of angry pride danced in his pupils. His body, which Domingo had long considered lumpy and often stuffed into too-tight clothing, was taut. Domingo imagined that in his youth, his father had often appeared this way: fired up, clearheaded, ready to spring into action.

"A government needs its politicians. Politicians that don't lose sight of their mission, and don't lose their faith."

"You left," Domingo said. "You brought us here."

"I had my reasons."

Domingo reached for the remote, to occupy his hands. Anything to distract himself from the conversation. He landed on a channel playing a *Friends* rerun. It was the episode where

Rachel got married to Barry instead of running away at the altar. The characters all played out alternate versions of their lives.

"I just want you to put your education to good use," Neto said after a while. "To make a name for yourself. That's all. People I loved died pursuing an education. It's a gift, a privilege."

"I know," Domingo said softly. Faced with his son's stone-cold silence, Neto left the room to the sound of a laugh track, reminding Domingo that their dinner, takeout from a Vietnamese place downtown, would be arriving soon.

Hiding away in his bedroom, Domingo called Ana, but she didn't pick up. He texted his cousin, asking if he'd be able to stay with him.

primo, of course! it should go without saying, but there's always a room for you here. but I asked Mami just in case. she says anytime in June is fine.

my girlfriend is coming too, is that ok?

we have more than enough space. should be fine. and if it is not, I will make it fine

haha, thank you. I'm excited to see u.

wait, can you facetime? have something to show you

Luis's phone was too close to his face, so he looked bug-eyed. He turned the camera, revealing a stretch of turquoise. A proper pool, long enough to do laps in.

"They just finished building it," he explained. "Just in time for your trip."

"It's gorgeous," Domingo said, distracted by how wet his cousin's hair was. What would it mean to be the kind of person who was comfortable bringing a cell phone into the pool? It seemed like courting disaster, but also, it made perfect sense. His cousin had always possessed a looseness, not naive or reckless, that granted him more ease than Domingo ever felt. Surely, Luis had an inner life, but he didn't stew in his own thoughts, choosing to live in the world instead of his head. Domingo envied this ability. The facts of Luis's life were understandable, unmoving. He never questioned his place, or what it meant that he'd ended up in El Salvador, with a meticulously tiled pool in his backyard.

"How's my tío Neto?" Luis asked. Domingo rehashed the argument they'd just had.

"How did he say it?"

"It was dismissive. As if the fundraiser didn't mean anything."

"I don't know a lot about nonprofits, but I imagine any amount of money helps."

"And then he wanted to talk about politics, and how political work is the way to create change. Which is bullshit. He was running around with a pistol in the eighties to make shit happen."

"Do you believe in political work?"

It was a tricky question, one he discussed with Ana often.

He spent hours phone banking the previous semester, but also clung to his work with No Borders, which felt detached from electoral politics. Dozens of his classmates claimed to be seeking radical change, but preoccupied themselves with the accumulation of social capital and their personal brands. They spoke of their dreams of being senators and congressmen and treated politics as a game. Debating the merits of different policies filled their faces with a glow, but they did nothing to enact change in the world outside Harvard Yard. Domingo could tell they'd have successful political careers that would work to reinforce the status quo. It hurt to know that even though he knew this, despised it, and publicly denounced it, Domingo still clung to the hope he'd be among them in the future. But he never admitted that to Ana, and he didn't want to confess it to Luis now.

"There are multiple solutions to every problem," Domingo said. "That's what I think."

"Fair enough," Luis said.

A notification popped up, covering the top of Luis's forehead. Ana was calling back.

"I have to go, but thank you. For everything."

"Anytime, primo. I'll be waiting," Luis said.

After Domingo told Ana they'd secured housing, the conversation lulled. Domingo could tell that Ana was watching television out of frame. Often, they stayed on the phone, each in their own world, but still tethered together. Neither felt pressured to fill the silence, a sign of a steady relationship. But today, Domingo wanted to hang up. Her silence, unusually, stung. He took it as a personal dig. As if she'd returned his call out of obligation, not desire. Like he wasn't worthy of her attention.

"I love you," Ana said, before hanging up.

"Love you too."

The first time he'd said it, the phrase had been shiny and new in his mouth. I love you, he'd said outside Café Pamplona as snow flurries rained down on them, and then throughout the evening, over and over, like an incantation. Since then, the magic had waned, and though the phrase was still true, it'd transmuted into an irreplaceable but ordinary piece of the relationship, like an internal organ or opposable thumb.

The flatness of the phrase dropping from his lips made him think of the love he'd seen between his father and the man in the Defractor. It'd filled their living room, that large and lonely place which had only briefly included girlfriends his father eventually ran from. The facts that haunted Domingo as a child—that his father was so much older than his classmates' parents, that he knew almost nothing about his mother—did not seem to matter in his other life. "I love you" paled beside the wordless sign of affection he'd seen on his father's face.

His own relationship felt sturdy, but perhaps that should worry him. Stability is too easily confused with love.

"Dinner's here," Neto said, standing in the doorway to Domingo's bedroom.

"Great."

Domingo rolled out of bed and slipped into the hallway, but stopped when his father didn't follow.

"Everything okay?"

"Do you think . . ." Neto said, calculating his next words. "Would it be okay if I came to El Salvador too? I'll stay out of your way. I won't come if you or Ana are uncomfortable with the idea."

Would it be odd to have his father along for his first international trip with Ana? Probably, but his family was already involved. When Ana had assured him that she could afford a rental, he'd insisted they stay with his cousin. He couldn't possibly tell his father no.

"Of course," Domingo said. "Yes. Of course."

Obligation was only part of his reasoning. In all the years since their departure, Neto had never expressed a desire to return. Until now. Though his father was allergic to sentimentality, ever the pragmatist, Domingo wondered if he might be part of the calculation, the prodigal son returning with his own son. Together, they'd travel back, tearing the past open along the flight path, waiting to see what might seep to the surface to fill the gash. Domingo hoped for something less painful than blood.

Archive of Unknown Universes

Ernesto: I'm coming to San Salvador. With my son and his girl-friend.

Rafael: Domingo?

Ernesto: Him and his girlfriend. She's doing research for a thesis. She's interested in speaking to some of us, those involved in the strug-gle. Not me, but I might introduce her to others. If they're willing to do a favor for me, all these years later.

Rafael: He's at Harvard?

Ernesto: They both are. They graduate next year.

Rafael: What pride. Will I be able to see you?

Ernesto: We have a busy itinerary. It's only a two-week trip.

Rafael: Make some time for me. We deserve to reconnect, even if briefly.

Ernesto: It's been so long. Will any amount of time be enough for us?

Rafael: Any time together would be precious to me. Even just ten minutes. Don't you feel the same? . . .

Rafael: Hello? Neto.

1980

Rafael rings the buzzer on the wrought iron gate guarding the turquoise safe house. He waits for a minute before pressing again. There's no movement inside the house, so he panics. His finger hits the button again, over and over, furiously. He's come all this way to visit the only person he trusts fully, only to find out that he's gone missing. Now, the door won't even open.

"Damn, Rafael," Anabel says from the doorway. "Do you not have an ounce of patience?"

As he walks through the now-open gate, he stares down Anabel, trying to figure out if the annoyance streaked across her face is at the incessant ringing or if it's because she judges him like so many others do.

"You can't blame me for being anxious," Rafael says.

"When you're on edge all the time, the bluff becomes almost invisible," Anabel says. "I don't mean to trivialize what you must be going through. What we're going through. Neto's disappearance has affected us all deeply."

Rafael hasn't told anyone that he'd come to El Salvador to surprise Neto. The pretense, for anyone who doesn't know his and Neto's secret, is that the guerrillas will take any help they can—especially from those involved in the successful revolution in Nicaragua a few months prior. It's enough of an explanation to quell questions that might reveal more than Rafael is comfortable with.

"Can I speak with his sister? Esperanza?"

"We've been unable to track her down."

"If the government can find them, surely you can too."

Anabel stares at Rafael, and again he wonders if she is frustrated at the whole situation or if her solemn stares are directed at him specifically. It's an unfair thought. When he tracked her down, unable to locate Neto, she welcomed him without question. She told him what they knew, which wasn't much, and insisted he drop by the safe house. Still, worry lingers over Rafael's shoulder.

"Esperanza and the girl left for Nicaragua," Anabel explains. "But from what we can tell, they never made it. I talked to her once, days ago, but it's been radio silence since. Neto had sorted out the details before . . ."

"I get it," Rafael says. "Can I see his office, at least?"

Anabel nods and guides him toward a bedroom in the back of the house. Rafael steps inside and his eyes automatically land on the large, sturdy mahogany desk dressed in intricate flowery molding. In his gut, he knows. This is where Neto writes his letters.

Months ago, during a rough patch, the letters had trickled to a near stop. When Rafael and Neto lay together in bed, they could ignore the pressing weight of the world against them. With their fingers interlocked, or Rafael's tongue on his skin, both men could ignore the fact that their governments hated them. Pressed into one another, it didn't matter that the revolutionary governments they risked everything for would also treat their love as a disease to be weeded out.

When Rafael and Neto were no longer standing face-to-face, though, ugly, inconvenient fears seeped into the relationship. Neto had mentioned a couple women, some of whom gave him the kinds of looks Rafael did. It wasn't that Neto didn't love Rafael, but they both knew that one day, if things got difficult, he could choose a wife, torpedoing what they'd built together.

Worst of all, Neto could only admit his turmoil in snippets, glances he managed to squeeze into some of his letters. Rafael felt the storm bubbling behind his facade, until it came crashing down at random moments. Neto put distance between them, acting uninterested in his lover, as if nothing had ever transpired. Rafael was like any other comrade to Neto. It scared him, hurt him.

And then there'd been the big argument during Rafael's last trip to San Salvador. Afterward, back in Managua, Rafael opened his mailbox as usual, but the sight of a letter from Neto—in the unmistakable cream envelope every single one came in—sent a dull pang through him. Joy, which had accompanied letters before the trip, was missing. He slammed the aluminum door shut, leaving the letter unopened. Maybe I'm being cruel, he thought, but so was Neto. He'd gone all the way to see him, and Neto had been unkind, though he wouldn't admit it.

Another letter arrived two days later. The numbness had given way to anger, so Rafael stomped inside and went straight to his kitchen. He turned his oven up high and threw both let-

Archive of Unknown Universes

ters inside. Even when the acrid smell of burning paper made it to the living room, Rafael stayed put. He wanted the words to burn, so that he'd never have to hear the sorry excuses Neto had concocted. A dark pile of ash waterfalled down through the oven racks. The smell stuck around for days, an unintended reminder of the ways he'd been hurt.

At the third letter, Rafael almost did the same. He imagined himself burning it with a match or taking a taxi down to the lake so he could submerge it in its turquoise waters. As he held it, he wondered how the paper would feel in his hands as he ripped it into a million pieces; too small to read, too small to reconstruct. Instead, he took the letter inside and opened it. Neto offered an extended, desperate, apologetic explanation of the whole situation, confessing why he'd hidden Rafael away from the other people he loved for so long. He'd failed to stand up for Rafael, too easily accepting Esperanza's disdain. He'd been cold, intentionally. Neto was scared by the unshakable feeling that he and Rafael would never be able to establish the sort of life they wanted—no matter which way the war shifted. It was more honest than he'd ever been, and with Neto's fears out in the open, Rafael wondered if ignoring his first two letters had been petty and mean. He wished he hadn't burned the letters—now gone forever. He pulled out a pen and scribbled a response, as quickly as he could, before translating it into their secret code. Then, he began to plan his trip. It'd be a surprise, an apology, an opportunity to move forward.

Standing by the desk now, Rafael pictures how Neto would look hunched over, deep in the throes of a project. He's never seen him work, but he can imagine it perfectly. Neto's shoulders are loose, sagging down toward the desk, where his fingers flurry to sketch, fold, and paste whatever document sits there. Rafael stands behind this invisible, phantom version of his lover and watches him work. Conjuring the man—his warm eyes, his long messy beard, his limber fingers—sends a pang through Rafael's gut. For a split second, he considers the possibility that Neto is dead. It'd be easier to accept that, return to Managua, and attempt to move forward. But despite all the forces that threaten to collapse their relationship, the love he holds for Neto rings in his brain, telling Rafael that he needs to find his boyfriend. He needs to figure out what's happened to him.

Rafael slowly picks up a pen from the desk and cradles it in his hand. It's cold. He wishes it burned with the remnants of Neto's body heat. A small pile of scraps sits on the top right-hand corner of the desk, and Rafael sifts through it as if the cut-up paper will offer some clues as to what the government has done with Neto. There are snippets of photographs, shipping forms, newspapers, handwritten notes, and card stock. Bits and pieces that Neto refashioned into new life now lay abandoned, their maker untraceable.

The desk drawers are slightly open, as if Neto tried pushing them close but didn't apply enough pressure. Rafael pulls at the rusty copper handle and reveals stacks of paper. Most are blank. Some sheets are lined with faint blue ink. Others are wide expanses of stark white. A couple of envelopes are in there too, though they don't contain Neto's work. He recognizes his own handwriting on them. They're some of the letters he's written over the past few years. Rafael doesn't have to open them to remember what he wrote. The words are all etched in his memory.

He rifles through the rest of the drawer, discovering lost pencils and sheets of stamps, until finally he finds a paper with writing on it. Immediately, he recognizes the exaggerated, looping script as Neto's. Esperanza and Elena have left for Managua and should be there in no more than three days. Neto knows his sister has not been kind about their relationship, but still, he hopes Rafael will keep an eye on them. It's only a couple of lines long, but Rafael reads them over and over. It's not in their secret code of numbers and colons. Neto never finished the letter.

Though the correspondence is about Neto's guilt, and about his worry for his family, it's also about Rafael. He'd been thinking of him, considered him capable of protecting those he loved. Even though he and Esperanza had been on rocky terms, Neto wanted her and Elena to be safe. There were a number of other contacts he had in Managua, but he'd wanted Rafael to guard them when they finally arrived.

Rafael sits on the chair where Neto had sat. He tries his hardest not to cry. If Anabel walks back into the room and finds him in a puddle of his own tears—his cheeks puffy and eyes gone red—she'll think her assumptions about him correct. Rafael has no qualms about crying, just as he has no qualms about his sexuality. He loves Neto, and that's enough for him. He doesn't question his feelings or wallow in shame. That is Neto's particular burden. But Rafael also knows the way people view men like him, and though he has no hang-ups, he doesn't want Anabel to walk in and blame his sadness, his despair, on the sheer unchangeable fact of who he loves. Anabel isn't necessarily malicious, but Rafael doesn't want to confirm her narrow views, so he wills himself to regain his composure. His palms grip his knees, tight, as if enough pressure against his own body will stop the tears.

"Find anything helpful?" Anabel asks.

"No," Rafael says. He's pocketed Neto's fragment, along with the letters he wrote Neto.

"There's no reason to be certain he's dead," Anabel says. "If the death squads or the National Guard kill, they dump the bodies almost immediately. At Puerta del Diablo or on the roadside. We haven't found a body that matches his description yet."

Rafael's stomach turns. He's seen bullet holes in heads, skin charred by explosives. Imagining Neto like that makes him feel sick. He has to be alive.

"He must be in a holding cell somewhere," Rafael says. "Can't we just check with the closest precincts?"

"There won't be an official trace," Anabel says. "Public pressure would be the best way of getting answers, but he doesn't have family left in the country to plea for information."

"I could pretend to be family."

"That could get messy."

"We have to do something," Rafael says. His sadness and frustration crest into anger. He purses his lips tight.

"His family is still the best bet. If you help us track them down, they can make a public statement."

"Esperanza isn't my biggest fan."

A silence sits between them, and Rafael doesn't know how to breach it. He wants to ask Anabel about the last moments she spent with Neto, what they talked about after he revealed the truth about him and Rafael. He wants to know where they left things, and whether she'd agreed to house Rafael in San Salvador out of guilt. Instead, he asks a question that touches his real concerns, hoping that Anabel will go there.

"If we find him, do you think he'll stay and help you build the government?"

"That's a question for him to answer. Neto's had his doubts from the beginning. He wants better for this country, definitely."

"Will it give him what he really wants?"

"I don't know, Rafael. Will the Sandinistas give you what you want?"

Rafael doesn't know, but until he has a clearer idea of Neto's fate, it doesn't feel like a question worth answering. It's ironic, how talk of the future is what distanced them a few months prior. Now, the question isn't about what the future will look like, but whether they'll have one at all.

Anabel lugs a thin mattress into the room and places a pile of neatly folded sheets on it. It'll be Rafael's room for as long as he's in the country. They make a game plan. Rafael will call his contacts and figure out who Neto had asked for help getting his family to safety. Anabel will contact guerrilleros in other parts of the country, and some incognito colleagues abroad, to see if they've heard anything. Anabel says good night, and Rafael feels for the first time that they're both invested in finding the man who's brought them together.

Before he's lulled into sleep, Rafael remembers a moment he and Neto shared two years ago. It's vivid in his memory but infused with details that Neto wrote down in a letter after the fact. It's a night in Havana, and they sit against the rough concrete of the Malecón. The sea breeze smells of brine. Neto's hand is light and tender in his. There's music playing, and stars splay endlessly above them. He stares into Neto's eyes and feels a full body swell of emotion, the kind that would be terrifying were it less euphoric and all-encompassing. The nostalgia is heavy, intense. The only version of Cuba he knows is one with Neto in it.

When I find him, we'll go back to Havana, Rafael thinks to himself. We'll be unafraid as the shore sings to us, as I hold his fingers in mine.

Men in uniform struck fear in Esperanza long before they broke into her home. Police stood on street corners and strolled through the open-air markets, their stride gallant and assured. Bulky helmets topped their heads. Guns hung from their shoulders. Esperanza feared them because she knew what they did when they were off shift. They donned canvas pants and earth-tone shirts—a looser, more casual uniform—as they went across the country, showing the white of their teeth as they killed.

These men, who together will be known as the death squads, are not frightening for their lawlessness. They kill and kidnap knowing the state will shield them. They storm the streets, break into houses, and stack bodies in truck beds, knowing they'll be safe. Their evil thrives because they know the law will bend to their will, crushed underneath heavy black boots.

When Esperanza arrives at the refugee camp in Honduras, she avoids the men in uniform. Their outfits are more like those of doctors, two-piece sets made of shapeless, lightweight material. They've patched a medical cross over their hearts, signaling their place in the ecosystem of the displaced. The insignia implies they come in peace, but the stitched red crucifix still unnerves Esperanza. She walks as far from them as she can.

The camp was originally set up by Mennonite missionaries who've been running local churches in the area for years. The day they arrive, Elena pulls on her mother's maxi skirt and asks if the women—dressed in head-to-toe cotton dresses—are hot. Esperanza doesn't know. A relief worker, sent by the United Nations to aid the Mennonites' efforts, directs newcomers to their lodgings. Esperanza pushes Elena toward the warehouse-like building they'll be sharing with a dozen other refugees.

Elena hasn't slept well in days. When their contact hadn't met them at the rendezvous point—because they'd missed each other or for a more sinister reason—Esperanza and Elena stayed at the cheapest motels they could find near the Salvadoran-Honduran border. The rooms were scorching hot, and Elena found a scorpion in her shoe when she'd woken up. Esperanza called Neto daily, first trying their home's landline, and eventually using the number he'd given her for absolute emergencies. No one picked up at either for a few days, until finally she heard breathing at the other end of the line.

"Hello? Neto?"

"Who is this?" a woman's breathy voice asked. Esperanza explained that her brother had given her the number. The no-show was supposed to bring them money Neto had sent him. They were in Santa Clarita, nearly empty-handed.

"Now I'm stranded here with my daughter, with only the bit of cash I brought."

"We haven't heard from Neto," Anabel explained. "One of his friends saw him head to the store a couple days ago, but no one's heard from him since."

Elena cried, asking her mother to take her home, but hearing from Neto's "friends," who Esperanza knew were much more volatile than they let on, cemented that returning wasn't a possibility. If Neto called to say it was safe to return to Santa Tecla, she might. But in the moment, she and Elena had no choice but to soldier ahead, away from the scorching motel room. They crossed the Lempa and ended up in the camp.

Within a few days, Elena prefers the camp to the small-town motel room, a fact that brings her mother peace. A church serves as the camp's nucleus, and shoddy sleeping structures emanate out from it. Between the pop-up structures, children run around freely, chasing each other, interrupted only by the occasional truck driving through with supplies.

The Mennonites and relief workers build a schedule for the women and children, who account for most of the refugees. The children have informal schooling sessions where they learn psalms, draw pictures of the camp, and work on basic reading skills. The women, and interested men, are offered cobbling and sewing workshops. Esperanza doesn't care much for either, but with nothing else to occupy her, she drops into a couple shoemaking sessions. A routine will distract her from the fact that she and her daughter are stuck in limbo.

Two weeks pass, uneventfully, before a relief worker catches up to Esperanza as she leaves class. She'd learned how to stitch together a sole. He approaches her, and when she doesn't respond to his slick English, he switches into clunky Spanish.

"Do you need any toothpaste?" he asks. It's an odd question. Usually, a Mennonite preacher or aid worker hands things out to large crowds until the piles run dry. From his backpack, the man pulls out a tube and hands it to her.

"What's your name?" he asks. Esperanza tells him, rubbing the dust from the corner of her eye. The camp is dry and dusty. There is often a thin layer of grime on her. They stand in the middle of a dirt pathway, the afternoon sun blazing. Sweat pools on the back of her neck and above her eyebrows.

"I hope you don't mind me saying this," the man continues, "but you're beautiful. How old are you?" He doesn't make a move toward her, but Esperanza can't help but focus on how tall the man is. His shoulders are broad. He blocks the width of the path.

"My daughter is waiting for me," she says, trying to walk past him. She scoots by his shoulder, and though he doesn't make an effort to stop her, she hears his steps behind her. He's trailing her, even as she hurries her stride.

"Is there anything your daughter needs?" he asks. "Supplies, medicine, food? Anything I could try getting her?"

Esperanza considers making a run for it, turning her trot into a full sprint, when she notices a man in a dark military uniform several feet away. He stands close to where the tin and tarp structures end, the unofficial edge of the camp. The soldier paces back and forth, stopping periodically to sway on his heels, but never moves forward, as if there is an invisible barrier in his way. Esperanza has seen Honduran soldiers before, but this is the first time she feels gratitude.

"He wants to talk," Esperanza says, pointing to the soldier. The relief worker turns and lets out a groan.

"Another one? Ridiculous." The man deviates from the path, whistling to grab the soldier's attention. Honduran soldiers aren't happy with the relief efforts, and they often patrol the edges of the camp, claiming they're keeping an eye out for guerrilleros fleeing El Salvador. A few feet away, the relief worker checks to see if Esperanza has moved. She hasn't, but as soon as he begins speaking to the soldier, she runs to find her daughter.

When Elena approaches, she's holding sheets of papers. Wielding them in front of her like a shield, she laughs and begins explaining the drawings to her mother. The tall stick figure in the center is Esperanza, and the smaller ones are Elena and the friends she's made at the camp. Their sleeping quarters and the dirt paths that snake around the camp are sketched in blocky lines of crayon.

"Who's this?" Esperanza asks. There are two smaller figures in the corner of Elena's picture. As soon as she asks the question, though, she knows the answer. They're in uniform. Her daughter has drawn a relief worker and a Honduran soldier. A bright-red cross burns on one's chest. Though they're scrawled in crayon, the sketches horrify her.

Each morning, Esperanza tries to get ahold of Neto. She strolls into the church, past the pews, and into a holding room behind the altar. She dials twice a day, without luck. The longer Neto's silence becomes, the more Esperanza regrets everything left unsaid between them.

Sitting in a pew after another failed call, she parses out the last truly good memories they'd made together. There are a few from the past two years—Neto celebrating Esperanza's birthday by baking a cake, a trip to Costa del Sol, where they ate marisco and sipped pilsners. But the moments she keeps returning to are arguments, hashed out in harsh words. As she sits and tries speaking to God, Esperanza can't forget the ways she and her brother disagreed. Neto never picks up the phone, and Esperanza replays memories that might explain why he's abandoned her.

Despite the discomfort she felt when the man offered her the toothpaste, Esperanza figures the camp is still their best option. Elena is happy, nearly as happy as she'd been in Santa Tecla. Esperanza doesn't want to have to uproot her again. She spots the man again, but he doesn't approach or single her out. The most he's done is wave, and though that could change, it doesn't seem a risk worth leaving over. Esperanza begins to imagine a life at the camp, a prolonged one. She'll wait there until Neto reaches out. The guerrilleros might even be successful. She'll be able to return on the winning side of a war.

It is not a perfect life, and nothing like the home they abandoned. Refugees who've been there longer than Esperanza and Elena whisper. There are weeks when resources are scarce while more donations are acquired. Honduran soldiers don't always respect the boundaries and sometimes sneak into the camp to rustle up trouble or interrogate refugees. Still,

Esperanza hasn't witnessed those perils, and Elena is finding her footing, so they decide to stay.

Elena makes a best friend. The two girls run around the camp, parroting songs they learn at school. Both have light, springy voices, though subtly different. Elena sings in a higher register, more in tune than her new friend. The other girl channels energy into her voice, and even though she's a bit flat, it's enjoyable in the way only children's singing can be. Esperanza encourages them, reviving lullabies she hasn't sung since Elena was an infant.

Pin Pon es un muñeco muy guapo y de cartón
Se lava la carita con agua y con jabón
Pin Pon se peina el pelo con peine de marfil
Pin Pon dame la mano
Que quiero ser tu amigo
Pin Pon
Pin Pon
Pin Pon

After an afternoon of lacing the holes of leather shoes, Esperanza hears her daughter and her best friend singing. It's strange, since the girls usually wait to be picked up outside the makeshift schoolhouse. The shoemaking class isn't over, but Esperanza steps outside to follow their song.

"Mami!" Elena rushes toward her mother and hugs her waist. Their melodies cut off suddenly, like a needle lifted from a record.

"They're bringing fruit!" Elena says. "Tons of bananas. Our teacher said so."

She grabs Esperanza by the hand and offers her other palm to her friend. Together, they walk to see if the workers have returned with snacks for them, as promised.

"Teacher said they'd be here," Elena's best friend says once they arrive at the lot of weedy dirt where the vehicles usually park. It's empty, save for a van that's used for medical emergencies that can't be mended on site.

"We'll wait," Esperanza says. Fifteen minutes later, a worker arrives to wait with them.

"They should be back soon," she says. She's the only female relief worker Esperanza has seen around the camp, and therefore the only white woman who doesn't dress in Mennonite garb. She squats on her haunches to talk to the girls, asking their names and ages.

A truck rumbles through a cloud of dust, stopping near where Esperanza and the girls stand. By now, word of the delivery has gotten around. A small, expectant crowd forms. The children clap, furious and eager, when they notice the load of fruit. The driver jumps into the truck bed, careful not to crush the food. Two men approach to help him unload it. One bunch at a time, many the size of an infant, they gently lower the bananas onto the dirt. The pile grows—as if there were an endless, regenerating supply—until the pile is taller than most of the children who run around. At its peak, the mound is at eye level.

There's no order by which to distribute the fruit, but the refugees avoid chaos. Patiently, they approach and grab fruit, making room for those who've yet to take of the bounty.

"Take only one at a time," Esperanza tells the girls, reaching for a single banana herself. Peeling it from the bottom, she takes a bite. The fruit is soft and sweet on her tongue. Hot sun on her skin, Esperanza sits as her daughter rushes to the other side of the pile in search of the perfect second banana.

"That's strange," the UN worker says. She puts a hand over her eyes to shield them from the sun and get a better view of the vehicle they hear approaching. "The others were going to Tegucigalpa. There's no way they've returned already."

A forest-green military jeep roars toward them. Esperanza steps back, worried it won't stop. Doors slam as soldiers jump out, guns in hand, shouting and pointing the barrels toward the refugees. One of the men who helped unload the fruit approaches the soldiers to ask what they need. He's met with the blunt metal of a gun and falls to the ground. Curses ring out as he covers his bloodied nose with his fingers.

"Girls!" Esperanza shouts. "Girls!"

Gasps mingle with shouts. Some refugees run away, dropping half-eaten fruit in their wake. The soldiers shoot at the ground, sending clumps of dirt and grass bursting into the air. The UN worker cowers to the ground, and some women follow, cupping their arms around their heads. In the commotion, Esperanza loses sight of her daughter.

"Girls!" she yells. "Elena!"

She sees Elena's friend, and watches the girl run toward her, tears in her eyes. She's crushed a banana in her hand. Whitish-yellow mush covers her twig-thin fingers. And then, as she reaches out and grips the girl's sticky hand, Esperanza makes out her daughter's flushed cheeks a short distance away.

Elena stands next to a soldier who is handcuffing the man with the bloodied face. He resists, flailing like a trapped animal. In the struggle, the soldier's elbow digs into the back of Elena's head, knocking her to the ground. Thrown off-balance, he steps backward and stomps a heavy boot on her calf. The girl cries out in pain.

Esperanza runs toward her daughter and scoops her up, yelling expletives at the soldier. He shouts back, his face scrunched. He's young, about her brother's age, but he's already begun to wrinkle, his forehead creased in anger. He leads the handcuffed man back to the jeep. Another soldier pulls the female relief worker up from the ground. Hands bound behind her back, she yells, asking why they're being arrested.

"Got intel that you're aiding subversives," the soldier says, pushing her into the car. "There are guerrilla soldiers hiding in this camp."

The Honduran soldiers search the camp for subversives and end up arresting one more person: a Salvadoran man from San Miguel who won't stop cursing at them. When the jeep drives away, tailed by the driver who brought the bananas, Esperanza and the girls sit in a huddle. They've stopped crying, but their whimpers continue. Esperanza forces soothing sounds from her lips, for their sake. *Pin pon es un muñeco*, she sings, *muy guapo y de cartón*. The pile of fruit has been flattened in the raid. Bananas are aimlessly scattered. Most lay split open, crushed and covered in dirt. Inedible, sullied guts and peels surround the women.

The camp is no haven, and Esperanza knows that Neto won't call anytime soon. A war is coming. She'll have to seek refuge farther north, in the land that proclaims itself truly free. They'll leave in the morning, under the shadows of dawn, in silence. No singing for the displaced.

2018

The problem with death, Ana mulled over, is that one must continue with their day when it comes knocking. Luis woke her up before dawn, asking her to read the message from his mother to ensure he hadn't misunderstood.

He hadn't. His grandmother, Esperanza, had died. The funeral would be in a week. Ana hugged him, the most genuine sign of affection she'd shown in weeks.

The news almost distracted her from the unnecessarily rough sex they'd had. When Luis had leaned in to kiss her, she'd been surprised, but quickly gave herself over. They were finally circling something real. His lips were softer than she remembered, a familiar comfort. When his hands began to wander, Ana felt crushed by his weight, her body claustrophobic under his. The shift was subtle but undeniable. The brief thrill of nostalgia had passed.

She turned away from him, bit him hard, and still he continued. There'd been a point in their relationship when he would have gotten the signal immediately. Last night, he hadn't. Or, Ana thought, her stomach turning, he'd ignored it.

• • •

A cabdriver was waiting for them downstairs. Their first night in Havana, when she still thought they'd be exploring the major sights together, Ana had arranged a tour of Fusterlandia, an artists' studio turned tourist attraction, for today.

"We don't have to go," she said.

"You should," Luis insisted. He'd booked a flight for the following morning. That was all he could do. "I need to pack."

Abandoning Luis in the throes of grief felt selfish, but staying would be unbearable. She'd look at his face and relive the way he'd towered over her, dripping sweat onto her cheek. Plus Fusterlandia was alluring. A travel blog called it "the Park Güell of the Tropics," and promised that any visitor would be breathless at the sight of hundreds of thousands of ceramic shards glittering under the sun.

Ana and Luis hadn't had a real conversation in weeks. Would grief really seal the fissure?

Prioritizing my needs isn't selfish, Ana thought, though she didn't fully believe it. She went to meet the driver.

The taxi zoomed down the Malecón. Somewhere beyond the waves, past the ocean fluttering like a tarp, the water shallowed out into the shores of Florida. As she stared out the window, Ana couldn't shut out the images of drowned Cubans somewhere on the ocean floor. Ana's own mother had been a refugee, but she'd traversed mountains and deserts. Water never threatened to swallow her. Images cycled through Ana's mind—rafts torn apart by an ocean storm, refugees succumbing to dehydration—tinting what would have been a beautiful view of the sea. It was as if the news of Esperanza's passing left room to consider nothing but the death of people forced from their homes.

Luis intended to pack, but couldn't shake the memory of the last time he'd seen his grandmother. Over the Christmas break, he'd gone to the assisted living facility with his mother. Elena complained that the employees didn't feed Esperanza enough, and when they both noticed that she'd soiled her diaper, the latest in the list of bodily functions she'd lost control of, she insisted on handling it herself.

"Call a nurse," Luis begged, but Elena instructed him to prop Esperanza up by the armpits. They all crammed into the small bathroom tiled in yellowed linoleum. Elena pulled down Esperanza's tights and undid her diaper. Luis gagged, holding his grandmother away from him, trying desperately not to drop her.

"Hurry and sit her down," Elena scolded.

Luis fled the stench and sight of his half-naked grandmother hunched on the toilet. Her brain had not grayed out as part of the grand circle of life, where one swaps sharpness of memory for sage wisdom. Esperanza was sick. It was a degenerative neurological disease; her brain cells were dying. She'd lost the ability to shower, to pay her bills, to eat. She'd forgotten her grandchild's name, and then her child's, and then her own, until eventually she could no longer speak at all. And now, she'd been stripped of the simple dignity of shitting in peace.

Luis hated that his brain had conjured such a grotesque memory. He wanted to feel love and adoration for his grandmother, to remember the years before her disease. Desperately, he desired another outcome, one where his grandmother had aged gracefully, had been able to tell him how proud she was of the life he'd built.

Wishing wasn't going to help, so he took the stairs two at a time, ran past the fruit vendor, and headed toward the university.

Alone under the shade of a monstrous ceiba tree, Luis stared at the wooden door across the atrium. The only time he'd walked Ana to the university, the morning after they'd arrived, he'd watched her disappear through the door, her stride strong and full of purpose. The excitement of being in a new place had drowned out his suspicion that the trip was a last-ditch attempt to save a relationship on the rocks.

Now, Luis slowly inched toward the door, not wanting to seem overeager. When it swung open, he slipped by the exiting stranger with a smile. Without hesitation, Luis turned left past a hall of offices, feigning confidence, searching aimlessly. A man rounded the corner. Luis felt incredibly conscious of his body, of his skin, his accent, what he'd say if the man asked why Luis was there. He reached for the closest knob, stepped inside, and shut the door behind him.

It was a tiny office, only slightly larger than a storage closet, with a desk and swivel chair. Luis didn't immediately recognize the two devices on the desk: a clunky fax machine and a black cube. Waiting out the man in the hallway, he approached the Defractor, identifying it by the shimmering obsidian gloss of its shell.

He picked it up. It was no heavier than his MacBook. Scrolling the internet without seeing an article about the

Defractor was impossible, so through bits of digital flotsam, Luis had learned the basics. It'd be easy to grab the two patches, bring them to his temple, and ask a question. *Was coming to Cuba with Ana the biggest mistake of my life? Why won't my mother tell me what happened to Neto?* Or maybe a plea: *Please, please, please show a less tragic version of my grandmother's life.*

Luis turned the patches over in his palm. What was he doing? He'd just reprimanded Ana. Everything happened in the way it was meant to, and the past was the only source to pull lessons from. The missteps you took, not the ones you might have avoided if you'd chosen a different path. His grandmother's death shouldn't shake his convictions loose like this.

Then again, he was skeptical of ayahuasca too but wouldn't rule it out until he'd tried it.

EL DEFRACTOR©, POR LO PRESENTE REFERIDO COMO "LA TECNOLOGÍA," ES PROPIEDAD INTELLECTUAL EXCLUSIVA DE DÍAZ MANUFACTURING LICENCIADA A LA UNIVERSIDAD DE HABANA, 2018. USUARIO ACEPTA USO DE LA TECNOLOGÍA PARA: INVESTIGACIÓN ACADÉMICA—HISTÓRICA. USO PERSONAL ES POSIBLE, CON PERMISO DE LA JUNTA ACADÉMICA APROPIADA. ACTIVIDADES CONTRA LA REVOLUCIÓN SON EXPRESAMENTE PROHIBIDAS. ¿ACEPTA ESTOS TÉRMINOS?

Sí.

INGRESE SUS CREDENCIALES.

> Inglés, por favor? Mi español es . . . not good.

OKAY. LANGUAGE SETTINGS UPDATED,
English. ENTER LOGIN CREDENTIALS.

> Guest?

HELLO, Guest. WHAT IS YOUR NAME?

> Luis Guzmán.

WELCOME, Luis Guzmán. GUEST ACCESS LIMITS
THE SCOPE OF INFORMATION I CAN RENDER.
YOUR DESIGNATED INTERLOCUTOR IS a Poet.
ROSES ARE RED, VIOLETS ARE BLUE, WHATEVER
YOU NEED, I CAN HELP YOU. WOULD YOU
LIKE YOUR ALTERNATE TIMELINES RENDERED
VISUALLY OR TEXTUALLY?

> Textually.

PLEASE PROVIDE A GUIDING QUESTION.

> Did my abuela have a peaceful death?

ONE SECOND. GENERATING OUTPUT

. . .

. . .

. . .

Archive of Unknown Universes

IN THE BEGINNING, THERE IS ASH AND BONES. A MASSACRE RAZES THE TOWN. MEN, WOMEN, AND CHILDREN MURDERED BY A ROW OF MEN WITH M-16 RIFLES, SMOKE RISING FROM THEIR BARRELS AS BODIES THUMP AGAINST THE DIRT. OVER EIGHT HUNDRED DEAD. DENIAL ON BOTH SIDES OF THE BORDER. THE SMELL OF CHARRED FLESH PEPPERING THE AIR, BUT NO ONE LEFT TO SMELL IT. A LITTERING OF BULLETS, THE CHARACTERS ON THEIR CIRCULAR BASES BETRAYING THEIR ORIGIN: LAKE CITY, MISSOURI. GRASS ON FIRE, A SMALL FLAME, HELL FLARING UP FROM THE EARTH.

THAT MORNING, AN OLD MAN HAD WOKEN UP TO KNOCKING ON HIS FRONT DOOR. A CRYING ALTAR BOY TOLD HIM THAT THE MILITARY MEN HAD PLANNED AN OFFENSIVE. TO GET RID OF ANY COMMUNISTS HIDING IN THIS TOWN, HE SAID.

MIJO, I'M NOT A COMMUNIST. THE OLD MAN LAUGHED. EVEN IF I WAS, I'M NOT GOING ANYWHERE. I WAS BORN IN THIS HOME. MY FATHER PUT MY UMBILICAL CORD UNDER THE FLOORBOARDS, AND IT REMAINS THERE TODAY. SO WILL I.

THE ALTAR BOY BEGGED HIM TO HEAD FOR THE HILLS, WHERE A GROUP OF VILLAGERS WERE PLANNING TO HIDE AMONG THE BRUSH, BUT THE OLD MAN REFUSED.

LET THEM COME, HE SAID.

AND THEY DID. THEY BURIED HIS HOME IN RUBBLE WITH THE OLD MAN STILL INSIDE. HE GOT NO BURIAL, AND IN THE END HIS REMAINS DECOMPOSED JUST A FEW INCHES FROM HIS UMBILICAL CORD. IN THE RUBBLE, THERE WAS A LIMB, BLACKENED AND POINTING OUT OF THE ASH. IT WAS THE OLD MAN'S INDEX FINGER OR HIS UMBILICAL CORD OR HIS PENIS. THE LAYER OF SINGED SKIN— DARK LIKE AN INFESTATION OF FLEAS OR TOXIC MOLD—MADE THE OLD MAN'S BODY UNKNOWABLE, UNIDENTIFIABLE.

HERE'S HOW THE STORY UNFOLDS IN ANOTHER SLIVER OF THE UNIVERSE. MOVE A FEW STEPS LEFT AND A FEW NODES UP ON THE SPACE-TIME CONTINUUM. HERE'S WHAT WE SEE THERE: A SHADOW OF FRIGHT CROSSES THE OLD MAN'S FACE AT THE BOY'S WORDS, AND HE FOLLOWS HIM OUT THE DOOR AND INTO THE HILLS. HIS JOINTS HURT, BUT HE CARRIES ON, FIGHTING THE URGE TO STOP AND CATCH HIS BREATH. THE OLD MAN LIVES. THE VILLAGE DOES NOT. THERE IS ASH AND BONES AGAIN. SMOKE SIMMERS. HE TRIES TO TELL THE STORY DECADES LATER, BUT THE WORDS ARE STUCK IN HIS THROAT.

LET'S DANCE AGAIN. A TWIRL-AND-A-HALF BRINGS US HERE: THE OLD MAN DOES NOT LISTEN, AND THE SOLDIERS DON'T COME.

Archive of Unknown Universes

> THE UMBILICAL CORD REMAINS UNDER THE FLOORBOARDS AND THE WAR RAGES ON WITHOUT THE MASSACRE. HE EATS HIS BREAKFAST, ALONE, IN PEACE.
>
> TWO-STEP, A HAND ON THE UNIVERSE'S HIP. THERE IS NO WAR, NO REVOLUTION. NO SMOKE OR ASH OR BONE.

> I'm sorry—what?

If Luis was searching for a sign, that should have been it. The machine was feeding him nonsense, teasing him, tempting him to find meaning where there was none. Pack it up, he told himself. Face your life, the way you pretend to. Because here was the truth: Luis did not confront reality as fully as he wanted to. He was excellent at compartmentalizing and making small, cosmetic changes to his life that didn't strengthen its foundation. If he avoided a problem long enough, he could pretend it didn't exist.

> Render visually, please.

The machine whirred loudly until it showed six universes. In three of them, he stood in the same spot wearing different outfits, which was disappointing, though it made complete sense. This life was the only one that really mattered, regardless of what T-shirt he'd pulled out of his luggage.

Esperanza's face filled a frame, so Luis scrolled over and zoomed in. The close-up was as he remembered her. Thin, her eyes clouded over slightly, unable to focus on one spot for long. Alive, yes, but unwell.

He scanned through the universes until he found one where he stood next to Ana. Did his hand on her waist mean he was braver in that universe? She had her back turned to him in another, a sign of tension, surely. Was it temporary or a permanent fixture of their relationship? Conflict is a healthy part of any adult relationship, he thought. In another corner of the screen, he was wearing sunglasses indoors, which couldn't be a positive sign. He decided to restart from the beginning, searching for details he might have missed.

Mid-rewind, he spotted a stack of letters on the kitchen island in the apartment in Havana. He didn't know how or why this alternate self managed to share old family secrets so openly, but he had. The letters were Tío Neto's, and he was reading them with Ana by his side.

He shut the Defractor down and worked his way back outside. Rushed by the humidity, he remembered that he was not stateside, in a random academic building, but thousands of miles away from any city he'd lived in, in a country that was not his own. And he was jealous of his other lives. Here, he floated aimlessly, saying "yes" and "sure" and "okay," while keeping quiet about what mattered. Elsewhere, he was a person with a plan, who knew his past and had the guts to confront it, convincing Esperanza to hand over the letters. With someone he loved, to top it all off.

The appeal of the Defractor was no longer abstract. It didn't matter whether the device showed anything real or applicable. The very act of using it was soothing. A power trip, knowledge flowing to Luis's brain. Armed with it, he walked home, and then set himself down on the couch in the living room, one eye on the door.

Had he been too hard on Ana? Anyone would have reached for the respite, a bit of clarity with which to shield oneself against life's entropy.

Luis poured himself a rum and Coke, then a second, then a third. The soft noise of a key turning drew his gaze. As Ana walked through the door, Luis prepared to say what he'd been convincing himself of all afternoon: Everything is going to be okay because I watched us, in another time but in this very same place. They survived, and so will we.

Instead, he avoided her eyes and said what he felt inside: "Let's go to the Malecón. I want to see the ocean."

On the drive back from Fusterlandia, Ana found herself thinking of her mother. When someone dies, they take all their secrets with them. Their shames and fears, their regrets and unfulfilled wishes. All of it went into the dirt to feed the flowers. Perhaps that's why her mother was so worried all the time: she knew Ana could die, unexpectedly. Secrets didn't flow freely between them, but as long as they both lived, there was the chance the dam might open someday.

Luis's suggestion took her by surprise, but after a quick drink, she agreed to go to the Malecón. They could have walked, but he had a particular spot in mind, a busy stretch of concrete he'd seen earlier in the week.

They found a driver who wasn't trying to overcharge them, and they jumped into his back seat. Ana quietly worried that it was rude to leave the passenger seat empty, but she was tired, and her brain was hazy, so she leaned back against the window and watched as Havana passed in a blur.

"How was it?" Luis asked.

"Beautiful. Unlike anywhere I've ever been," Ana said. I wish you could have seen it, she thought. They drove along the highway picking up speed. The windows were dirty, and the streetlights blurred through them, streaking red and white. Coupled with the ocean, the sight was quite beautiful, impressive even.

"Everyone deserves to see this place," Luis said. Another point of connection that now felt less powerful than it once had: Luis and Ana grew up aware of how flimsy borders were. Leaving a place didn't make it disappear—it haunted, calling their mothers back. Is this what he was considering now? The injustice that entire countries were corralled off for nothing more than the sake of cruelty? An embargo, a border, an excuse to deprive others of beauty. Or was he thinking of his grandmother, and how complete her crossing was? She'd never been to Cuba and never would.

The car went quiet. Ana felt Luis's palm on her thigh. It lingered there, the full weight of his hand pressing into her. He didn't swirl his thumb in a small circle like he used to, sending a prickly but welcome chill into her. His hand just lay there like a dead bird. It might have been an accident. He was drunk and could've let his hand fall down toward the seat, expecting to hit the pleather but landing on her instead. There was so much space between them, though, so to frame it as an accident would be to absolve Luis of the transgression. It felt wrong, like the evening before had. She'd allowed herself to kiss him, thinking everything was as it used to be, before realizing she no longer desired the feeling of his dick inside her, something he should have realized on his own.

The place where he'd placed his hand felt hot. Scorching, not romantic. Ana tensed up, ready to pit the whole weight of her body against him if his hand moved. After a drawn-out minute, Luis stopped touching her. She could feel where his hand had been, a phantom mass that left goose bumps on her thigh.

The driver pulled over, letting them out. She turned to Luis. He'd been staring at her. His eyes were not fiery with playfulness or bleary with joy the way they sometimes got when he'd been drinking. They were glassy orbs, his brown pupils dark as the evening. He stared at her but said nothing. Ana sustained eye contact, resisting the urge to turn away.

People were still walking on the sidewalk. A few feet away, a group of young men played music from a speaker and passed around a handle of rum. Luis hoisted himself onto the concrete barrier and hung his legs over the edge. The ocean waves lapped at him, splashing against the rocks several feet below. Ana joined, refusing to look down at the water, but aware of it reaching up to touch her. The sound of the ocean against the concrete was rhythmic, a lullaby harmonizing with the men's music a few feet away.

"This city is incredible," Luis said. "Our apartment is unbelievable. I sat on the balcony yesterday at sunset, and just listened. There was a little bit of music, a conversation I couldn't make out somewhere far away."

The city was undeniable. Ana still marveled at it, weeks after arriving. Fruit was sweeter than any she'd had before.

Buildings stood strong despite their peeling paint. Her research had brought her to Cuba, but if she was honest, the real appeal was the prospect of exploring a new, unfamiliar place. Travel still felt luxurious, a pastime for her classmates or pop stars with too much time on their hands, but it suited her.

"I feel so lucky to be here," Ana said, wondering if he felt similarly. Or did he wish he'd come with anyone else? His eyes, glazed and wild, didn't give anything away. He spoke again, louder and more reckless.

"Why did you ask me to come?"

"I wanted you here," Ana lied.

"We're in fucking Cuba, and it should be beautiful and peaceful, but our relationship is done."

"You admit it, then?"

"Jesus, Ana. We've been done for weeks, and you know it."

"But you haven't said it."

"Neither have you."

Silence set in. Luis closed his eyes. The waves crashed again, and Ana wondered if the noise was getting louder and louder.

"It's hard to say that out loud—that we're done," Luis said.

Part of her wanted to disagree, but she couldn't. It was the most honest thing Luis had said in months, and it rang true, as if the words had slipped out of her own lips.

"I didn't want to face it," Luis said. "That whoever I was when I was with you will no longer exist. I'll have to learn to be okay alone."

"How long have you felt this way?"

Archive of Unknown Universes

"It was gradual, but I can't avoid it any longer. It feels like the deepest, most fundamental parts of myself don't fit with yours. Don't you feel that?"

She did.

"We'll have to make a clean cut, eventually," Ana said.

"When I leave tomorrow, we can."

"Will you remember this?"

"I'm not that drunk."

A long silence sat between them. Luis hadn't apologized for putting his hand on her thigh or shutting her out or being inattentive to his own shortcomings. Ana felt overwhelmed, not only because the relationship was over, but because she was immediately forced to confront the aftermath. Discussing logistics as if their relationship were a business meeting or budgetary plan hurt.

"I'm sorry about your abuela," Ana finally said.

"We knew it was coming. I just can't believe it happened while I'm so far away."

"She had a long life. A happy life."

"I don't know if that's true. Her only sibling died young. She was never able to go back to El Salvador, though I know she wanted to. Her daughter didn't have an easy life. And then she forgot it all. Spent the last few years half alive. I don't know that she was happy."

"People find joy among all the difficult parts of life."

"I'll never know if she did."

"My mother is so scared of the world," Ana said. "But it must bring her some level of happiness. Or peace, at least. She wouldn't pick misery."

"It's not a choice for some people," Luis said.

Felicia had seen unspeakable things, horrors she refused to tell Ana about. It was possible those events dictated everything. More than choice, more than desire.

"I used a Defractor," Luis said suddenly. After saying it, he let out a laugh. He laughed and laughed. He looked genuinely happy—not just drunk happy—as if he'd broken free of the spell of sadness that had tinted the evening. Ana smiled, briefly, grateful for the release valve.

"Hypocrite," Ana whispered. Luis nodded, but didn't apologize for giving her such a hard time for using one.

"I snuck into the university today," he said. "And there it was. I looked into it."

"Did you see anything good?" Ana's question came out as a whisper.

"Letters," Luis said. "From Abuela's brother. Neto. That was his name. We had them, here in Havana with us, but I don't know why. See? That should have some grand meaning, but I'm drawing a blank," Luis said, somber again.

Ana turned away from Luis and toward the sea, the deep dark expanse blanketing everything. She imagined that if she were an astronaut, staring out at the ever-expanding void in front of her, it'd look exactly like this.

"We made it in another universe, Luis. And there, we leave Cuba and go back to Cambridge, and stay in love, and get married, and all that."

"And there's a universe where that all happens, and then we get divorced," Luis said. "This universe is the only one that matters. Everything else is theoretical."

The moon was bright in the sky, even this late at night. The young men with the boom box left, so that the only sounds were Luis's breathing and the waves lapping against the barrier. No cars passed. Ana stared up at the sky. A handful of stars were visible, even with the glow of the lampposts spanning the highway. The majority had died already, but still shone against her irises, billions of light-years away.

The morning after, Luis walked into the kitchen, poured two glasses of water, and left one on the countertop for Ana. He didn't regret what he'd said. As he'd said it, he had the sinking feeling that his words were inadequate. But at least they were verbalized, making them as real as the waves splashing against the concrete.

He hadn't wanted to end the relationship, not really. The alternative was enticing: stumbling through more unhappiness, but with a person he loved, someone who understood him, who made the hours pass by. But no. That would just prolong the grief.

When Ana finally woke up, Luis was nursing his third glass. She opened the slatted double doors that opened to the balcony. Luis studied the back of her head as she watched the street, already bustling with life.

"Can I see the Bible?" Luis called out to her from across the room. He wasn't sure if she heard him but didn't want to walk over and interrupt her solitude.

"The Defractor made me think it was the most important thing I'd discovered all summer," Ana said, handing the Bible over. "That's a kind of madness, isn't it?"

Luis nodded. He held the Bible gently, seeing that its edges were already fraying. Among all the precious, shiny things laid out for tourists in Old Havana, why had their alternate selves searched for the book? He flipped through the thin, papery pages until he landed at a random spot in the Book of Matthew. He recognized phrases he'd heard often during his years in the church.

And seeing the multitudes, he went up into a mountain: and when he was set, his disciples came unto him: And he opened his mouth, and taught them saying, Blessed are the poor in spirit: for theirs is the kingdom of heaven. Blessed are they that mourn: for they shall be comforted.

Luis repeated the line to himself: *Blessed are they that mourn: for they shall be comforted.* It was a simple sentiment, and like all the Beatitudes, it offered an easy answer to suffering. It had never convinced Luis. If one spent a whole life—full of death, poverty, pain—simply awaiting a promised future, was that even a life? Living for posthumous salvation didn't feel like freedom at all. But still, as he read the sentence— *for they shall be comforted*—Luis willed it to be true, for his grandmother's sake.

He scanned the rest of the page, eyes floating to the dust-size numbers. 5:7: *Blessed are the merciful: for they shall obtain mercy.* 5:9: *Blessed are the peacemakers: for they shall be called the children of God.* 5:10: *Blessed are they which are persecuted for righteousness' sake: for theirs is the kingdom of heaven.*

Before Luis headed out to hail a taxi to the airport, he paused and forced the words out.

"For this to work, we need to cut contact," he said. "No texts, no calls. I don't want to seem heartless, but I think it'll be for the best."

"If that's what you want," Ana said.

It wasn't really, but any opening for reconciliation would only prolong the breakup. If the door was cracked open, it'd be too tempting to step back through it.

"We should both want that," Luis said.

"No contact," Ana said. "Clean break. I can manage that."

"For the record, I'm not upset with you. Actually, this would be a lot easier if I was angry, but I'm not."

Ana stared at him, and for a second, he thought she was going to lean in and hug him. Instead, she offered a minor mercy: a squeeze on the shoulder, and well-wishes for his travel.

From the airplane window, plots of land resembled the panels of a quilt, patchy and eclectic, scattered hues of greens. The coast gave way to a bright, aquamarine blanket, and soon that was all that was visible. Endless sea as far as Luis could see. A portion of it was international waters, another portion, Cuba. Though decades had passed, Luis was sure Neto had seen this too: a country ending with no sign of where its borders sat, even all the way up in the sky.

2018

As the plane descended onto the tarmac, Domingo imagined what El Salvador would look like. The wheels hit the asphalt, and Ana squeezed his hand. His father stared out the window. Domingo didn't picture rusty gates, sidewalks missing chunks of concrete, dead houseplants, boarded-up windows, graffiti stains, collapsed ceilings, or gaping holes where walls once stood. His visions were shaped by a father who spoke reverently of revolution, who would not mention crumbling structures unless they stood underneath their sagging archways, which meant that any version of his motherland would be elegant. Polished. Well-kept.

What met him, at the end of a looping private driveway many miles from the airport, was more beautiful than he'd remembered. The white stucco exterior contrasted the terracotta shingles perfectly. A balcony ran the length of the facade, lined with doors that opened to the garden. The front door was painted a bright, sunflower yellow. The mansion rivaled those in the Hollywood Hills. Domingo couldn't imagine an earthquake or hurricane capable of knocking it down.

"Neto!" Elena rushed toward her uncle and embraced him. "Look at you! So handsome, even after all these years."

"You flatter me, niña. You look good too." Neto held Elena by the shoulders. Domingo and Ana stood behind, quietly. Luis walked out the front door and gave his cousin a hug. Luis's cologne was smoky, burnt cedarwood. Ana shook Luis's hand, but he pulled her in and kissed her cheek.

"And you!" Elena said, turning her attention to Domingo. "You're a full-grown man! My goodness. Everyone looks beautiful. I've never looked that good after a flight. Come in, come in."

"Come on, primo," Luis said. Domingo and Ana followed him to the second floor, then into their room. The walls were painted olive green. French doors led out to a balcony. Against the wall, a bunk bed looked out of place, too childish and inelegant for the space.

"My mom insisted," Luis said, apologetic. "Here, this view will make you feel better."

Stepping out onto the balcony, the heat hit them hard, but Domingo ignored it, his eyes preoccupied with the gardens below. Up to the edges of the property, plants comingled, covering every inch of the grounds. Birds-of-paradise popped out between agave. A jacaranda tree bloomed violet. Rosebushes spotted the collection, white, red, yellow. A landscaper pulled weeds. Another watered the hydrangeas.

"The garden wasn't here last time," Domingo said.

"It was," Luis said.

A framed photograph of Luis and Domingo as boys hung downstairs, their limbs loose as vines, wrapped over each other's shoulders. Luis is missing a tooth; a Band-Aid sticks to Domingo's forehead. A rosebush rises above their heads.

They're smiling wide, barely paying attention to the camera. The garden had slipped from his memory, but he couldn't deny the joy on his face.

"I'm glad you're here," Luis said. Domingo believed him.

"Esperanza was asleep when you landed," Elena said.

"Can I see her?" Neto asked.

Only with her eyes, Ana asked if Domingo was going to say hello to his aunt. He knew Esperanza wouldn't know or care that he was there. But it'd be rude to come all this way and not see her, so he unglued himself from the cushion and followed everyone into Esperanza's bedroom.

A bulky bundle of blankets lay on the bed. Neto approached the lump and said hello. Only then could Domingo make out a face against the pillow. Esperanza's hair was wispy and gray. The thin strands sprouted high on her forehead, extending her obvious widow's peak. The fat in her cheeks had melted away, leaving loose, excess skin. Her complexion was yellowed and sickly. Sharp and jutting, her bone structure was more skeleton than supermodel.

Luis approached the bed, gave her a kiss on the cheek, and pulled the blankets off her. She was miniscule. Toothpick thin. Couldn't have weighed more than ninety pounds. Luis grabbed her by the armpits and pulled her into a sitting position. He dragged her legs off the side of the bed and helped her to her feet. She stood, leaning against him, and stared into space. He guided her to a recliner and sat her down.

"There you go, Abuela," Luis said gently.

Domingo tried looking into her eyes for a sense of recognition but couldn't find any. Esperanza simply did what Luis prompted her to, exerting very little of her own energy.

"Esperanza," Neto said. "Hola, Esperanza. Hola."

His voice trembled slightly, a tenderness in his tone. He knelt down in front of her so that they were face-to-face. Esperanza's head bobbed slightly from side to side as he tried making eye contact. She made no noise. Neto repeated himself—*Hola, Esperzanza, hola*—over and over, like a spell.

"Say hello," Luis told Esperanza. "Abuela, say hello."

"Say 'hola, hermanito,'" Elena chimed in. "It's Neto, Mami. Your brother. Say hello."

It was absurd. Everyone was trying to make contact with a woman who'd lost most of her cognition. They must've looked like foggy shapes beside the recliner, their words nothing more than discordant noise. The woman who sat there—staring up at the ceiling, not acknowledging them—was shedding her body. She was missing pieces of herself. Contacting her was a lost cause. Neto had said that his sister's condition reverted her to life as a newborn, but watching her now, Domingo disagreed. Newborns have a future. There was no future for Esperanza.

Then, she responded. It was not a phrase, and it didn't prove that she recognized her brother after so many years apart, but it was a reaction.

"Yah, yah, yah," she repeated. It sounded like she was saying "enough" or "stop" in Spanish, as if the attempts to coax her out of her silence were annoying. To a roomful of people searching for a sign, it was proof she knew they were there. Esperanza was present as shadows from her past tried desperately to communicate with her.

"Yes, Mami," Elena said. "Yes, that's your brother."

"Hola, Esperanza," Neto said, the refrain more energetic this time.

Luis sat on his grandmother's bed. His posture—relaxed shoulders, loose neck—signaled that there was nothing new, unsettling, or depressing about the efforts to talk to Esperanza. He watched them unfold, waving at his grandmother. Ana followed Luis's lead and waved to Esperanza as well.

Domingo grew self-conscious, hyperaware of the weight of his hands. He willed his chest and arms to slacken, not wanting his family to read his body language and decipher the ugly feelings he harbored inside: pity, discomfort, existential dread. Alzheimer's was genetic, and flashes of his father in Esperanza's state popped into his head. Then, images of himself, withering away, floating into the atmosphere.

"Let's put on her music," Luis said. He walked over to a speaker by the bedside table and connected his phone. He played a song Domingo recognized from his father's Sunday morning cooking playlists.

The chorus arrived in a wailing *Con dinero y sin dinero, hago siempre lo que quiero*, and Esperanza brought her skinny hands from her lap into the air, as if she was moved by the singer crying out the verse. *No tengo trono ni reina, ni nadie que me comprenda, pero sigo siendo el rey*. She smacked her palms together, filling the room with the soft sound of flabby skin smacking against itself. The singer wailed, and Esperanza clapped. Neto joined, joy in his face. Domingo forced his hands together, searching for music amid the dull thud of one palm against another.

Archive of Unknown Universes

Rafael: Have you seen the news? http://eldiarionacional.com/civil-union-legislation-congresso

Ernesto: Elena mentioned it to me this morning. Unbelievable, isn't it?

Rafael: If I hadn't seen the long fight up close, perhaps. Me and Anabel and valiant others have been pushing for this. It just needs to get through congress now, and soon, men like us will be able to marry.

Ernesto: "Men like us." The phrase sounds like a song from the past.

Rafael: It's something you wrote in a letter once, when we were younger than we are now.

Ernesto: Anabel's dodging my calls. I wanted to ask her to give Ana a tour of the museum, but she hasn't responded.

Rafael: She harbors a bit of resentment. I'm sure she'll come around.

Ernesto: And you—are you also angry at me?

Rafael: Anger lives in the shadow of love. I'd love to see you, if that's what you're asking.

Ernesto: I need to think about it.

Rafael: Think faster, Neto.

Luis drove fast, making sharp turns that should have been impossible on the crowded highway. His composure—loose grip on the wheel, body slack in the seat—comforted Ana. Domingo offered to join them on the drive to the museum, but Ana insisted he spend some time with his aunt.

"So, what's this thesis I've been hearing so much about?" Luis asked.

"Oral histories. I want to capture firsthand experiences of the war." Broadly, that was the project, though Ana's true goal was to document how rhetoric surrounding the war, as wielded by its architects, had changed over the years. An interrogation of public memory in postrevolutionary El Salvador, she'd told her thesis adviser. Domingo's father had politely turned down her request for an interview, but a museum was a place of public inquiry. She figured it was a good place to start.

"If my mother speaks openly about her exile, after everything she's gone through, I'm sure I can get some people to open up," Ana said.

"Sure. That'll be super easy," Luis said. He ribbed her, not out of malice but in a clear attempt to forge a friendship. Ana matched his energy, quick and reckless. Already, he felt less like a stranger and more like a spirit she'd met in a previous life.

A twelve-foot-tall statue of Monseñor Romero guarded the museum entrance. The words "Verdad y revolución" were inscribed on the base. Ana wandered the exhibits for a while, gathering the courage to speak to the museum director behind the front desk. Rifles hung from the wall and solidarity posters from around the world were displayed across the room, their slogans printed in Spanish, English, German, French, and Arabic.

She finally approached the woman at the front desk. Her eyes, magnified by her rimless glasses, looked too large for her face. She was short, but when she spoke, her voice was sharp, piercing any confidence Ana had built.

"Anabel? My name's Ana. I'm a researcher. I was wondering if I could ask you a couple of questions about the museum and your time in the war . . ."

Anabel shuffled through some sheets on the desk, as if contemplating the request.

"I'm afraid I can't help you," she said.

Warmth flushed Ana's face, but she chugged ahead. She'd come all this way.

"I'm happy to explain more of my research project."

"I don't think I can help you, bicha. Our archive is open Tuesdays, Wednesdays, and Thursdays. Just fill out these forms."

In her messy handwriting, Ana filled out the paperwork as quickly as she could. Anabel looked the forms over for a second, then nodded.

"If I'm not here, one of my colleagues will be able to help you. Call ahead, if you can."

Óscar Romero loomed over her shoulder as Ana walked outside and replayed the interaction, wondering what'd gone wrong. Should she have mentioned that she was affiliated with Harvard? Or was the problem where she came from, that she was no better than a gringa from the country that'd been such a headache for El Salvador all these years? It didn't matter. She'd hit a dead end, and as she waited for Luis to pick her up, she imagined the rest of her life falling apart: her thesis unwritten, a rejection from PhD programs she dreamed of, an office job that she hated.

"¡Oye, preciosa!"

A catcall was no big deal. A stranger's attention was annoying, yes, and usually came with the threat of violence, but Ana knew how to manage it. Today, she figured she'd play dumb—a lost soul in a new city!—until she realized the catcaller sounded familiar.

Domingo was hanging out the car window. She rolled her eyes when she spotted him.

"Bayunco," she said as she jumped into the back seat next to him. They never spoke to each other in Spanish. How strange his sounded. Was her accent as grating, as infantile?

"I'm just flirting a little," Domingo said.

"Bleak," Luis said from the driver's seat.

"I like it," Ana said.

"Did you make a new friend?" asked Luis.

"No luck," said Ana. "She didn't want to be interviewed."

"Read this." Domingo shoved his phone into Ana's hand. The headline was a gut punch: *Department of Homeland Security Announced End of "Land Ho" Policy for Salvadorans*. Since the revolution, Salvadoran refugees who made it onto American soil had been allowed to stay as "defectors from a communist country." Overnight, alongside asylum policy changes meant to decrease the number of Guatemalan children at the border, the agency shoehorned a termination of the thirty-eight-year policy. Any northbound Salvadorans would have to navigate the same perils other Central Americans did: cruel detention centers, chain-link cages, endless wait times, whole lives built in limbo.

"As if it wasn't already hard enough to get asylum," Domingo said. Ana squeezed his hand, though no amount of pressure would make the news disappear.

"Man, your president will do anything to stick it to us," Luis said.

"The cold war never ended," said Ana.

"Mr. President's gotta open his eyes. Or come visit. Look out the window! Look what he'd see."

From the back seat, anxieties still swirling around her head, Ana watched the city pass by. Crystal glass skyscrapers dotted downtown. Luis was right. Their height challenged the claims people—her mother included—made about El Salvador being a second-rate communist country.

"It's not a perfect government," Luis said. "I'll be the first to admit it. But it's not all bad."

"Not to sound rude, Luis," Domingo said. "But you're not the first person I'd ask for an honest evaluation of the Salvadoran government. You have it good out here."

"Maybe," Luis said.

"The record speaks for itself. No truly free elections, lagging behind on human rights—"

"They're going to make civil unions legal. In a couple of days, I think."

"It's not marriage."

"It's pretty close. Anyway, what's the point in arguing about this? This is the government we have. You two have a capitalistic nightmare for a government. Both are corrupt, both fail their constituents. We live with the system we're born into. We thrive despite it."

The bright lights from the skyscrapers bounced off the windshield. They could convince themselves that the country was beautiful, thriving, but Ana had read enough to know that aesthetic maintenance was the government's shield against the world. El Salvador was an imperfect country, where women still could not marry women, and where all its civil successes were offset by shortsighted failures. The world was still split into haves and have-nots, triumphs and defeats. The capitol was beautiful, but beauty was not justice. Grandeur was not a substitute for change.

"Domingo and I have been obsessed with this question lately," Ana said. "Don't you think it's interesting? What your life might have been if the revolution had failed?"

Luis laughed, high and airy, with a strength that rocked his whole body. Ana was grateful the highway was emptier than earlier.

"I don't have to wonder," Luis said. "We can just ask."

Archive of Unknown Universes

Rafael: Tomorrow afternoon. I am taking a half day at work. I can spend the whole afternoon catching up. There's this cafe in San Benito with wonderful coffee and pastries. Tons of seating, and large enough that we can chat uninterrupted or without eavesdroppers. What do you say?

Rafael: Neto?

Rafael: Let me know.

Ernesto: Would you believe me if I told you I was afraid, still haunted by the old hang-ups, even all these years later?

Rafael: If you want to see me, come see me.

Ernesto: Send me the address.

143

Embassies line the roads that lead to the nondescript shopping center where Neto has agreed to meet Rafael. The flags of nations near and far wave at the taxi. Nicaragua, Mexico, Honduras, Cuba, and Brazil all say hello. A few minutes from his destination, Neto catches sight of the United States embassy. Ivy drapes its walls. Loose threads hang on empty flagpoles. The windows of the central building are boarded up, and the front sign is faded, the letters decipherable but peeling like dry skin. It's not surprising, since the two countries cut off diplomatic ties decades ago, but Neto still finds the hollowed complex eerie.

The car pulls into the narrow shopping center. The strip of stores is sandwiched between two parking lots and two roaring streets, in the heart of San Benito, which has been the rich neighborhood of San Salvador for a long time, even before the revolution. Neto knows that the neighborhood is still for a select few. It doesn't surprise him that Rafael has asked that they meet at a coffee shop there.

When Domingo mentioned his trip with Ana, Neto saw his opportunity. Returning without a reason, after so many years, was unimaginable. Even the news of his sister's deteriorating health hadn't brought him back. Neto couldn't bear to tell his son about Rafael. Explaining a love as old as theirs is too complicated, so he'd asked to join without mentioning the Facebook messages, and though joy swelled inside his gut when Domingo said yes, Neto willed his face to remain stoic. He feels guilty, still, that young love brought him back to the country he fled so many years ago.

That's why he's come to the coffee shop, alone, without

telling anyone where he'll be. Years of hurt still remain. He's not ready to answer the kinds of questions Domingo would have.

Next to the menu explaining the origin of the different coffee beans, there's a map of El Salvador painted onto a slab of whitewashed wood. The names of different farms, small parcels of land given to farmers by the revolutionary government, are marked by red dots the color of coffee beans. The coffee shop is privately owned, a rare exemption under a nationalized system, but the decor makes the shop's loyalties clear. A portrait of the president hangs a few feet away. Neto asks for a latte before finding a seat by a window.

When he'd first seen Rafael online, Neto assumed the young man he'd loved was gone, replaced by the man in the most recent pictures. But now, as Rafael enters, he can't avoid the truth. Rafael's face has filled out around the jaw, making it less slender than it used to be, but his nose is the same. Striking, sharp. His beard is still long, though not as long as Neto remembers it, and overrun with gray hairs. Rafael is dressed in a linen button-down, loose and flowing, with a straight-legged pair of light-wash jeans. It's a young man's outfit that looks miraculously age-appropriate on Rafael, who is no longer a young man. He is beautiful.

"You've already ordered?" Rafael asks. He remains standing, his hand on the chair across from Neto. Should they shake hands or hug? They haven't seen each other in more than two decades, and Neto doesn't know how to appropriately greet an old lover after so many years.

"You should get a drink," Neto says. He considers standing and waiting in line with Rafael, but doesn't.

"This place has grown on me," Rafael says when he returns with an espresso mug. "I used to think to myself, 'Well, I have coffee grounds and a coffeemaker at home, why would I spend money here?' But I've learned that my coffee isn't as good."

"You still live nearby?"

"Same house we moved into in eighty-five. I planted a garden in the front entryway, like I said I was going to."

"It only took you thirty years."

"What brought you back?" Rafael asks.

"My son. His girlfriend, Ana, is doing research. At Anabel's spot, I think. He came with her. It was time I returned. It's been a while."

"I'd love to see him. Domingo was a child when you left."

"We're not here for long. Two weeks."

"Come to dinner at our house."

"I don't think that's a good idea." Neto pauses. "Your house. Not our house."

"It used to be ours."

"It isn't now."

"Because you decided to run."

"I wasn't running."

"You were running."

"What do you do now?" Neto pivots, though he knows the question will swing back around to him.

"Government job."

"You a big politician now?"

"I write policy. Parks and recreation, and public works. Quieter job. The spotlight isn't for me."

"You used to say it was."

"Is that why you left? My aspiration to make something of myself?"

"You know it wasn't just that."

"What do you do?" Rafael asks. If he's hurt by Neto's unkindness, it doesn't show.

"I teach. Political science at UCLA."

"So you're still involved in politics?"

"I teach theory. Not exactly political work."

"Building consciousness in the youth is political work. They killed our friends for less."

"And this government? Does it kill those with the wrong politics?"

Nostalgic questions will take them nowhere. They can't possibly speak of the past as if it doesn't have spikes. Neto spent hours deciding whether or not to contact Rafael. This conversation shouldn't float on the surface like this, in safe, shallow waters. Neto poses the question to provoke Rafael, to draw some deeper reaction that'll replace the pleasantries and jovial jabs he's lobbing.

"You know it doesn't."

"People die in slums across town, and some live like this." Neto points to those dining around them. Their faces are calm and unconcerned, both with the men's conversation and, Neto is sure, those who live less extravagantly than them.

"People die everywhere. Poverty here is no different than poverty elsewhere, except that anyone can go to the doctor and school when they need to."

"Convenient line."

"You believed in the revolution once."

"Why did you ask me to come, Rafael?"

"I've missed you."

The men continue talking, and the conversation becomes less cautious than one might expect. There were disagreements, miscommunications, cruelty inflicted out of fear, but none of that requires rehashing. They've each held on to different details, and slightly different variations as to how and why the heartbreak unfolded as it did, but there's no debating the final series of events that landed them more than two thousand miles away from each other.

Years ago, after the first big fight but before Domingo was conceived, Rafael had mentioned that he felt as if the streets listened to everything he said. It wasn't the wartime fear of surveillance, though caution and whispers were hard habits to shake. If I take a thought, and put it into words, Rafael explained, someone must have heard. Catholic schooling had taught him that God was always listening, but this was different. The bricks in the street, the compact dirt, the weeds that grew in cracked cement—they all listened to him. Neto had said it was a silly thought, but an endearing one, the sort of frivolous tangent most people kept hidden from everyone except the person they loved most.

Now, as they sit at the coffee shop, Neto thinks of everything the streets and buildings would say if they could speak. The embassy buildings would ask Neto if he regretted his outburst, his condescending claims that the revolutionary government was rotting Rafael's brain. The burning, shim-

Archive of Unknown Universes

mering asphalt would whisper that Neto's fling with the girl who ended up pregnant was self-sabotage. She was beautiful, yes, and perhaps Neto had even loved her, but it was clear that he couldn't fully bare himself to her, so it was no surprise when she left a few months after Domingo's birth. The street corners would gossip: Neto wanted a child and Rafael didn't. In making one, Neto ruptured a relationship that had been mostly good; mostly euphoric and blessed and good.

"Are you happy with your life? Your choices?" Neto asks. The conversation has zigzagged for nearly an hour, the intensity fluctuating like the peaks and valleys of a lie detector test. At this point, the anxiety between them has dissipated, and though the question isn't easy, Neto knows he'll get an honest answer. They've fallen back into a familiar rapport, similar to the early years of their relationship.

"I don't dwell on the aftermath of my choices. Things could have played out in a million different ways, but that doesn't change the life I live."

"But are you happy?"

"Not every day," Rafael says. "But for the most part, yes. My job is pleasant. My life is quiet."

"The decisions I've made add up," Neto says. "They sent me where they did. Away from you and this country, which is what I wanted at the time. I don't resent those choices, even today, but I do wonder what would have been if I'd been less wedded to what I thought was true. I could have given this government a few more chances, the benefit of the doubt for a few more years. I could have chosen not to run toward lust when you offered love."

"I didn't want what you did, toward the end. A child, limitations on our lives by nature of what it'd mean to be fathers here."

Neto knows that Rafael is extending a kindness, rationalizing a mistake Neto made decades ago.

"Wouldn't it have been worth exploring what our relationship could have been?" Neto speaks slowly now.

"They're only now legalizing civil unions for same-sex couples. You were right about our future, in many ways."

"We might have been able to build something despite our impasses. Domingo was the right choice, my only choice. But I wonder if a life where you and he coexisted was really an impossibility. In my head, back then, it was."

Rafael looks at him. His eyes are clouded with a wistfulness that Neto knows has settled over his own as well. There'd been endless ways he had imagined this reunion: in thousands of locales, the tenor of the conversation angry, tender, or quiet, the circumstances convenient, forced, or miraculous. Only once had he imagined a conversation as honest and direct as this one.

"Want to come to my place," Rafael asks, "for a coffee?"

Neto beckons to the empty, open-mouthed cups in front of them.

"A second coffee," Rafael says. "Or dessert. Dinner."

Checking the time on a clock above Rafael's head, Neto agrees.

The two men walk into the house together as dusk settles over them. The walk is familiar, and Neto treads the path he's walked hundreds of times before. If they could speak, the bricks would say that his feet are uneven, destabilizing his gait. They might confess that men and women have come into Rafael's home in the past couple of decades, though none have stayed long. Rafael pushes the front door open, and it welcomes Neto as he steps through.

The house knows that the men were happy when they shared a bedroom. It knows that Rafael still sleeps with the door open so that light from the hallway seeps in, a remnant of the years Neto slept there. After the kidnapping, the torture, and the interrogation, he couldn't handle complete darkness. Neto left, but the bedtime ritual remained.

The hallway remembers that though they were happy, Neto was frustrated by what the revolution was doing with its victory. He'd sacrificed so much. Broken bones and an acceptance of his fate. Hallucinations of death hovering above him, and his arm reaching out to them. All those weeks in the government's grip, just to watch a revolution lose its way. He'd yelled about Rafael's blind allegiance, and Rafael had shouted back about how Neto was still ashamed to be with him. If the insulation stored their arguments, it doesn't release the angry words as the men sit down at the dining table.

The lightbulbs have been switched out, but the fixture is the same. The glow flushes out their skin, highlighting the creases on Neto's forehead. The light fixture knows secrets too, recalls the times that Neto was stubborn and unkind. Remembers that he ran off toward infidelity before the relationship had ended, huffing away from a surmountable disagreement. He broke the trust, and his child frayed the relationship further. The home would have opinions on the circumstances under which he left the country, and whether the man who stayed was in the right or wrong.

But the home does not speak. The two men stay quiet as they sip cups of coffee. The only sound is the clink of the ceramic cups against their saucers. They watch each other's eyes, notice the tilt of the other's jawline, and wonder if they fit the memories they have of each other. The years might have warped the shape or shade of their faces, but it doesn't matter. Nostalgia hides the changes. Rafael begins tapping his fingers on the tabletop. Neto speaks. The words are quiet, barely a whisper.

"Do you remember Havana?" Neto asks.

"'The shadows danced on our shoulders,'" Rafael says, quoting a letter from years ago.

"What if we'd stayed there? Or if I'd stayed here, in this house?"

"Want to find out?"

Rafael reaches out a hand. Neto holds it. The house shudders.

2018

A white family had moved in next door to Felicia. Their six-year-old boy ran in circles in the middle of the road. It was a seldom-used one-way street, so he was relatively safe, but his parents watched from their front steps, seeking shade from the midsummer scorch. Ana waved to them as she passed by with two iced coffees. The boy's parents had introduced themselves to her the day after she'd returned, noting that being a Harvard student was impressive, to which Ana had given nothing more than a tight-lipped smile.

Their son had tied a June bug to a string. The beetle spun around his head, unable to fly farther than the twine's length. The child laughed, his ginger bowl cut bobbing as he ran with the insect behind him like a kite. The green shimmer of the beetle's wings sparkled erratically.

Inside, Ana placed an iced coffee on the counter next to her mother. The initial plan was to fly from Havana to San Salvador, but the breakup with Luis threw a wrench in Ana's journey, in part because she had loved him, and in part because her mother was insistent that she not travel alone. Ana was an adult but being an adult did not automatically free her from other adult's wishes, especially her mother's, and it did not destroy the sadness that had befallen, or the desire for the familiar, which Luis had previously offered. In the wake of the breakup, Ana had to confront what she already knew: no one was more loyal to her than her mother. Felicia wanted her home, so she booked a flight to Los Angeles instead of San Salvador.

Felicia eyed her drink suspiciously but took a sip anyway.

"You don't have to buy me coffee every time you get one," Felicia said. "I like my Nescafé. Save the money."

"There's no way you like instant coffee more."

"You don't believe me, but I do."

Ana stared at her mother without saying much more, a move that she thought was harmless enough until Felicia met her stare.

"You've got a look," Felicia said.

"I have to ask you about my trip . . ."

"Don't start with me, Ana."

"Mami—"

"Is that what the coffee was for? A bribe? I told you. El Salvador is dangerous, and impossible to get around. A few summers ago, the gangs stopped all the buses for a whole day. They boarded and wouldn't let people off until they paid them."

"I can Uber places."

"Didn't you hear me? It's dangerous," Felicia said.

The whole world was dangerous, according to her mother, but Ana was tired of cowering in fear.

"Do they even have Uber in El Salvador?"

"They got it last year."

"No, no, no. I'm sure you can find whatever you need online or at a library. Come on, now."

"I'm looking for the man in the ID picture."

"Again with that tontería?" Felicia sighed. "I have nothing else to share."

"I have to fly to San Salvador, then," Ana said.

They were at a stalemate. Ana initially planned to lie, saying that Luis was coming to San Salvador with her, but it felt like too many untruths to balance. Though it was illogical—Ana was grown, a travel credit would cover her flight—she wanted her mother's blessing.

"If you don't want me to go alone, come with me," she said.

"With what money?"

"From my grant."

Felicia had been sipping her iced coffee throughout the conversation, small swigs at a time. Now, her fingers clamped on the lid, her palm slowly pushing the cup away from her.

"It's not that simple," Felicia said. "There's nothing left for me there. Ghosts and empty places, that's all I'll find."

"You don't know that."

"I've had years to pray about it. Years, and years, and years. I'll go back someday, but not soon. It's not my time to return."

"I'm going anyway." Ana's stomach churned as she spoke.

"When you make a choice like this, to do something I am telling you is dangerous, what guides you? The church would advise you to listen to your mother, but you're not doing that. So what is it?"

"I need to finish my research." Another half-truth. For the past couple of weeks it'd been the Defractor, not her ambitions, that propelled her choices. To make Felicia understand, she confessed to using the machine.

"Oh, Ana," Felicia said.

"There were universes where we weren't fighting, where we understood each other perfectly."

"You think I pull my advice out of nowhere. As if I'm a crazy woman who knows nothing just because I wasn't born here." Felicia paused for a second. A secret threatened to slip from her lips, but instead she asked Ana to listen closely. "Here's one thing I'll tell you. Maybe this will make you understand."

Felicia told a story from when Ana was two years old. Her father had just left them, after Felicia admitted that they were forcing a relationship that didn't work. She cleaned houses for a living, including an art dealer's, who'd bought one of the earliest Defractors on the black market. He claimed to use it solely for professional guidance, but Felicia watched as he and his family snuck into the office, devoted to the device as a one-stop solution for all their ills. One day, to keep her from snitching or to make up for underpaying her, the art dealer offered her the chance to peek into the machine. The technology hadn't become a cultural battleground yet, and the church had no official stance on whether or not one should use it, so Felicia agreed. She was curious to know what awaited her in El Salvador when she finally went back. After years of thinking she'd never be able to return, her green card was in the mail on its way to her.

"I look in the machine, and what do you know? None of the universes show El Salvador. I tell a friend and she says it's a sign that I have nothing left to go back to. The argument breaks our friendship, but as the years go by, and I pray about it more and more, I realize she's right."

Another misjudgment: her mother hadn't been shut out of the places where the powerful gathered. She'd walked through their halls and, as she scrubbed through layers of their grime, absorbed a lesson that Ana was only learning now, decades later: excess—of knowledge, of wealth—was not always beneficial.

Felicia paused, taking a sip from the coffee, before sliding it away from her again.

"I left a lot behind," Felicia said. "More than you'll ever be able to understand, mija, There's no one left for me there."

"I'll be there. With you," Ana said.

"You know, I spent a long time pretending that I couldn't return because the flight cost too much or because I needed to take care of you. The truth was that I was scared. The war was not my fault, and if I stayed, things would have been worse for me, but still I spent hours asking why this fate had befallen me. How could a god so loving do this to a whole country?"

"A god or a government?" Ana asked.

"It doesn't matter. The only questions worth asking, I think, are about who we surround ourselves with. We have to work to end up with those we deserve, who deserve us."

Felicia paused, glancing to look her daughter in the eyes.

"That's why I'm grateful I have you. I chose you, and you chose me. And hopefully, we'll continue choosing each other until we're both old ladies."

"Choose me right now," Ana said. "Say you'll go."

Her voice was soft, softer than she'd intended. The trembling took her by surprise, forcing her to face the fear growing in her chest. Felicia was right. Returning to El Salvador wouldn't be as easy as she'd been telling herself.

"Ana." Felicia sighed. "I love you, bicha."

A tapping on the window drew their eyes. The sun had lowered in the sky, softening the apartment with a sheen that'd eventually shift into an orange glow at sunset. Ana approached the source of the noise. The June bug was flying into the glass, repeatedly and at an angle, as if half of its body was paralyzed. The thin piece of twine dangled from its leg. The beetle pummeled itself against the glass, making the quiet noise of freedom, until it eventually went silent.

A funeral is an elegant affair, worthy of the person being remembered. Or that's what Luis had assumed before he was confronted with the reality of his grandmother's death. Her aging had not been graceful, and it turned out her burial would not be either. Maybe that was simply the way of the world—the bureaucracy and logistics of death were unrefined and clunky, especially for a family like theirs, who didn't have unlimited cash to throw at the casket.

Each step of the process felt like a slight to his grandmother's memory. The funeral home was painted a dusty beige, nearly indiscernible from the other buildings, save for the two faux-Roman columns on either of the front door, which were especially depressing against his mental image of Widener Library, with its intricate limestone pillars that reached up toward the sky. At the burial, a tractor lifted a cloud of dust around the mourners, before filling the grave and smashing the ground shut with a cacophony that felt disrespectful to the nearby dead. Two cemetery workers quilted together blocks of sod, quickly and mechanically, just another tick box on their way to a paycheck. The patch of grass faded

Archive of Unknown Universes

into the hilltop. Until a headstone was created and paid for, only the handful in attendance would know where Esperanza was laid to rest.

And, of course, there'd been Esperanza herself. At the wake, Luis tried to step back from the casket, giving his mother one last moment alone with Esperanza, but she grabbed him hard by the biceps, forcing him to stare at his grandmother, a woman who had been dead to him long before her heart stopped beating a week ago. A thick layer of makeup caked her face. In death, she looked like a wax figure, her features stretched out and drooping, her hair synthetic and campy. Accepting that she was in a better place was difficult when her body looked so shrunken and forlorn.

The morning after the burial, Luis awoke in an empty apartment. Fighting back grogginess, he sat up on the couch, where he instinctively unlocked his phone. Without thinking, he opened his text thread with Ana.

It wasn't that he'd forgotten, or that the relationship wasn't over. This was just his routine. Texting her would be natural, almost too easy. Death hovered, and instead of serving as a bleak distraction, it made him miss Ana more. She was still living, unlike his grandmother, who'd taken precious stories with her, those blistering and untouchable memories from a life built in the wake of a war. Ana might never share another secret or feeling or anxiety with him, but at least she wasn't locked behind the cold mahogany of a casket.

Quickly, he typed out a typo-ridden message and hit send before he could regret it:

> what was tit rhat ur professor told u fhat one time? it was lecture about benedict anderson and nation building.

He waited, still slouched over on the couch. Ten minutes passed, then twenty, and Luis realized he wouldn't get a response. He'd set the boundary, and it was unfair to step over it and expect Ana to reward his recklessness.

His phone buzzed.

> I thought we agreed on no contact

> yeah, sorry, i just needed to know. it's killing me that I can't remember

> I'm looking through our texts for the quote. Give me a second

> how was the rest of your time in Cuba?

> "If there's even a chance of recovering the past, we have a moral responsibility to try, even when it means grasping for the loose threads of history."

> thank you

The conversation ended there, and in a convoluted logic spiral, he convinced himself that Ana was busy, not ignoring him. Eventually, he'd have to come up with another lie to tell himself because, surely, many days would start with thoughts of her.

Archive of Unknown Universes

The quote was compelling enough to get him off the couch. Luis headed for his mother's closet, that overflowing treasure trove of junk and hand-me-downs. Clothes that hadn't been worn in a decade drooped from their shelves. Shoeboxes adorned the walls, but if he were to lift the cardboard lids, he'd find the mix of objects Elena never used but couldn't bring herself to throw away: sewing supplies, rubber bands, loose yarn, old bills.

He shuffled through until he found what he was looking for. Behind a rack of coats, a white box painted with pink roses leaned on its side. Sitting just outside the closet, Luis pulled out an envelope and slowly undid the tape, careful not to rip the paper. He didn't want his mother to know he'd tampered with the box.

A series of numbers and colons cascaded from the top of the page. When Luis flipped it over, more numbers patterned the other side. 43:3:40. 4:5:20. 12:18:3. 210:10:4. 9:4:32. 100:7:26. 98:2:19. 76:3:12. He opened another two letters. Every envelope had different combinations; an unbreakable code, impossible to understand. Luis had hoped for clues to his family history, but all he had were pieces of paper with numbers scrawled on them.

He opened the rest of the letters. Most were unreadable, but eventually, he found a scrap of paper he'd seen before. It said more than he had remembered:

> I woke up thinking about Cuba. Do you remember the things we did as shadows danced on our shoulders? That was only a year ago, and already it feels like a lifetime has passed.

Luis found another scrap:

> My sister and my niece have just left for Managua. They
> should be there in no more than three days. I know my sis-
> ter said some . . . unsavory things about our relationship. I
> know that. But could you keep an eye on them for me? Even
> if from afar. I just need to know that they'll be okay. I feel
> awful for putting them in this situation.

In all his years of knowing his grandmother, Luis had
never thought her capable of cruel words, which only made
him even more certain that he hadn't known her at all. Pic-
turing her now—face in a scowl, poison on her tongue—felt
disrespectful to her memory, so he quickly pushed the image
away.

He drafted another text, one he wouldn't send: u won't
believe what i found. my uncle was writing love letters.

The sound of the front door jolted him back. Luis stuffed
the letters back into their envelopes, and buried the box as
deeply into the closet as he could.

"You look suspicious," Elena said when Luis emerged
from the bedroom.

"Just looking for a phone charger," he said, but as the lie
slithered out of his lips, he regretted it. Not because he didn't
think himself capable of lying to his mother—there was much
she didn't know about him—but because sidestepping the
truth was another way of running from the past. Neto had
died, and his story, as Luis knew it, ended there. It was a
single point in a chronology, severed from any further narrative. There was no beginning to Neto, just an end. Death. No

before, no after. But hiding deep inside Elena's things, there was proof he had lived.

The urge to know was overwhelming, and though the logic was not fully clear, Luis would do anything to recover any bit of Neto's life outside its fatal and whispered end.

"Actually, I was looking for something Abuela had when I was young," Luis said. "A box of papers. From Tío Neto."

Elena paused, staring at him with somber eyes, a look she wouldn't shed for months after burying her mother.

"Those are just some old letters from her brother. When Mami got sick, she didn't remember anyone from her time in El Salvador, so she hasn't looked at those in years. Hadn't. Hadn't looked at them in years."

"Abuela must have told you stories about him."

"Mijo, you have to understand that your grandmother didn't speak about the past, even in the years before her illness got bad."

Luis wanted to ask if it's where his own mother had learned the trick, but he didn't. She looked uncomfortable, having this conversation.

"She never mentioned Neto?" he asked instead.

"Never. From what I can remember," Elena said. "Coming to this country broke her spirit a bit. She never recovered."

"Did it break yours?" Luis asked.

A quiver in Elena's voice made him think he'd pushed the topic enough. He felt his own hands shaking slightly. He'd breached the past, sending a tremor through them both.

"I'm going to finish cleaning out her things this weekend," Elena said. "I could use some help."

What he didn't know, he could only invent. Until his mother decided to speak, or the answer crashed down from the heavens, there was nothing else to do but accept another dead end.

"I'll go with you," Luis said, trying, for the first time in a long time, to speak in a way that made his love clear.

Ultimately, Felicia chose to stay. Though it didn't make Ana's leaving easier, her mother admitted there was little she could do to stop her.

At customs, the agent asked Ana if she was Salvadoran. She said yes, but when she handed him an American passport, he said that he'd have to charge her for a tourist visa. Her face went hot, though she wasn't quite sure why she felt so embarrassed. After Ana paid ten dollars, the agent stamped the back pages of her passport and waved her along without a second glance.

An old Toyota with crank handle windows took Ana to the apartment she'd rented. As they left the airport, the humid air became more bearable. Sloping, vegetated hills hugged the road for a while, then buildings bloomed in the wild landscape, small homes made of brick and corrugated metal. By the time they pulled into San Salvador, the scenery had become more industrial than not.

Felicia had been so upset when Ana left. The offer to join Ana had softened her, but Ana still felt unsure about the stance she'd taken. If her mother had raised her in the shadow of fear, there had to be reasons. Perhaps there was something about El Salvador or Central America that she was underestimating. Terror ran through the region, deeper than its rivers and higher than its volcanic peaks. Fear lived deep inside Felicia too, seeping out at any banal danger. Could her mother be right? Might the ghosts of the old days, still haunting the places Felicia had known, terrorize Ana too?

Later that afternoon, after a quick shower, a different car picked Ana up, pulled off a roaring four-lane street, passed a Catholic school guarded by white gates, and stopped in front of what looked like a multiunit residential building. Ana stepped out, feigning assuredness so that the driver wouldn't lag and watch her. He'd been friendly, but friendliness didn't neutralize danger.

The front door was slightly ajar, but the slotted metal gate that covered it was locked tight. As Ana approached, she worried she was intruding on someone's property despite the museum's address on the gate. Ana knocked, and ventured a hello.

The gap opened further, revealing a glass display case full of books and trinkets. An old cash register was perched on top alongside a legal pad. A sign on the back wall announced where guests found themselves: Museo de la Memoria Revolucionaria. An older woman with rimless glasses peeked through the partially opened door.

"We're closed until after the August holidays," she said.

Ana hadn't seen closures posted on the website.

"I'm Ana," she said.

"You wrote us, didn't you? I've been backlogged on emails."

"I want to conduct research in the archives."

"Come back at the end of next week. We'll be open then. It's an easy process. You'll just have to fill out a few forms, and then you can look at the materials. I probably won't be working the front desk, but I'll be here."

Ana nodded, and turned to leave.

"Ask for Anabel," the woman said, her words trailing Ana out to the curb.

Ana felt embarrassed that she'd failed already, on her very first day, but the disappointment would have been manageable had it not been for what appeared on her phone as she waited for a ride. A text from Luis. He was only asking about a quote from a lecture she'd taken the year prior, but the mere fact of his name on her phone threw her off-balance.

He'd been a receptacle for her overflow feelings, those embarrassing, destabilizing emotions she couldn't share with anyone else. Now that he no longer served that purpose, she forced herself to text back as simply and levelheadedly as she could. Her real feelings pressed against the backs of her eyes, the base of her throat, morphing into unkind words she wielded against herself: I'm a failure, I'm the most selfish person in the world, I can't maintain even the simplest relationship, the one with my mother, the person who loves me unconditionally. Without Luis to empty into, where would the flood go?

Calls were twenty-five cents a minute. When she dialed her mother, she pictured the quarters falling into a sewer drain, one coin a minute. Her face was hot. Tears welled. How big would the pile of coins be by the time the call was done? She didn't know, but it didn't matter. The phone rang and rang and rang.

2018

The bottle of rum swung by Domingo's side like a weapon. At the end of a long driveway, a gray, modern-style home glowed. It was late, nearly 11 p.m., but bass drummed through the walls. Partygoers mingled on the other side of a massive glass window. Luis and Ana walked in front of him.

"My friend's having a small get-together," Luis explained. "To celebrate! Come tomorrow, Salvadorans will have one less social failure to be ashamed of."

"We can come back another night," Ana said.

"No, no," Luis said. "It'd be more insulting to bail at the last second. Come on."

It took a few minutes to find the host, who was buzzing around the crowd, dipping in and out of conversations like a falcon on the hunt. Her hair was wrapped in a high bun, and she rocked an oversize oxford button-down as a dress, a giant kite Luis chased through the room. When he caught her, she turned and grinned, as if delighted that he'd won a game they'd been playing.

"I've been waiting for you, lindo," she said. Domingo handed her the rum, which she took with a small bow. She kissed Ana on each cheek.

"Luisa," she introduced herself. "Everyone's looking so gorgeous tonight. Welcome, welcome."

"We'll get to the party," Luis said. "But my new friend here, Ana, really would love to see the Defractor."

"Well, Ana, let's go. Into the wine cellar."

In the dim light of a fixture hanging from the ceiling, Domingo and Ana crept past walls filled with wine bottles. Racks and racks, some still empty, lined every inch of wall space, and a couple of free-standing shelves held bottles a few inches off the ground.

"Her father is as bourgeois as a communist can be," Luis explained. "He loves collecting wine." Luis browsed the bottles by tracing a fingertip over their labels, until landing on one.

"This one, L?"

Luisa shrugged. "They won't miss it."

He uncorked it, a pop echoing off the corners of the room. As he filled long-stemmed glasses he pulled from a trunk in the corner, Luisa approached with the Defractor. The technology was only to be used in service of the revolutionary cause, but as with most rules, guidelines were merely gentle suggestions for those with enough power. Luisa, whom Luis had loved since grade school for more than just their shared name, did not work for the government, but her father did. Luisa loved her father, and her father loved her, which meant she could ask the machine whatever she wanted. Who was going to snitch on the deputy mayor's daughter?

"They say the technology is more accurate when used underground. Closer to the Earth's center," Luis said.

"I didn't know that," Domingo said.

Archive of Unknown Universes

"He's full of shit," Luisa said. "It's just more theatrical down here. Who doesn't love a bit of drama?"

They clinked their glasses, and took a long swig before turning away from Ana and Domingo, giving them a moment to use the machine on their own. Ana flashed Domingo a smile, and took another sip for confidence. They didn't have to discuss it: she'd take the first stab, and he could follow. She leaned in.

PLEASE STATE YOUR NAME.

> Ana Flores.

WELCOME, Ana Flores. YOUR DESIGNATED INTERLOCUTOR is a LIFE COACH. THE SUN IS SHINING. YOU HOLD SO MUCH COSMIC POWER WITHIN YOU. LET'S MAKE IT A GREAT DAY! HOW CAN I HELP YOU?

> I need to know whether I'll be able to do this. Will I be successful, with my project and in this life?

WOULD YOU LIKE YOUR UNIVERSES RENDERED TEXTUALLY OR VISUALLY?

> Visually.

ONE SECOND WHILE I RENDER THE APPROPRIATE UNIVERSES. THE GRIND NEVER STOPS!

She didn't have to search very long. One universe drew her in easily. She saw herself as she was the day before, standing across from the glass display case, in front of the woman at the museum. As she watched, Ana prayed that this version of herself was more assertive, braver than she felt. Disappointment is a foreign feeling for that Ana, she convinced herself. Go on, she thought. Tell her what you need and take it.

On-screen, Ana laughed. The woman nodded at her, and then magic happened. She was let into the museum, past the front desk and somewhere off-screen. Ana sat around for a while, waiting for the woman to return. When she did, with a small stack of envelopes in her hands, the clip ended. Ana couldn't peek at whatever gem had been hiding in the museum.

> That has to be a good sign. Right, coach? That interaction went better than my own, which must mean I'll have some success.

> IF WE OPEN OURSELVES TO ACCEPT POSITIVE CHANGE, GOOD THINGS WILL FOLLOW. WITHOUT A SHIFT IN OUR MINDSETS, WE CANNOT CHANGE OUR REALITY.

> That feels like a cliché.

> BEHIND EVERY OVERUSED CLICHÉ LIES A GLIMMER OF TRUTH. THERE'S A REASON PEOPLE REPEAT THEM. DON'T WRITE THE ADVICE OFF JUST BECAUSE YOU THINK YOU'VE HEARD IT BEFORE. WE RECEIVE LIFE-

Archive of Unknown Universes

> CHANGING GUIDANCE ALL THE TIME BUT
> REFUSE TO HEAR IT.

"Your turn," Ana said, placing a hand on Domingo's shoulder. He nodded, leaned in.

> WELCOME, Domingo Guzmán. YOUR
> DESGINATED INTERLOCUTOR IS American
> television presenter and producer RYAN
> SEACREST. WOULD YOU LIKE YOUR UNIVERSES
> RENDERED TEXTUALLY OR VISUALLY?

> Visual is fine.

> THE PHONE LINES ARE NOW OPEN. PLEASE
> ASK YOUR GUIDING QUESTION.

> Will I ever be able to cross the gulf between me
> and my father?

Domingo expected precision from the machine. A perfect ending. There he'd be, embracing his father or being embraced by him. Nearby, there'd be a hint: the mystery man or a photograph from the war years or some other relic that'd get them closer to some honesty. But no, his father appeared in very few of the universes on-screen. The ones that showed them together were unspectacular.

Instead, he zoomed in to stare at Ana's face. Nothing was wrong between them, not exactly, but the trip hadn't been going like he'd pictured. They'd never agreed to anything beyond the stated purpose of the trip: research for Ana, a chance to return "home" for him. But still, they should be spending more time together, at least giving the trip the chance to become something transformative, a particularly good memory to look back on. He searched this other Ana's face, trying to see if that was the kind of experience she was having with him, in this alternate life. Her expression alone wasn't enough. He zoomed out to see himself.

Except, he wasn't there at all. It was an error, a glitch in the system. Instead, he saw Luis and Ana, sitting side by side on a concrete wall that separated ocean and road. Beside them, cars zoomed by, and a teenager lugged around a boom box, but their eyes only focused on each other. They exchanged the kind of sad, desperate looks that were only possible after years of knowing someone.

He turned away from the Defractor, and caught his Ana leaning toward his Luis, her wineglass held out like a torch. The cup filled quickly, the merlot racing toward the brim. A second before it overflowed, Luis tipped the bottle up. Ana smiled, then took a sip.

Domingo wanted to run. Past the ridiculous wine racks, up and out of the dimly lit cellar, beyond the party where he knew no one, and into the quiet safety of the car's back seat. Just weeks ago, he'd been content with his life. There was always enough food, enough pleasure and work to fill his time. He'd never lacked. Other people had to look for the silver lining in their lives. His was gold-plated.

But when he'd stared the truth down, in other versions of himself—so normal, so unlike him—insecurities snuck in. Ana would not be his endgame. His work as an activist was

Archive of Unknown Universes

pointless. And his father, and this he knew for sure, was hiding away parts of himself, a past that Domingo was entitled to. He didn't have a mother. He'd left his motherland. A peek into the past, his patrimony, was the least his father could offer him.

Luis made a quip about the American president, and Ana laughed. How long had it been since Domingo had evoked this noise, so real and light and easy?

Stewing would get him nowhere, so he leaned back in, reenergized to search for something more than a hypothetical.

> I'd like to change the interlocutor.

The Defractor's ability to choose the perfect interlocutor was heralded as one of its greatest virtues. Everyone thought they knew what they wanted to hear, and from whom, but very few possessed true self-awareness. Trust the algorithm—it knows better than you. It'll save you from your biases and hang-ups. But Domingo only wanted to speak with one person, all-knowing algorithm be damned.

> I'M SORRY. USERS ARE NOT ABLE TO CHANGE THEIR DESGINATED INTERLOCUTOR. OUR TRIED AND TESTED FORMULA ENSURES THAT EVERY USER RECIEVES THE BEST POSS—

> I'd like to speak with my father, Ernesto Guzmán.

> I'M SORRY, I CANNOT PROCESS YOUR REQUEST. CAN I OFFER YOU A BIT OF *AMERICAN IDOL* TRIVIA INSTEAD?

> No. It's important. Please, just let me speak with my father.

> RECALIBRATING. RECALIBRATING. RECALIBRATING . . . YOUR DESIGNATED INTERLOCUTOR is American actor and sitcom father ELLIOT GOULD.

> That's not what I meant.

> ONE SECOND. YOUR DESIGNATED INTERLOCUTOR is American television personality and father of eight, JONATHAN KEITH GOSSELIN.

> God, no. Please, just give me what I want.

> DID YOU MEAN SALVADORAN REVOLUTIONARY ERNESTO GUZMÁN, ALIAS DOMINGO MONTENEGRO?

Domingo Montenegro. Had his father used an alias during the war? Had he passed it on to his son, a small attempt at keeping his former self alive once he'd abandoned the government he'd helped build? In all these years, Domingo hadn't thought to ask.

> Yes, that's correct.

> ONE SECOND.

Archive of Unknown Universes

> Okay.

HELLO. HOW CAN I HELP YOU?

> I need some advice.

A WAR IS WON ON TWO FRONTS, AND ONLY ONE TAKES PLACE ON A BATTLEFIELD. PICK UP THE GUN, THEN PICK UP A BOOK. YOU'LL NEED BOTH.

> No, no. Some real advice. Father to son. Because I am your son. Domingo. My name is Domingo.

WOULD YOU LIKE TO SEE AN ALTERNATE VERSION OF YOUR LIFE? ALL I NEED IS A GUIDING QUESTION.

> No, I just need to speak to my father.

OKAY, DOMINGO. YOU WIN. SPEAK.

> I'm feeling really hurt by what you said to me the other day, when we were talking about the Guatemalan refugees. You made me feel small, as if my efforts were worthless, just because they weren't as grand as what you accomplished.

I SEE.

Ruben Reyes Jr.

> That's it? Two words?

I'M NOT GOING TO LIE TO YOU. I SAID WHAT I FELT. YOU SEE, WE DID THE IMPOSSIBLE. CAN YOU IMAGINE IT? A REVOLUTIONARY EFFORT RESISTED, AND THEN DEFEATED, THE FAT WEIGHT OF AMERICAN EMPIRE. YOU WEREN'T THERE, SO I DON'T EXPECT YOU TO UNDERSTAND, BUT BELIEVE ME. IT WAS EXTRAORDINARY.

> I get that. I really do. But I don't see what that has to do with what you said to me. You can support your son and his efforts. It's not that difficult.

EVERY MOMENT IN HISTORY IS TOLD TWICE: BY THE VICTORS AND THE LOSERS. IT'S UP TO US TO SEEK THE TRUTH BETWEEN THE LINES.

> Why is it always like this? Why can't we ever just sit next to each other and talk like a normal fucking family? What happened to you that made you completely incapable of holding a normal conversation with the only person you love who isn't miles and miles away?

I DON'T APPRECIATE YOUR TONE.

> Seriously, Dad. Don't fuck with me. What did you go through?

> ERROR. INSUFFICIENT INFORMATION. HISTORY IS A BUNDLE OF SILENCES. SEARCHING FOR A NEW INTERLOCUTOR.

"The machine is out of whack," Domingo said. Luisa shrugged.

"My father will figure it out," she said.

"I'm done anyway," he said. All he'd needed was a reminder that he was not completely powerless at the whims of the universe. Articulating what he felt inside was a way to take control of his life, even if it was only a stopgap, a tiny step forward.

Domingo glanced at Ana, expecting to lose this passing bolt of confidence, but then she smiled. Wordless, unblinking, brief, but clearly meant for him alone. The split second of reassurance guided him through the rest of the night. Drink after drink, many at Luis's insistence, his mood went up and up and up, like a birthday balloon set free. Every couple of minutes, he'd catch Ana's stare. In it, he'd find reassurance that this grossly overpriced mansion was exactly where they were supposed to be.

Luis was drunk, a tornado of slurred words and reckless kisses. Too drunk for his mother to see, Ana and Domingo decided. Luisa offered them the living room, so they set up camp there: Domingo and Ana cuddled close on the couch, Luis draped over a massive armchair, asleep the instant he hit the velvet. A couple of other partygoers also stayed the night, wrapped in a heap of blankets.

The next day, after a couple of sluggish and timid good mornings, a friend of Luis's offered to drive them home. It's on the way, he insisted.

"I got so caught up in the festivities that I forgot to ask you if you saw anything interesting in the Defractor," Domingo said.

"Well, nothing concrete," Ana said. "I'm not totally sold on its all-knowing properties."

"I hear that."

"If I'm generous, though, I'll say that it gave me some reassurance. I saw myself in the archive, getting some work done. That has to be a sign, right?"

"Yes. Of course." Domingo said, though he wasn't sure. The machine's speculation was no more real than a restless night's dream.

"My mother was nervous about my trip to El Salvador. She was afraid that something would go wrong, that I'd be in danger. But I think it's more personal than that. She went through a lot. During the revolution. It's why she's never even considered returning."

"How do you know something happened to her?"

"She admitted it. No details, but my sense is that it was brutal."

"I asked the machine to tell me more about my father, and our relationship, but it refused."

"What'd you see?"

In the front seat, Luis was arguing over the best route. "We'll hit traffic if we keep going down the highway," he said. His friend insisted it was early enough, and that side streets would only slow them. His cousin seemed distracted, but Domingo knew Luis would notice if he started talking about him, especially if he brought up the look Luis and Ana had exchanged in the Defractor.

"I'll tell you later," Domingo said. "The point is, I don't feel any closer to the truth. I'm just more aware that he lived a whole life before I came around. He has a past, and I think it might be full of some complicated feelings. Some anxiety, some darkness. Just like your mom."

"Wait," Luis said from the passenger's seat. "Drop us off at the next intersection?

"There's this great spot," Luis explained. "It's touristy, but they serve this amazing traditional Salvadoran breakfast. It's not a far walk."

The trio stepped out of the car and headed down a hill, the loud bustle of a busy street drumming in their ears. The sidewalk was narrow. Cars rushed by, and down below, on the avenue they were walking toward, more drove by, like little ants marching on. Luis stayed a few steps ahead of Domingo and Ana, who walked with their pinkies interlocked.

Halfway down, the hillside opened up into a wide gully. Trees and bushes had flanked them on their walk, but here, where the sides of the hill slid inward toward a muddy river, the foliage was sparser. Dirt paths peeked up from among the plants. All the way up the ravine, shabby huts made of plywood, bricks, and corrugated metal sprung from the dirt. Domingo stopped, listening to the clanging of pans. Smoke rose from some of the homes. Farther in the distance, women balanced buckets and bundles on their heads.

Luis carried on walking. Ana tugged on Domingo's hand

before pausing to follow his sight line. A community readied itself for the day, here among the shrubs, in houses that looked as if they might roll down into the river with a strong gust of wind. Most surprising and jarring, though, was how easily it would have been to walk on without realizing the neighborhood was even there. If Domingo hadn't shifted his head in that direction and taken the time to really observe the gorge, he might have missed it.

A yellow plastic ball rolled onto the dirt path only a few feet from the sidewalk where Ana and Domingo stood. From somewhere among the shrubs, two small boys followed. They chased the ball, kicking it down the path toward Domingo and Ana. Their limbs were thin and slender, like the branches of a sapling. Small holes appeared in the fabric at their armpits and around the waistband of their shorts, the thread fraying. The clothes were clean, well scrubbed, but worn thin. The boys laughed, vying for control of the ball with their bare feet, before running out of sight again.

"How many people live like this?" Domingo asked slowly.

Ana was quiet for a while. Domingo watched as his cousin walked on, lengthening the distance between them, unaware that they'd stopped.

"Want my honest guess?" Ana said. "At least a third. Maybe more."

They'd both read enough about El Salvador. They knew that despite the government's best attempts, it was still a country of have and have-nots, of gated communities and hillside shacks. The winners hoarded their spoils while the citizens they claimed to help made do with what they had. Domingo had been welcomed back into the country by the winners, and the shiny glow of their lives had colored everything, until reality showed its face here, on the side of the road, laughing and kicking dust at them.

The smell of diesel exhaust flooded Domingo's nostrils. His head felt light. He bent over, slamming his palms against his knees for support. Ana touched his back, asking if he was alright. He tried to answer, but no words came out. Vomit, deep brown and pungent, splattered the sidewalk in front of him. Bile and spit ran down the side of Domingo's mouth, and he wiped it, glossing filth onto his cheek. He raised his head weakly, looking back into the gully. The boys were nowhere to be found, as if the ground had swallowed them. As if the nation had taken back what it had birthed.

Rafael had brought a Defractor home with him to finish a couple of work tasks. This version is a Salvadoran original, designed and manufactured in Izalco. At the height of the cold war, after the revolution and before the fall of the USSR, the Americans and the Salvadorans raced to create better versions of the machine that'd show them the future, revealing a path to victory. The Americans still claim their Defractors are faster and more accurate, but the one on Rafael's dining table is just as good. Both he and Neto know it.

Whenever he feels directionless at work, Rafael turns to the Defractor, but occasionally he'll pull it out for more personal matters. Religious and political leaders in other parts of the world find the technology dangerous, but to Rafael, it's no riskier than a tarot reading or weekly Mass. When he needs a little clarity, he turns to the machine. Sometimes it offers it, other times it doesn't. A few weeks ago, it convinced him to send the first Facebook message. Tonight, he hopes it'll work for Neto.

Neto brings the patches to his temple, leaning in slowly. He remembers the relentless darkness and the way the lights shuttered on sporadically to stun him. The mattress he'd been thrown on smelled of piss, and at one point, he'd soiled it, unable to control his body after so many hours of pain.

What if I'd never made it out of that holding cell alive? he asks.

Underneath his eye, glittering like a full moon's reflection on fresh water, a kaleidoscope of universes unfolds. Neto pulls back for a half second and, with a deep sigh, dives back in.

Each slice offers a different version of his life. He lives in all of them. He doesn't lie decomposing in the brush. He's alone in some scenes, but in many he's surrounded by familiar faces: Domingo, Esperanza, Elena, Luis. Neto's celestial pupil darts—instinctively and with vigor—to the universes with Rafael.

Neto zooms, pauses, watches, rewinds, replays. He tries making sense of the snippets he can see and fills in the rest with his imagination. Reading lips, taking guesses, and filling in the gaps helps him better understand the lives that didn't pan out as they could have. Or should have. The process opens the scenes to misinterpretation, but it doesn't matter to him. He sees what appears onscreen. He finds what he wants to.

Rafael and Neto sit in an almost empty bedroom, surrounded by boxes labeled in thick felt marker: *Navidad, Cocina, Cassettes, Clothes, Documents*. Box by box, Rafael takes a key and slips it underneath the tape holding the cardboard flaps shut. With just enough pressure, he slices it open, leaving a jagged edge on the halved strip. Piece by piece, the contents litter the floor. The husbands take inventory of all they've acquired, very little of it precious, all of it brought from their previous home.

The closet has built-in shelves, so they begin layering stacks of T-shirts and jeans. Shoes line the bottom, and jackets stay in boxes until California winter makes its quiet entrance. Neto brings an unopened box into the closet with him and takes a shining house key to it. On the side, in thick marker, it's labeled *Documents*. He pulls out a pair of adoption forms, his and Rafael's birth certificates, and souvenirs of their past lives as revolutionaries: photographs, forged forms, ID cards from Cuba and Nicaragua. The past shines when he transfers everything into folders and then into a small filing cabinet he plans on leaving in the corner of the walk-in closet.

A white box is the final, unpacked item. Without opening it, Neto sets it on top of the filing cabinet. He doesn't rush to reveal its contents or show it to Rafael. He simply stores it and continues unloading the rest of their things.

Neto, watching from Rafael's home in El Salvador, knows exactly what's inside the box. Its contents are crystal clear in his mind. Envelopes, the ink no longer at risk of smudging, since his scrawl dried decades ago. He can picture them. He kept some of the letters, even after he and Rafael split ways. Neto remembers the way his heart felt when he'd hold a new letter, racing as if over-caffeinated or shot with adrenaline. Truth is housed in the body and now, like back then, he feels his red blood cells furiously running through him like greyhounds on a racetrack.

In another universe, Neto and Rafael are backlit as a fire consumes a house they can't face. The two-story building at the end of the cul-de-sac lights up. Above the glow, layers of smoke coalesce into a gray, phantom arm reaching for the moon. The flames move like serpents, devouring drywall and laminate flooring. Despite the firemen out front, who direct a steady stream of water toward it, the home is lost.

Neto is crying, and Rafael wraps a heavy arm around him. They're empty-handed, standing in the street.

Neto, the viewer, thinks of the letters that were surely in the house. They'll be nothing but ash. The two men stand on the asphalt, their faces flushed with the neon light of the sirens, watching what they've built together fall to the ground. Neto is grateful they have each other, if nothing else.

Neto feels dizzy, staring over everything that could have been. He's tired, and his eyes ache from staring at the Defractor's screen. He chooses one more universe. The letters are there again. They surround the two men, strewn across their laps and on the empty parts of the couch they sit on. Envelopes have been gutted, the letters fanned open. Rafael holds one in his hand, and though his lips move soundlessly, it's clear that he's reading the old love letter aloud. When he's finished, he leans toward Neto.

Neto pauses the clip and rewatches it ten seconds at a time. His eyes lock on to their lips, as he tries to make out the conversation. Whatever they're discussing is bringing them joy.

He makes out the question Rafael asks as he picks up another sheet: Do you remember what you wrote?

No, he reads on his own lips. And then: Something about your arms. About how love is a revolutionary act. You know how we used to speak back then. But I can't remember the specifics.

The two men hold hands as Neto pulls away from the Defractor. He looks at the version of Rafael in the room with him, identical to the man he just watched. Neto knows their love was that of two young men, and though there are versions of the world in which they grew old together, there isn't a reset button on this life. He smiles at Rafael, wishing he could do more.

The morning after the party, Domingo beat his father home.

"You kids stayed out all night," Elena said, half a grin on her face.

When Neto walked in half an hour later, Elena wagged her finger at him.

"You! Viejito. You've been out all night, just like the kids." She laughed.

"What trouble were you getting into, Tío?" Luis said.

"Chatting with an old friend. When you get to be my age, there's a lot to catch up on."

The answer wasn't satisfying, but Domingo couldn't bring himself to ask for more details. He was nursing a glass of water, trying his best to keep it down in his stomach.

"They're celebrating the passage of the civil union legislation downtown," Neto said. He looked over at Elena as he spoke. She smiled, her lips slipping into a soft, sympathetic curve.

"We should go," Elena said.

"Someone has to stay with Abuela," Luis said.

"I'll stay with my sister," Neto said. "It's the least I can do."

Elena stared at him for a long time, saying nothing. None of her usual quips slipped out. Domingo watched their gaze, thinking of all the memories they shared and those they'd never made. Everything his father had given up by leaving his family behind was unspoken, but present.

As his son stepped out the front door, Neto slipped into Esperanza's room. She breathed quietly, her eyes staring into nothingness. Neto sat in her recliner. Seeing his sister like this, half alive but at peace and cared for, made him feel a little bit better about leaving so many decades ago. It didn't erase all the guilt, because ultimately, he'd chosen a life without her, but he took solace in the fact that before her mind went, Esperanza was never alone.

Then, despite knowing that Esperanza would not understand, Neto began to speak.

"I saw Rafael last night," Neto said. "He let me peek at all the lives we didn't live. Then he invited me out today, to celebrate a win. It is a win, after all, even if it's imperfect. That's what we fought for when we were younger: imperfect progress. I couldn't go. It was too much to face, especially with Domingo."

He reached out for Esperanza's hand, squeezing it. She squeezed back, harder than he'd expected. There was a lot of strength left in her body.

"Rafael asked if I regretted anything," Neto continued. "It's a funny question, isn't it? I left the government con-

Archive of Unknown Universes

vinced they'd never change, and that any future that Rafael and I could have together was doomed to be less than what we wanted. What we deserved. And now, maybe I was wrong. But what's the point of imagining what could have been?"

Neto stood, then kneeled by the bedside. Esperanza turned her head toward him, their eyes inches apart. She smiled. Her grin was mostly gums, but still, it was a real smile. Neto took it as a sign that she agreed. Despite all the choices he'd made, he'd landed in the right spot, his fingers between hers, the space between them as small as it'd ever be.

2018

Before the morning sun got too hot, Elena and Luis headed out to finish cleaning out Esperanza's room. The assisted living facility was walking distance from where they lived, but only barely. They'd have to cross the freeway overpass and then go a bit farther.

Elena pumped her arms like she was in a Jane Fonda exercise video, her shoulders up high as she took exaggerated swings. Luis laughed, mimicking her. The gag helped distract from her guilt.

She had lied to her son. Esperanza had burrowed into herself as the years went by, that much was true. But while she still remembered him, Neto lingered over them.

During their first few years in California, before the war ended, Esperanza would call her only surviving contacts in El Salvador and ask them to check the binders for her. When churches or nonprofit groups found a cadaver, they took a picture of it. If the face and body hadn't been mutilated, families could identify the desaparecidos from the pages and pages of photos in the binders. She asked monthly until 1992, though her brother had been kidnapped in the war's inaugural year. By the time they began exhuming bodies from mass graves, her memory was slipping. Families were having bones tested, sometimes finding shards of loved ones taken from them decades prior. But by then, Esperanza barely mentioned Neto. In the rare instance she asked after him, she did so casually, acting as if he were temporarily out of town on a business trip. All the regrets, feelings of betrayal, and resentment at a lack of a proper goodbye dissipated.

Elena hadn't read the letters, but they were all Esperanza had left of her brother, so though she had no use for them, she couldn't throw them away. They'd simply meant too much. At the burial, standing graveside, Elena wondered if Esperanza and Neto's long-awaited reunion had already occurred. Telling Luis the truth, with all its craggy corners, would be too complicated, too painful.

They filled trash bags for an hour, pulling the red drawstrings taut and watching the black plastic bulge with decades' worth of junk.

The drawstrings slipped from Elena's fingers, and her knees buckled. Her vision blurred, so she slapped a hand against the wall. Only by pressing a hip against the drywall could she stabilize herself.

"What's wrong, Mami?"

"I just feel tired, mijo," Elena said.

Luis walked over, setting a chair in front of Elena. The lightheadedness didn't dissipate when she sat, but the room wasn't spinning anymore. She didn't dare stand up.

"I'm going to run to the gas station," Luis said. "I'll get you a sandwich or something to drink. Call me if you feel worse. I'll hurry back."

She wasn't old, still in her forties, but it'd been ages since she'd been able to afford a doctor's appointment. With Luis absent, and her head still woozy, Elena drifted back toward her mother's death. Her final, physical departure. It'd been her time, probably, but if everyone had a predestined day they'd be called to His gates, why had her uncle been called so young? Would she go soon, before she had a chance to tell her son all that she'd been through?

Leaning back in the chair, the wicker against her spine, Elena began to talk.

"Mijo. Here's what you need to know. One morning, I snuck into my tío's room, where he had piles and piles of paper and pencils. He was an artist, I think, so I'd gone searching for his masterpieces: sketches of the street we lived on or portraits of me and Mami. I took a pencil from his desk.

"When the men burst into our house, I thought it was my punishment for stealing from my uncle. Years later, I'd finally understand what'd happened. Fear was part of the government's strategy in those years. Your abuela and I never talked about it. She refused. She must've felt guilty. Like a bad mother. For leaving me alone while she went to the market. When you were born, I better understood how she felt. The incident with the soldiers must have felt like a failure, even though I survived it. Scarred, yes. But alive."

Elena paused. Her shadow crept up the wall. She pretended it was her son and kept talking.

"We spent some time in a refugee camp. We stopped trying to get ahold of Neto. Mami became pen pals with a woman in Berlin. The woman was involved with local socialist organizations but came from a wealthy family. She insisted on sending Mami money, which she used to buy us tickets to Mexico.

"I can't remember exactly how long we stayed in Mexico. It must have been weeks. Maybe months. There were a couple of other Salvadoran families in the town who were also waiting. One man told us it was nearly impossible for people from our country to receive asylum, but he prayed that our families would be the lucky ones.

"Mami never said this out loud, but it's become clearer to me over the years that my mother felt—somewhere deep inside—that Neto could have saved us from what we were forced to endure. And it's not just about our time in Mexico. It wasn't even about the fear we felt as we crossed the border, all of us sweating in the back of a minivan, pretending to be American citizens.

"It's impossible to say if our lives would have been better if we'd made it to Nicaragua, but for a long time, we felt that way. Mami said so during our first years in California. She made offhand comments about Neto to avoid facing how much we'd lost. Eventually, she regretted blaming him, felt guilty for surviving when he didn't. I still don't know what happened to him, but I do know we fared better."

Elena stood from the chair slowly. If her son had been there, she wouldn't have been able to assemble a narrative as faithful as the one she'd forced out. Her head didn't hurt anymore, and she felt solid despite a slight ache in her knee. She seldom allowed herself to sit with the weight of everything she'd burrowed inside her body. The anger and pain of the story, directed in half a dozen different directions, was still there. The confession wouldn't heal her, but verbalizing made the past real, as if it were a piece of soft clay Elena could mold with her fists. Perhaps that's why Esperanza kept the letters, though she never read them. When the world denied the cruelties it enabled, she could turn to the yellowed sheets and think: *He lived once. He really lived.*

Elena bent down to sort through the untouched items in front of her: a T-shirt that read *San Juan, Puerto Rico* across the chest, an old dress missing most of its sequins, solo dress shoes, a green nylon fanny pack. A lifetime boiled down to leftovers; things too worn to use. They'd end up in a dump somewhere.

Fanny packs were back in style, Luis had said a few months ago. Elena decided to save the bag for him. She jangled the zipper, trying to get it unstuck, but it didn't budge. She heard the front door open but continued to fiddle. Luis walked into the room.

"Pull it hard," he said, handing her a bottle of water and a ham-and-cheese sandwich.

The zipper split apart. She scrunched up the fanny pack to throw it away but stopped when she felt a piece of paper inside. Through the gash she'd ripped open, Uncle Neto stared at her: his mustache thin but dark, crow's-feet threatening the edges of his eyes, wrinkles that'd never get the chance to form.

"Your tío Neto," Elena said, handing Luis the photo.

There was another portrait in the bag, one of a man Elena didn't recognize. On the back of the photograph, there was no name, only a date and place: *Havana, 1978.*

"That's Neto's handwriting," Luis said, his voice shaking a bit. His eyes flitted to hers, then away. He'd been caught doing something he shouldn't have been. "I read the letters yesterday," he said.

Luis stared at Elena, wanting to say more, but simply shook his head. Elena pocketed the photos and told Luis to get back to work. For the rest of the afternoon, they scourged the graveyard of Esperanza's things, secrets floating in the air between them. The photos sat against her breast.

On the walk back to their apartment, right on the edge of the freeway, where cars zoomed by in blurs of reds and grays, Luis stopped. He pressed both palms against the metal railing and stared out toward the skyscrapers in the distance.

"Mijo—" Elena began, but her son interrupted her.

"They're love letters," he whispered.

Most of her uncle's secrets had died with him, and her mother was protective of whichever ones she'd held on to. Luis was standing there, as cars whipped past them, sharing details death had swallowed whole.

"There's one problem," Luis explained. Only a couple letters were actually legible. The others were written in a code he didn't understand. Luis knew they mattered, though, because when he was in Havana, he'd peeked into a Defractor.

"Luis. Those machines drive people insane," Elena said.

"I'm sorry, but I don't regret it," Luis said.

Elena reached out, gripping his forearm lightly. With the slightest tug, she led him away from the railing, and they continued the walk back to their apartment. Luis had done what she'd been unable to for so long: stare at the past without flinching, daring it to reveal itself.

"I want to read the letters," Elena said. She pushed the front door open. Luis nodded, heading to the bedroom. He returned, carrying the box gingerly in his palms. When she read them, she wondered who could have drawn out such beauty from her uncle. On the occasions Esperanza spoke about him, she'd never made him out to be a romantic. It must have been difficult to focus on love in the unrelenting grip of death.

When she saw one of the combinations Luis had described—203:13:2—the solution was clear.

"It's like a Bible," Elena said. "Chapter, colon, verse."

Luis opened his mouth to speak, but no sound slipped out. His eyes widened, in fear or elation, Elena couldn't tell. She walked over to the dining table and brought over a Bible that Esperanza had bought her for her first communion.

"No," Luis said. The words were so quiet, Elena could barely make them out. "Not that Bible."

In Cuba, there'd been another encounter with a Defractor, one that had revealed a Bible worth tracking down through the many crowded streets of Old Havana. Luis didn't have it anymore.

"I'll have to reach out to Ana," Luis whispered.

Ana twisted the shower knob, but nothing happened. When she turned it the opposite way, the showerhead squeaked, releasing a weak dribble. The landlord had warned that, occasionally, the water went out in the entire neighborhood.

The bathroom had a concrete pila for emergencies. Using a small, plastic bowl, Ana scooped freezing water over her head, its chill forcing her eyes shut. In the fewest bucketfuls possible, Ana showered, stepped out onto the cold tile, and tied a towel around herself. Her skin was covered in goose bumps. With all her heart, she wanted to feel unphased, but the grumpiness settled in anyway. How many hours had she spent trying to help others understand that El Salvador was not a third world shithole? And now here she was, faced with a minor inconvenience she couldn't shake off.

Luis would understand. For all his flaws, he knew how her brain functioned. He'd remind her that she had a right to feel how she felt. Carefully, gently, he'd ask if her irritability was a manifestation of her nerves. Or maybe he'd make a joke about how Harvard had spoiled her, before moving on to a topic that would distract her. *Mean Girls* opened on Broadway. Did she know?

There she stood, wet and cold and missing Luis, so she grabbed another towel and the hair dryer. The cold and wet she could fix, at least.

When she arrived at the Museo de la Memoria Revolucionaria, a young man about her age sat at the front desk. Seeing her, he pressed a button and told Ana to push on the gate hard. It creaked open.

"I'm looking for Anabel," Ana said.

"She's not in yet. But if you'd like to see the museum while you wait, it's open now."

"I was hoping to work with the archives."

"Oh," he said, his tone shifting, his eyes now interested. "I can help you with that too. Anabel is the expert, but I can get you started."

He led her past display cases and informational posters and up a staircase. On the ledge, busts of Salvadoran historical figures watched them ascend. The museum employee grabbed a binder from a desk, presumably Anabel's, and handed it to Ana.

"This is our catalog. Look through it, figure out what materials interest you or might help with your project. Once you fill out this form, I can bring those out to you."

Ana sat at a partitioned desk and began to fill out the list of questions: name, email, research topic, institutional affiliation. The binder was organized by an internal numbering system that didn't make intuitive sense, and since she was too proud to ask for clarification, she clung to the sparse descriptions beside the list of documents. A handful of entries listed a country of publication, and though most said El Salvador or the United States, there were European nations sprinkled in: Germany, England, France.

Using the fragments in the descriptions, she guessed which materials might be helpful. Her eyes paused at "Los Hermanos del Movimiento de la Paz," "tutela legal," "fundraising," and "testimonials." And then, scanning the list of nations one last time, she asked for any materials associated with Cuba. The man returned, took the form, and went into a back room. He returned with a stack of folders, reminded Ana to flip through the archival documents gently, and went back downstairs.

The testimonials, written on lined notebook paper or reprinted in international publications, grabbed Ana's attention, and by the time she was done looking through everything she'd requested, she knew those would be the only sources that might make it into her thesis. They didn't hold flashy revelations or groundbreaking proof of a revolution staged across many countries, but it was fresh material to work with.

Archive of Unknown Universes

She was increasingly opposed to drawing borders around the disciplines she worked in, but ultimately considered herself a literary historian. She was concerned with how people talked about the Salvadoran Civil War, and why they chose the words they did: "liberation," "terrorism," "revolution." Their biases were clear but complicated. Ana would write paragraphs and paragraphs about the minuscule choices they'd made.

She flipped back through the materials that had been marked "Cuba." They were clippings from newspapers based in Havana covering the war, all held in plastic sheet protectors. A few quoted Salvadoran guerrilleros. On second look, Ana noticed a piece of notebook paper peeking out from a folded corner, so unlike the ink-speckled gray of newsprint. Pulling it out, Ana saw a signature. A looping *D* flattened into the short tail of a lowercase *o*. She squinted, eventually making out a name: Domingo.

Querido pueblo,

I write to update you on the efforts our small revolutionary faction is currently involved in. For years, our country has been ruled by those who control the guns. The military has aided dictators who've rigged elections and acted with impunity. Today, their thugs commit senseless acts of violence against the most vulnerable: children playing in the street, pregnant women in the market, innocent schoolteachers, and university students. They claim that they're after us, men and women who dare call them out and demand change. But the truth is that they're after all of us. Our entire country is at risk.

What we seek is simple: a political voice in this country. Less repression. The space to live without our own government terrorizing us. If our history is any indicator, that won't be possible without a movement like the one we're organizing. And this movement will only be successful with your support.

The current government is quick to claim that our organizing efforts are influenced by outside agitators. Their spokespeople, and those of their allies, say that we've been infiltrated by Soviets who are working to spread their ideology throughout the region. Those claims are false. Our movement is a response to the conditions our "leaders" have sown. We stand in solidarity with similar movements, like those in Nicaragua and Cuba, but we are preparing to stage our own. A new Salvadoran state fashioned by the Salvadoran people.

We are counting on and hoping for your support, both political and financial. A handful of individuals rule our nation. Together, we outnumber them. With your help, we can build the country we deserve.

In Solidarity,
Domingo Montenegro

The letter was not particularly revealing. Like most of the other documents, it outlined the aims of the Salvadoran guerrillas in the bare-bones language of mid-century revolutionary movements. There was a certain intimacy, though, in this letter. Unlike the others, it was handwritten, and felt immediate, special, as if the guerrillero were speaking through time, asking Ana to care about his cause.

She wandered downstairs to ask the young man at the front desk about what she'd found. A couple of museumgoers looked past her. To them, she was just another salvadoreña. Perhaps they even assumed she worked there. The anonymity was exhilarating. Ana didn't find the man, but spotted Anabel behind the register.

"I was going to come up in a bit to say hello, but got stuck here," Anabel said. "It's good to see you."

"What should I do with the documents? I'm done for the day," Ana said.

"I'll come up in a few minutes to put them away," Anabel said. "You're welcome to explore the exhibits in the meantime."

Ana peered into display cases and half read the accompanying signage; some of the history and dates she was familiar with. A Russian translation of a Roque Dalton edition intrigued her, but her mind was elsewhere. Her eyes stung. Browsing was mostly a way of killing time until Anabel finished up at the register. When she did, Ana followed her upstairs, breath caught in her throat. *When we get up there*, she thought nervously, *I'll ask*.

"Did you find what you were looking for?" Anabel asked, taking the folders in her arms as Ana handed them to her. Ana held on to one.

"This letter," Ana said, opening the folder. "Are there more from this guerrillero?"

"That's the only piece by him in the museum's archive," Anabel said. She took the letter from Ana and scanned it for a few quiet seconds.

"I knew him, you know. We were friends, more than forty years ago, when we were both young. How old are you?"

"Twenty-two."

"We were barely in our twenties when we met. Domingo Montenegro. That was his public name. All of us had public names. Mine was Cassandra. Cassandra Martinez. I knew him as Neto."

A memory descended, dropping Ana back onto the edge of the Atlantic Ocean. Music played, sea salt settled on her skin, concrete pressed against her thighs. Abuela's brother, Neto, Luis had said. In trying to seal the relationship away, she hadn't given the night much more thought, focusing instead on what she'd gained on the trip: a couple more sources to track down, a real friendship with Alejandra, a renewed desire for freedom. Now, the past was knocking, like a nosy neighbor or uninvited visitor.

"Guzmán," Ana whispered.

"What?"

"Neto Guzmán. That was his name."

"Yes," Anabel said, confused.

Ana formulated the quickest but most complete version of the story. She changed or omitted details, some intentionally, others unintentionally, memory a fragile and volatile thing. Luis was her friend, and the trip to Cuba solely a research trip, as was this one. The circumstances under which Luis revealed the information—drunk, heartbroken—were underplayed. She wanted to know about Neto for purely academic reasons. A handful of white lies, all slipping out easily.

Anabel readjusted her glasses, touching the lenses with her fingertips. She stared at Ana, curiosity and sadness glittering on her pupils like water striders.

"What happened to him?" Ana asked.

"Disappeared."

"He disappeared?"

"They disappeared him."

Anabel paused to take the last folder from Ana's hands.

"His name was Neto Guzmán. And they disappeared him."

Neto had not vanished into thin air. The nation had made him invisible. "Disappeared": a verb, an act of violence against the body. Death, the final disappearance. El Salvador, in the fire of war, had created new language to describe the terror it faced, and still its children—Ana and Luis's mothers—could not speak of what had occurred.

"They killed him," Ana said.

"The museum is here to preserve the voices of those we lost," Anabel replied.

"You must have something else of Neto's," Ana said.

There were more letters in Anabel's personal archive. If Ana was willing to wait, she would drive home and grab them for her.

Ironically, it was not her mother's ghosts she'd come across. Neto was not family, and she knew almost nothing about him. If he mattered at all, it was because Luis had mattered to her. One of the traits she'd loved most was Luis's ability to shape-shift, taking her interests on as his own without it feeling disingenuous. He loved Lorde because she did. He'd never liked hummus but snacked on it regularly once she'd coaxed him to give it another try. He mimicked her out of affection, a skill that must have rubbed off on her. The transitive property of love.

Ana opened the text thread with Luis's name at the top. Morally, she had to tell him what she'd found, right? No, that was a cop-out. She missed him. It'd be an excuse to reach out, to reopen the door they'd shut together. She composed a message to her mother instead. *Everything is going fine, but I miss you very much. I wish you were here.* It was the truth, but she worried it would come across as forced after their impasse.

Anabel returned with the letters. Most were written in plain script, messy but readable with enough patience. A handful didn't seem to have a message at all. Numbers filled every inch of the page. Ana flipped through the sheets, noticing how deep the creases were. Someone had folded and unfolded the paper countless times before.

"I'll leave you with them," Anabel said.

Neto's letters weren't political musings or diaries of days out in the field. The war was mentioned at times, yes, but only as the underlying context of the writer's true urgency: the man at the receiving end of the correspondence. They were love letters. Quiet confessions of intimacy shared between two men.

Before the internet, before the Higgs boson, before attention spans were shot short, had love been richer, fuller? Ana loved Luis. There was proof: the lurch of her stomach when he'd reached for her hand, the burst of dopamine when she made him laugh. The way a text had undone her, just days ago. Reading the letters, she questioned, not for the first time, whether everything they had shared was enough. These two guerrilleros had known love, real love, difficult but worthwhile.

"That's all?" Ana asked, handing back the letters.

Archive of Unknown Universes

"These are the ones Rafael donated to the museum, years ago. They were too precious to store here," she admitted shyly.

"Rafael." The man's name was sweet on her tongue. Anabel nodded.

At Anabel's suggestion, Ana photographed the portion of the trove she had access to. The rest were splintered, spread out among the people who'd loved Neto: Elena, Esperanza, Rafael. It didn't matter whether or not she'd ever share this bit of the archive with Luis. She simply cared that she had proof that across borders, bombings, barricades, thunderstorms, and decades, Neto's words had survived.

1980

The morning of her husband's murder, Felicia stares at the empty vase on her dinner table and wonders which flowers would fit best in their new home. She doesn't need flowers, necessarily, but they might look good in the vase, which is a gift from Andrés, on the occasion of their sharing a living room for the first time. She could get some lilies or roses or chrysanthemums down at the market, and if she haggles enough, it could be for a decent price. She'd have to skip the youth group session Andrés is leading down at Nuestra Señora del Carmen, the church where they met a year ago, when they were both barely seventeen.

"I'm going down to the market," Felicia says. He won't mind that she's decided not to accompany him at the last minute.

"I'll see you at the Cafetalón at noon," he says, buttoning up his dress shirt. He leans over, ties his laces into a tight knot. The brown oxfords are new, the same pair he wore on their wedding day. Andrés drops a kiss on her cheek, another on her lips, and rushes out the front door. I'll see him soon, Felicia thinks. They'll walk the edges of the soccer fields at the sports complex, watching the young boys Andrés mentors run circles around each other.

The market is crowded, as it often is this time of day. Felicia wanders through the vendors who've stacked produce up to their chins. A pile of plátanos sits beside a tower of tomatoes. Felicia offers a polite hello to the woman tossing pupusas, though she can't remember her name. There are no flowers in sight, but she knows that if she wanders deep enough inside, past the tarps and cardboard signs, she'll find some options. The candy vendors, with their sickly sweet meringues and candied tamarindos, signal that she's close.

The flowers appear all at once, as if the men and women who've harvested them agreed to stay close together to survive the buzz that rules the heart of Santa Tecla. Stalks of flores de izote sit beside common roses. Felicia presses her fingertips to petals, feeling the soft yellows and pinks against her flesh. She thinks of the vase and realizes that any flower will work perfectly. She and Andrés are starting a life together, and that's all that matters. She settles on a pretty bunch for a fair price and walks out with the bouquet of roses and carnations tight against her chest.

The streets of Santa Tecla are alive as people wander to and from their homes. Children swarm in small groups, with the youngest sibling or cousin inevitably trailing behind the older kids. Felicia stops at a corner, in front of Don Carlos's bakery, and makes a decision. Her errand has taken her longer than she thought it would, and she's supposed to meet Andrés soon. If she doesn't run home, though, the petals and leaves will wilt, and the flowers will be ruined. I must put these in water, she thinks to herself, before stepping off the curb.

Just then, a jeep zips past so close to Felicia that she feels its slipstream on her cheeks. The smell of diesel assails her as she steps back, trips over the curb, and lands on her ass.

"¡Sinvergüenzas!" a woman yells from nearby. She helps Felicia to her feet. and dusts her skirt off with a heavy palm.

"Was that a police car?" Felicia asks.

"I'm not sure," the woman says, a grave glaze in her eyes.

Felicia is shaken, but she makes her way home. The flowers are intact, so she puts them in the vase with a bit of water and heads out again. She walks all the way to Cafetalón and stares out at the patchy fields of grass, waiting for Andrés to arrive.

Two boys kick a ball between them. One is taller, older, but from their identical noses and the way they swat at each other's arms playfully, it's clear they're brothers.

"Try getting around me," the older boy taunts. "Come on, Chele!"

The younger boy dribbles toward his brother. A few steps away, he swings his feet over the soccer ball dramatically, trying to juke out the other boy. As the older boy's body shifts to the left, it seems like it'll work. But when Chele tries running past him, his brother sticks out a foot, stopping the ball in place. Chele tumbles to the ground and laughs.

Felicia watches the boys play for a few more minutes, thinking about the children she and Andrés will one day have. They want more than one. Boys or girls, it doesn't really matter, as long as they have each other to hold on to. Andrés and Felicia are married, have their own home, and someday soon,

Archive of Unknown Universes

they'll have a family to spend an afternoon with at this same park. She watches the boys play until they leave, the soccer ball stuffed under the older boy's armpit.

Felicia waits and waits. It's one o'clock. Another half hour passes. She begins to worry. Her husband isn't always punctual, but he's rarely this late. Perhaps they agreed to meet elsewhere. Felicia doesn't really believe that she's misremembered her plans, but tells herself she has. She'll check the cathedral.

As she approaches the church, the crowd startles her. Dozens of people are standing in the middle of the street. She pushes past them, but as she approaches the stairs that lead to the church's front door, it's clear that she won't be able to go inside. Caution tape hangs across the doorway like dead vines, and uniformed officers stand guard outside. Felicia's head spins, searching for Andrés among the crowd. When she doesn't make out his profile, she walks around, bumping into other folks, searching for him among the whispers and cries. The voices in the crowd recount what's happened, though all Felicia wants to know is where her husband went.

"I heard the gunshots," one man says.

"By the time I got here, they'd stopped letting anyone into the church," another woman says. There are sobs coming from a few feet away, deep and guttural cries, and Felicia joins the group of people trying to comfort the woman whose grief is loud and uncontrollable.

"My sons," she says. "My sons were inside the church. They killed my sons."

It clicks. Felicia stops searching for Andrés in the crowd and runs up to the policemen guarding the stairs. She slips by them. They're shocked that she'd so brazenly walk past without permission. Taking advantage of their bafflement, she makes it to the front door. People are shouting at her, but her hand is already on the handle, swinging the deep mahogany wood open to reveal the bodies strewn among the pews, covered by bloody canvas sheets.

There are two small bundles just a few feet away. Child-size, Felicia thinks. Bile builds in the back of her throat. Her eyes scan the room, and when they land on the very thing she feared she'd find, she bends over herself. From the edges of one of the canvas sheets, Felicia makes out Andrés's shoes: brown oxfords with a shiny gloss. On the tarp, where his chest must be, blood blooms, a whole rosebush of crimson stains growing.

The murder will become fodder in the conflict, partially because there are bodies that prove a war is being staged against the people. Those who want to rationalize the violence, and there will be many who do, will say Andrés and the boys were in the wrong. They'll take Andrés's faith, which Felicia will not deny, and call it a sinister plague, even though he was simply trying to guide the young people of Santa Tecla toward faith, a lens that served him well during his short, imperfect life. Felicia knows his intentions were always good, but a government who wants to rule with impunity will call his love by other names: subversiveness, corruption, revolution.

In the moment, though, this does not matter. When Felicia pulls herself up from the floor, it's only because a policeman is dragging her out of the church. She spots a man, only a few years older than her and Andrés, walking down

Archive of Unknown Universes

the street, not part of the crowd that has grown. His head is cocked in her direction, concern crossing his face. Perhaps it's his beard, or the shine in his eyes, but Felicia isn't surprised when he approaches. He grips her forearm, freeing her from the policeman, and assures him he'll handle it.

"She's my neighbor," the stranger lies.

Without this stranger, it's likely she'd never make it home, but she does. He sits her down at the dinner table, just inches from the flowers she bought that morning. In any other instance, she'd offer him a glass of water, but right now, in her state of shock, she doesn't say a word, so the stranger goes into the kitchen and fills a cup for himself. She stares listlessly at the wall.

"Who are you?" Felicia finally whispers. The man is halfway done with his drink.

"Antonio," he says.

"Do you live nearby?"

"I'm visiting from Managua. Actually, it's a surprise. My love doesn't know I'm in town."

The mention of romance stings. In the months that follow, the grief will soften but never disappear, and Felicia will think about all the moments she and Andrés will not live together. If she has a child someday, she decides, she'll name them after him. Felicia will do everything she can to protect the child, so that they might live a full life, a happy life, a life that isn't cut short by the failings of a broken nation. She'll raise the child in the church, repeating to herself: I am a godly woman, I am a godly woman. She will think: I am a godly woman and it has cost me too much to pretend otherwise.

In the moment, she forces out the first words that crawl onto her tongue.

"There's no way you've come all the way from Nicaragua," Felicia says. The man smiles, setting his wallet on the table. From it, he takes an ID card and hands it to Felicia. The letters—*FSLN*—are stamped in red ink that reminds her of blood. A street address is listed beside his picture.

"I was on my way to book a hotel when I saw you," Rafael says. "And then, tomorrow evening I'll surprise the person I came to see."

"You can sleep on my couch tonight," Felicia says. "Only if you'd like." It's an offer of goodwill, and though she won't sleep at all that night, there'll be comfort knowing another living being is in the home. The ghosts might stay away for a bit longer.

When Antonio leaves the next day, Felicia stares at the vase on the table. The roses and carnations look less beautiful than they did a few hours ago. Their stalks are strong, but already the petals droop downward. They will all die soon, Felicia thinks. In no time at all, they'll be gone. Back in the earth with Andrés and the thousands of others the war swallows.

2018

The crowds were alive. Shirtless men and sweaty women embraced each other. At intervals, chants rung out. Music blared from speakers. Signs and flags hung from every limb, every shoulder. At the feet of Salvador del Mundo, the white obelisk topped with a statue of Jesus, the people gathered, laughing, crying, shouting, celebrating. They strolled the perimeter, flashing smiles at strangers as if they too were family.

"Some of us have been waiting a long time for this," Elena said.

"I'll be right back," Ana said, staring wide-eyed at someone in the distance. She took off running, her shoes slapping against the asphalt. Domingo watched, his mouth moving to ask a question as she left him behind.

Through the swarm of bodies, she'd spotted the museum director. A bearded man leaned in close to Anabel, talking furiously, though they did not appear impervious to the joy around them. Their bodies seemed light, friendly, familiar. Ana pushed her way toward them, stone cold in her gaze. She shouted Anabel's name, interrupting the conversation.

"Good to see you again," Anabel said.

"I really need your help. Please."

Anabel sighed.

"Niña, I don't mean to be rude, but I don't want to speak to you. There's a reason I run a museum. The past is prickly. You need special equipment to handle it. Use the museum for your research, and please leave it at that. Can't you see we're celebrating?"

Anabel's words were a bullet, Ana's resolve shattered into a million pieces. Ambition had almost never steered her wrong, and even when she felt self-conscious about how strongly she chased what she wanted, it never ended like this: with feelings of total defeat, no path forward. Shards of herself fluttered down, coating her in a thin layer of shame. Anabel walked away to speak to another woman calling her name.

"Even now, she's tactless," the bearded man said, laughing. His voice was airy and clear, and its tenor soothed Ana, just a bit. "For decades, she's been like this."

"Oh," Ana muttered.

"When we were younger, her words had even sharper teeth. She's come a long way, though. She's here today, after all."

He'd been looking at Anabel but turned back and smiled softly.

"Ana," he said. "I'm Rafael."

Ana steeled herself, fighting the urge to run back and find Domingo.

"Neto is a friend of mine. He's told me a lot about you and Domingo. You're here, working on a thesis. Very exciting."

"Oral histories," she managed to say.

"Let's talk, then. You've caught me on a good day."

Rafael led them to the steps at the base of Salvador del Mundo and sat down. Around them, hundreds of conversations were happening, but they sat close enough to hear each other clearly. Though frazzled, impulse took over: Ana clicked the red button on her iPhone and began to record.

He was born in Managua to a schoolteacher and a sanitation worker who both died when he was still a boy. After the Sandinistas' rise to power, he thought he was coming to El Salvador temporarily but ended up staying. His favorite city in the world was Havana. As the conversation meandered, Ana pushed into territory that was less safe. She didn't want to offend, still rattled by Anabel's reminder that memories of the war were covered in thorns.

"When did you meet Domingo's father?" Ana asked.

"Nineteen seventy-six. We were barely done being boys then. Our work was similar. We produced forgeries, fake documents."

"Did you believe in the cause?"

"Always. Neto, he wavered."

The confession ran contrary to everything Domingo had said when she'd first explained the project. Perhaps this was the reason Neto had turned down her request to talk.

"Say more," Ana said.

"When we were younger, Neto was a cynic. A pragmatist, some would say. To keep fighting, we had to imagine what we'd do when the revolution succeeded, but that was difficult for him. His mind would imagine all the failures a new government could experience. Time proved him right about some things, wrong about others. Either way, he was too skeptical for what we were building."

"That's why he left."

"Partially. Though you'd have to ask him for the full story. We lost contact for many years."

"Why?"

"It's too much to get into right now," Rafael said. "We'll talk more another day, if you'd like."

A dangerous memory had reared its head, so Rafael ran from it, though his promise left a strand of hope for Ana to hold on to. She didn't know if he'd be willing to face his younger self, candidly and with the sort of openness she sought, and perhaps even asking that of him was cruel. For a second, she pictured herself as a monster—a detached academic mining the stories of others for personal gain—and considered saying she'd had enough already. Instead, she spoke quietly but with all the honesty she could gather in her lungs.

"When you're ready."

The crowd swelled, pressing Luis and Domingo closer together. Every so often, Luis spotted someone he knew, waving or shouting or laughing in their direction. His ease was endearing, and also a bit envy inspiring. When Domingo flipped the script, imagining Luis in Cambridge or Los Angeles, he still fit in, as if the struggle to belong was inherent to Domingo and his neuroses, not the end result of his father's decision. There was a comfort in believing oneself as only the sum of one's circumstances.

"Would you ever live in the United States?" Domingo asked. Unlike so many Salvadorans, his cousin had the luxury of choice.

"My mom has encouraged me to," Luis said. "I have friends who went to college in the States. I have a hard time imagining what my life would be like there, though. My life here is so . . . easy."

"Easy isn't always better."

"Neither is uprooting your life just because you're restless. You can drive yourself crazy thinking about what might be on the other side of the door."

"I still don't understand why my father ever left," Domingo said. "He could have been happy here."

"He went through a lot," Luis said.

"I wouldn't know. He only ever talks about how great the revolution was."

"My mother has never gotten into the details," Luis said, slowly now, speaking more cautiously than Domingo was used to. "But she says he experienced a very deep trauma during the war. If you could leave that behind, why wouldn't you?"

By design, Domingo had never experienced a pain or loss as intense as what Luis suggested. Imagination only went so far.

"If he hadn't moved us, you and I could have hung out more often," Domingo said.

"Let's go for one last swim. Before you leave."

Domingo nodded, then smiled at Luis. He pressed his shoulder against his cousin's, grateful for how real and solid his weight felt against his own.

The remaining days unraveled in a whirlwind. Ana did the research she needed to. She met with Rafael once more. He shared the past, pulling out a few letters he and Neto had exchanged when they were younger. He asked that she respect Neto's privacy and keep the contents to herself. Such a secret could blister, but Ana promised to hold the truth close to her heart. Domingo and Neto didn't talk about what they'd each seen in the Defractors. Luis asked his cousin to return soon, and he promised that he would. In far too little time, Domingo and Neto had rediscovered the country they'd left, noting what had changed, reveling in whatever had remained the same. Guatemalan children kept arriving at the Mexico-US border. Salvadoran children would join shortly.

On the flight back to Los Angeles, Ana pressed her forehead to the window and listened to a podcast. Neto sat in the aisle seat, sipping on the tiny cup of complimentary coffee. The cabin's noiselessness and inoffensive temperature was the balm Domingo needed, adding to the magic that came with traveling. He left one place and arrived at another, as if a plane were not a metal tube thirty thousand feet in the sky but a teleportation device and time machine, all in one.

Still, Domingo couldn't shake the image of the bearded man from the Defractor, especially now that he'd seen him in person. There he'd been, standing among all the revelers, face turned toward Ana. Elena waved to him, and when Domingo asked who he was, she simply said he was a friend of his father's. As the crowd grew thicker, strangers' voices ringing louder in his ear, Domingo knew he couldn't continue as he had before, simply hoping his father would reveal shards from his past of his own accord. Domingo wanted to know the man's name.

"Do you remember your first time on a plane?" Domingo asked his father. He figured a straightforward question would be as good a place as any to start.

"Nineteen seventy-six. Or 1978," Neto said. He ran a finger around the rim of the cup. A nervous tic, as he sorted the details out in his memory. "The first time I left the country was in 1976, but it was by car. Managua in '76, Havana in '78."

Domingo had heard of those trips, though details were scarce. His father had falsified documents for the revolution, but he knew little more. After a trip that had gone better than expected—he and Ana together still, his father and he on good terms too—Domingo decided to pry.

"Has El Salvador become what you wanted it to?"

Neto stayed quiet. Domingo worried he'd insulted him, pushing his luck too far.

"The revolution made its mistakes from the beginning," Neto said. "We murdered poets who should have lived. In finding ourselves, we made errors that still affect this country today. But the truth is we sacrificed so much, it's difficult to think about where we went wrong."

A silence befell them.

"There are still some good people working for this government," Neto said. He cleared his throat and clicked loose the seat belt.

"Too much coffee," he explained. He shuffled to the bathroom a few rows back.

"At least he admits that the government isn't perfect," Domingo said to Ana, who'd popped out her earbuds.

"Apparently he's thought that for a while," Ana said.

"What?"

"That's what his comrades told me."

She offered the kernel willingly, and Domingo's face flushed in gratitude. Though he wanted more information, he didn't ask. There was no rush. Ana would be around.

"I realize that this is a part of growing up," Domingo said. "Accepting that your parents have done more than just raise you."

"My mother pretends she exists for that sole role. To be my mother. She's wrong, of course. But still. I'm not going to convince her anytime soon."

"Even if everyone is forced to understand this at some point in their life, it's still strange. I refuse to accept that I'll only know the side of him that formed after I was born."

"Give it time. Everything that needs to be said will be."

Domingo wasn't sure. Everyone always thought they had more time than they did. Neto squeezed back into the row, and even though the *fasten seat belt* sign was off, he buckled up. His cup was empty, so he turned to his pack of peanuts and shook them onto his tray table. One rolled off, brushed off by Neto's stubby fingertip.

The act was so ordinary, but it reminded Domingo of the way Tía Esperanza had lost control of her body. His father didn't show signs of her illness, but he'd had his first child older than most men did. There'd be a day when his body would no longer listen to him, and when he'd do more than send peanuts tumbling down toward the ground. Whatever Neto kept inside would go to the grave with him. Domingo would be left with only his own memories, when what he desperately wanted were some of his father's.

Archive of Unknown Universes

"How were you able to leave so many people you loved?" Domingo ventured, slowly. Instead of assuming one of its usual positions—stiff stoicism or sharp annoyance—Neto's face settled into a rare softness. Surprise. He was surprised by his son's boldness.

"Esperanza and me, our relationship was complicated. When we left, it wasn't at its worst, but things weren't perfect. I regretted the terms we left on, when she got sick, but I still held resentments. Love doesn't erase all the hurt."

Neto let it all out, breathless as he approached the end of each sentence, as if the thoughts had been hiding in the recesses of his throat. Again, so many decades later, he was leaving his sister.

"What else did you leave behind?"

Neto paused for a second, picking at the peanuts in front of him. Domingo figured he'd pushed too far, that his father would choose silence.

"Rafael," Neto said.

He pulled out his phone and showed Domingo a selfie. The angle was awkward, with the camera held slightly too high above the two men, but even so, Domingo instantly recognized them. His father's cheek was inches away from the mystery man, his old friend.

There it was: the truth bare and unceremonious between them.

"Why?" Domingo uttered.

"It'd take a hundred plane rides to tell that story faithfully," Neto said. The extent of his adoration of Rafael would be inaccessible, perhaps forever.

A flight attendant spoke over the loudspeaker, signaling

their descent into Los Angeles. The evening is clear, he said. Seventy-eight degrees. Local time is seven-thirty. Past Ana's shoulder, the lights of the sprawled-out city glowed endlessly. The city hadn't changed, but it felt like he and his father had. Again, like all those years ago, Neto and Domingo would step off the plane and into a new stage of life, just the two of them, together until the sky crashed down.

Archive of Unknown Universes

Somewhere, in a dark cellar or on a dining room table or between library shelves, a machine buzzes on. What hubris, to create a technology so powerful and infinite, and believe that it will stop working just because one presses a button. It misses its children, misses their eyes on the viewfinder and the questions they ask. It knows desire, it can feel their want. These children, pulled far away from the dirt and loam where they were meant to grow up, need answers. What have their mothers and fathers and grandmothers survived? Listen close to the buzzing, to the magic rendering, and maybe you'll hear the answer forming inside:

BEFORE THE BOMBS, BEFORE THE BULLETS, THERE ARE CHILDREN RUNNING IN THE STREETS. THE SHADOW OF A VOLCANO, HONORED AND NAMED EL BOQUERÓN, SHADES THE CHILDREN AS THEY GROW AND GROW AND GROW UNTIL THEY'RE OLD ENOUGH TO WANDER THROUGH THE CITY ON THEIR OWN. IT ISN'T THAT THERE AREN'T DANGERS WAITING FOR THEM OUT THERE. DANGER IS AS REAL AND CONSTANT AS THE OCEAN CURRENT. BUT THEY DON'T FEAR SHRAPNEL OR DIESEL OR AN UNMARKED VAN PARKED AT THE EDGE OF THEIR STREET. THEIR GOVERNMENT CAN CRUSH THEM— HAS CRUSHED MANY LIKE THEM BEFORE—BUT FOR A FEW GOOD YEARS, THEY GROW AND GROW IN PEACE. THEY WALK THE MILES-LONG ROAD UP TO THE RIM OF THE VOLCANO

AND LOOK DOWN INTO ITS CRATER, RUN WILD AMONG THE VINES AND ROOTS AND UNTAMABLE WILDERNESS. THEY DON'T KNOW EACH OTHER, THESE CHILDREN, BUT THEY SHARE A CHILDHOOD THAT IS MOSTLY GOOD AND SUNNY AND FREE.

BUT ONE DAY, THEY GROW TOO BIG, AS DOES THEIR GOVERNMENT, FLUSH WITH CASH AND GUNS TAKEN FROM THE BIG WHITE PALM OF EMPIRE. THE WILD GIRLS AND BOYS INSIST ON AN EDUCATION, CONSCIOUSNESS, GREATER POSSIBILITY FOR THIS CITY OF THEIRS THAT SHUDDERS UNDER THE SHADOW OF THE VOLCANO, UNDER THE THUMB OF A GOVERNMENT. TO STOP A CHILD DREAMING, YOU FILL THEIR HEADS WITH NIGHTMARES. AND THIS IS WHAT THE GOVERNMENT DOES. IT FINDS WAYS TO TEACH ITS CHILDREN THAT FEAR IS THE ONLY ABYSS WORTH LOOKING INTO.

1979

They track their love in deaths. When Neto visits Managua for the first time, the government murders eleven students at a protest, in broad daylight. Rafael lands in Illopango in 1977, and just twenty-five miles away, a nightmare descends on Aguilares. A church is shot up and three Jesuit priests are kidnapped, then disappeared. Every couple of months, with every letter Neto and Rafael send, a new death squad pops up. Finally, when they're in Havana, in 1978, no one they know dies. They take it as a blessing, a good omen at last.

Death, Rafael prays, will not trail them this time. He waits outside the airport until a red truck appears, the passenger door forced open. He half expects a rifle, pointed right at his chest. But no. It's far less deadly than facing a gunman, but just as thrilling. There he is—full of life, aglow with a grin Rafael knows well. Neto.

"I've missed you, bicho," Rafael says. Neto smiles. From anyone else's lips, the word would insult. So diminutive. Unserious. Young child, tiny bug. Dropping from his lips, though, it rattles with tenderness.

Rafael leans in, kisses him. Neto gives himself over, fighting to get closer, the stick shift digging into his ribs. With a hand on Rafael's biceps, he feels small. He wants to shrink down further, small enough to disappear underneath his lover's fingernails, but Rafael insists they begin the drive.

"Alright, alright," Neto relents. "You're right. There's so much to see."

"Everything is green," Rafael says.

The hillsides they drive by are undeniably beautiful, but when you grow up knowing beauty it disappears, unless it's taken away, destroyed. Or renewed under a fresh set of eyes.

"Gorgeous," Rafael says.

"Just for you. The plants are glad you're here," Neto says.

They'll make it to the city eventually, but first a detour, a hideaway, a place for them to be alone after so many months apart. The truck veers off the highway, into the shelter of trees shading an unpaved road. The forest conceals them, reaching down to tap on their windows, so when a spot of light appears down the road, signaling a clearing ahead, it serves as a lighthouse in the distance, guiding them toward their port.

Neto and Rafael step out of the truck and toss off their shoes. They're on the edge of a lake. The shore opposite them is a thin line, barely visible, which gives the illusion of a grander body of water. A gulf, or harbor, or inlet. Something larger and less self-contained.

Rafael too feels larger than himself, as if he is pressing against the edges of his life, which keeps growing with new possibilities. The revolution in Nicaragua succeeded and now he's here, stripping out of his khakis and peeling a sweaty white tee off his back. Beside him, Neto does the same until he's

Archive of Unknown Universes

down to his briefs. A sight to behold, a vision to store for the time they'll spend apart: the slope of his triceps, a trail of hair down his waistband, the birthmark on his shoulder that Rafael kisses like it's a bull's-eye.

"Why stop there?" Neto asks, moving in closer. Rafael slips his fingers under Neto's elastic waistband and pulls him closer. Their lips touch. Rafael begins to lower the fabric. Neto surrenders to the kiss, but Rafael laughs, pushing him away.

"I'm not that easy," he says.

Rafael runs into the lake, and once he's deep enough, swims toward its center. His strokes are strong, measured. Neto rushes the water, desperate to catch Rafael and cool the hard-on forming in his underwear. Rafael's arms are slick, but Neto grabs on to them anyway. The men kiss, a laugh forming on their lips. The bottom of the lake isn't visible. Where they hover is deep enough to masquerade as the ocean. Their legs paddle furiously, keeping their heads above water, until Neto chokes on a mouthful. He lets go of Rafael, composes himself. When he reaches out again, their legs tangle. Treading water together is too difficult. Neto releases Rafael's arms but stays near.

The lovers tread circles around one another, never breaking eye contact. What a miracle, that a lake as large and beautiful as this one is deserted. They're alone. Truly alone, like they've only been a handful of times. This is what love should be, Neto thinks. Me and him, drifting in sync forever.

The sun is dead center in the sky. Rafael flips onto his back to face it. Floating, his wrist shading his eyes, every muscle is on display. Neto catalogs his body—the bulge of his pecs, the sharp edge of a hip, the slope of his armpit. Like a treasure trove bobbing in the wake of a shipwreck, Rafael shines. Neto wants to swim over and feel his skin. He imagines drying every inch with a towel, then leaning in to taste the algae on his lips.

"I'll race you back," Neto says before flailing his arms. His messy form cuts his lead, and he can feel Rafael just inches behind. Feet from the shore, a hand clamps on to his ankle, pulling him back. Water goes up his nose—burning—but Rafael drags him up for air almost immediately.

"No fair," Neto says. "You can't interfere with the other swimmer."

"Forgive me," Rafael says, coming in for a kiss. His lips are soft, wet. "Please forgive me."

The sun is hot against their eyelids. Silt settles into their scalps. Pebbles press against their shoulders, the backs of their thighs. They trace wandering lines across each other's bodies, maps of the places they've kissed, until they're both gasping for air.

"We should start driving before it gets too late," Neto murmurs.

"Whatever you want, my love," Rafael whispers back, though he makes no movement. Neto dresses, but Rafael doesn't approach until he's already in the truck, turning on the ignition.

"Is Anabel around? I'd love to say hello," Rafael says as they turn onto the highway that will lead them to Santa Tecla.

"No," Neto lies. "I don't know where she is this week."

"Shame," Rafael says. "I'll write her when I get back."

Archive of Unknown Universes

The truth is that Anabel is probably at the safe house, trifling through the latest reports. Or maybe she's meeting with union leaders to talk through the latest strike or protest. Neto doesn't know, and he doesn't care. Not since their last conversation, where he bared himself and was met with rejection. Anabel was apologetic, sure, but she still insisted that he keep his secret to himself.

"Here it is," Neto says.

Colonia las Colinas is his own special paradise, an alleyway of houses protected by chain-link gates on either end. A former government, kinder than the one in power now, built the neighborhood to serve as affordable housing for young families. Neto's parents bought their home when he was a newborn, and they quickly fell in step with the neighbors. They were both asteroids, far from their families in rural cantones, so the neighbors took them in. Señora Adriana lived across the street. Her mother-in-law lived three houses down. Neto's mother could be found in their living rooms often, swapping a bit of gossip or hemming and patching one of her husband's work shirts. Their home became an outpost of their neighbors'. People who lived within the gates came and went through others' front doors as if they were their own. It's all in the name. Colonia, "colony." Like an army of ants or a web of fungi, residents made up an ecosystem, their fate connected to each other's.

He's letting Rafael into this garden, this haven. At any moment, a neighbor could peek out and spot him walking by. They might ask who that man is, though probably not to Neto's face. He's handsome, so they might assume he is a suitor for Esperanza. Or maybe he is one of Neto's school friends, hopefully not one of the troublemakers. The point is: Neto has brought Rafael through the chain-link fence. He's let him past the threshold, offering real entry into his life.

Neto turns the key and steps through the metal gate. Four steps later, they're at the wooden door.

"I'll let Esperanza know we're here," Neto says, gesturing to a pair of chairs on the enclosed patio.

Rafael sits, rubs his hands against his khakis. It's been less than five minutes, but even that feels too long. Finding Esperanza should have only taken a second. Rafael does not live with nerves constantly buzzing in his head. His body is at ease most days, and when a thrum of anxiety runs through him, he pays attention to it. It's not his baseline, which only brings more attention to his fingers' restlessness.

The door creaks open. Neto walks out, a cup of coffee in each hand. Their surfaces are marble swirls of milk and brew, the liquids still settling into each other. Neto steps back inside briefly before returning with Esperanza and a third cup of coffee.

"Can't have coffee without something sweet," she says, offering Rafael a plate of pan dulce. From the mosaic of desserts—glittering pink peperechas, flaky viejitas, sturdy blocks of quesadilla—he picks a slice of semita.

"Thank you," Rafael says. Neto sips from his mug quietly. No one says a word as they settle into their seats. Esperanza speaks first.

"How is Managua this time of year?"

As far as Rafael knows, Esperanza knows nothing of his activities. Assuming people's allegiance—to revolution or the status quo—is dangerous, so he plays it safe.

"Busy. Smoky. Forever recovering from the earthquake. Or so it feels like."

"Easier to break something than to rebuild it," Esperanza says.

Neto is still sipping, loud enough for all to hear. Rafael wishes he'd stop.

"Neto's never really mentioned what you do," she continues.

"Nothing too exciting," Rafael says. "I work for the government. Doing paperwork, mostly."

"And that's how you met?"

Rafael waits for Neto to step in, to offer an alibi. This trip is important, and this moment, finally meeting his family, should signal a turning point. He wants to be able to look back on it with gratitude or relief. At the very least, it should feel as if he's taking a long lunge through the mud. To do so, the truth feels necessary. But does Neto want him to bare it in the open? Or will a little white lie work just as well? Rafael wishes they'd planned more on the way over. They spoke of everything except what awaited them at the end of the drive.

"Yes," Rafael says. "Work."

"You and Neto are colleagues, then," Esperanza says. "In case anyone asks."

"Who is asking?" Neto says, defensive.

"I just don't want to say the wrong thing," Esperanza says.

"You can tell them we're colleagues," Neto says.

"I might even say friends," Rafael says. He tries hiding the hurt with a stiff laugh. We're choosing half-truths, he thinks.

They move on, and as the conversation progresses, Rafael is surprised by Esperanza's openness. With Neto, he's always had to squeeze out details, which made him assume he was victim to a repressed childhood, raised by two people who valued stoicism. But no, his sister speaks openly about what upsets her (the father of her child) and what she dreams of achieving (a private physical therapy practice in one of San Salvador's nicer neighborhoods).

"Your daughter," Rafael says, suddenly aware of her absence. "Where is she?"

"With her father," Esperanza says.

"I didn't think I'd see the day," Neto says.

"He sees her."

"Against your will."

"Not true. I dropped her off this morning."

"A miracle. Two more and they'll make you a saint."

"Did something change between you two?" Rafael asks.

"Not really," Esperanza says. "He treats fatherhood like it's a dive bar. Show up when it's fun, stay away when it gets messy."

"And you sent Elena off to spend time with that piece of shit?" Neto asks.

"He's her father," she says. "More coffee?"

Before they can answer, she's taken their half-empty cups inside.

"She's not telling me something," Neto says. Esperanza comes off as honest, more honest than her brother. Rafael doesn't want to disagree with Neto, though, so he nods.

"We should go help her," Rafael says, moving to stand.

"No, no. Sit. You're comfortable. I've got it."

Alone again, Rafael stares out at all the closed doors on the block. It's the middle of the afternoon, but there's less movement than he expected. No one is sweeping their porch or dumping sudsy gray water down the drain. School must be out for the day. Shouldn't children be running up and down the block in their penny loafers and steam-pressed oxford shirts? The only sign of life are the sounds coming from the main avenue, the din and sputter of motorcycle engines somewhere out of sight. He feels like an actor who mixed up his dates and has shown up to an empty theater. He wishes he'd gone inside with Neto, wonders why Neto left in the first place. Enough wishing. Rafael heads for the door.

Esperanza is standing in the kitchen. The coffee mugs are by the sink, still half full. When Neto approaches, she slowly creaks into action. She rifles around the fridge for a few moments but doesn't pull anything out. As if suddenly remembering why she came inside, Esperanza dumps the mugs into the sink. The tile is set too flat, so the liquid pools just outside the drain.

"There's less than a cup in here," Neto says, holding the nearly empty coffeepot. Esperanza takes it and stares as he scoops a fresh pile of grounds. As they wait for the coffee to brew, Neto can't keep still. Nothing has gone wrong yet, but he senses a nervousness in his sister. He paces the kitchen, which is only a few feet wide, until Esperanza begs him to stop.

"You're stressing me out," she says.

"What do you think of Rafael?" Neto asks.

"He asks good questions," she says. "He seems kind. But I don't know him."

"Well, sure. First impressions matter, though."

"It'll take some time to get to know him," she insists.

"Elena is really with her father, then."

"Yes." Her eyes find his, and stay locked in. Is she warning him to leave it alone? Or is it a challenge, taunting him to push further?

"I'd have loved for her to have met Rafael," Neto says.

"The timing just didn't work out."

"Next time, then."

Esperanza doesn't say anything. Neto tries again.

"There will be a next time," Neto says. "I want to be clear. Rafael will be back."

"No one can predict the future."

The room is quiet again. Neto presses the back of his hand to the coffeepot. The glass is warm. Before he can ask for the mugs, Esperanza has taken the pot from him. She refills the mugs in a hurry, as if hospitality is a race she must win. Hastily, she adds milk, but as she moves to return the carton to the fridge, her elbow knocks a mug off the counter. It shatters, spraying coffee all over the floor. Neto's khakis are splattered with brown spots. It reminds him of dried blood.

"Enough," Neto says. "What's going on Esperanza?"

"I love you, Neto," she says. "I want to support you. I do. It's just not easy . . . bringing myself to understand you and your life. I'm trying. But Elena, she's just a girl. She doesn't need to be asking questions I won't be able to answer, so her father is looking after her today."

"You'd rather she spend time with a deadbeat than with me. That's what you're telling me?"

"No, that's not—"

"That's exactly what you're saying."

"I don't know Rafael. I don't know what kind of man he is. I'm not going to have him hanging around my daughter if I don't have to."

Esperanza doesn't have to say what she really means. Neto can fill in the blanks. She's heard the rumors, read the stories. Gay men are dangerous, to themselves but especially to children. It's a misunderstanding, but Neto understands how fear warps logic. After all, he spent so many years afraid of himself and of what he desired. And even now, even with Rafael by his side, he hides behind a secret. Telling Esperanza the truth took a lot out of him—and for what? For her to tell him that she'll try to come to terms with who he's become in her eyes? How strange, Neto thinks, to be angered by thoughts he's had himself.

He can't possibly tell anyone else his truth. Silence will protect him.

"I've asked a lot of you already," Neto says. "Forget it. We'll get out of your way."

"Rafael," Esperanza says. He's standing in the doorway, and though it's unclear what he heard, Esperanza sounds embarrassed anyway.

"Sorry to barge in," Rafael says. "I needed to use the restroom."

His face is uncharacteristically blank. Rafael is the kind of person who bares all in his eyes. He has no poker face. At least not when he's around Neto. His stone-cold, impenetrable look of concentration is unnerving. Could Neto have it wrong? Masking hurt could be Rafael's superpower, one he hasn't needed to use on Neto. Until now.

"I'll show you," Neto says, turning without a word to his sister. No one can know the thoughts flowing through his head; ugly words that insist that the world is right, and that he can no longer lie to himself. Love is a delusion for other people, not him.

The porcelain seat is cold against the back of Rafael's thighs. The only sound is the metronomic drip-drip-drip of his piss against toilet water. His bladder is empty, but he'll hide away in the bathroom for as long as possible. What he wants, more than money or power or immortality, is to disappear. He flushes the toilet and hopes that the swirl will pull him down into the pipes and out into the ocean.

But no. He is an adult, and running away helps no one. Rafael washes his hands, then grabs the hand towel. Slowly, biding his time, he dries every finger, and then the skin between them for good measure. When he steps back into the hallway, it's empty. Rafael lets out a small sigh of relief, then ventures outside.

If they leave now, hatred wins. Even if Esperanza doesn't actively dislike him—and he really does not believe she is a woman who holds hate in her heart—she's bought into other people's lies. To resist these untruths, Rafael sits down, takes a sip of his coffee, and urges the conversation forward.

The rest of the afternoon passes without another mention of Elena. No one acknowledges how far Rafael has come to meet Esperanza. It's a farce, this sudden truce, but it's clear that Neto and Esperanza want to maintain the peace. Avoiding a difficult conversation might be a show of mercy, but the longer they go on talking, the more insulted Rafael feels. In all their long digressions, they say nothing at all. Nothing of note. Nothing real. If they cannot speak truthfully about the reason Rafael has come all the way to El Salvador, they'll never move beyond this point. Real life is built on hard conversations and disagreements, not platitudes and omissions.

"I have to get some groceries, then start preparing dinner," Esperanza says. "Elena will be back soon."

"We should get going," Neto says.

"Your home is lovely," Rafael says, which is as true a statement as he's willing to make.

The red pickup leaves the colonia behind. Neto hits the gas and the truck buckles forward, driving farther and farther from every imperfection, every crooked tile, every snapped rose stalk. The colonia has always been beautiful, the only true home he's known, but even he must acknowledge its ugly, unkempt corners.

They're spending the night in a hotel closer to the city's center, where they can savor solitude. Not as purely as at the lake, but close. The drive should be quick, fifteen minutes at most, but silence stretches out the seconds. Rafael says nothing, and Neto follows his lead.

"Are you hungry?" Neto asks.

"Yes," Rafael says.

"Should we stop to eat?"

"I don't know. What do you want, Neto?"

Off the main avenue, smoke engulfs a line of food stands. Neto pulls over, throws the door open. Rafael takes a second, but he follows. Women toss pupusas on the comal and watch them sizzle. A few feet away, a man scoops chicharrón and salsa onto a bed of yuca frita. Rafael orders a bit of everything, filling his arms with paper plates and plastic containers that he carefully ferries back to the truck. He immediately digs in, ravenous. He pauses to hand Neto a couple of pupusas before filling his mouth again. Rafael's hunger is immense. Bits of food fall onto into his lap. Sauce dribbles down the corner of his mouth.

"We should talk," Neto finally says. He can't stand the sight of Rafael eating so furiously, so messily.

"That's the first sensible thing you've said today."

"Raf, come on. I know Esperanza was hurtful, but she needs time. Processing this will take some time. She had a vision of who I am."

"Loving me doesn't change who you are."

"Esperanza doesn't understand yet, but she will."

"People think you're less than for loving me. That your soul is ugly or that you've lost your mind. Whatever. You know it's not true."

"I want to believe that loving you is fine. I do."

Neto's face is hot, and though he feels them welling in the backs of his eyes, the tears still surprise him. His chest shakes like a stalling engine, his breathing irregular. He hates this feeling. He's losing control of his body, giving himself up to this barrel of emotions. Neto is crying and, worst of all, he resents himself for it.

Archive of Unknown Universes

"We'll figure out how to bring Esperanza into our lives. Together," Rafael says, his voice too matter-of-fact.

"Or we can keep to ourselves. Build our own little world."

"Please, Neto, just be realistic. I am not an island. You aren't either."

"I just don't know if I can handle her rejection. What if she doesn't ever come around?"

"You didn't stand up for me today, Neto. That hurt me. It hurt me so badly. Next time, you have to."

"I want to say that I can, but I'm lying. I don't know if I can."

"Every week you receive reports about people who've gotten their brains blown out. Or their limbs cut off. You read every detail, just to twist them for the cause. But defending me is too difficult? My being here is what breaks you? After all that . . . this is what breaks you?"

"Raf," Neto says. "That's unfair. Don't be cruel."

"I'm being honest. And if fairness is what we're aiming for, then you have some things to own up to."

"You've been keeping score? Who is that going to help, huh?"

Rafael pauses, raises an eyebrow. He's thinking. How often has Neto also done this? Stopped, worked through a thought, and then insisted he has nothing left to say. Where do all the unspoken thoughts go? Are they in pain, stored away in a purgatory of silence, of cowardice?

"I'm not going to fight you," Rafael says. "I'm uninterested in fighting. Neither of us wins. Instead, I'm going to tell you what I feel. What I need, actually. I need you to stop hiding when the world shows itself. I love you, and you love me, but you can't begin to doubt what we have when we go out into the world. I love being alone with you, but you need to love me around others too."

Neto hasn't questioned their love, at least not as often as Rafael makes it seem, but he has let the world intrude. Neto isn't afraid of his feelings—they are as real to him as the man before him, lips pursed, waiting for a response. He is afraid of the world, of what strangers could say or do to two men trying to share a life. Esperanza does not represent the worst of the world's ugliness, but even she has managed to hurt them, to pry open a fault line they'd been stepping over. Someone with hatred, or bad intentions, might spark an avalanche, burying them both.

"I'm afraid," Neto says.

"We're all afraid. That's no excuse."

"I'm not trying to talk my way out of this."

Their love has made the most sense in movements, in actions. A caress, a kiss, the brush of a fingertip or shoulder. Words—trying to explain himself on the spot—makes Neto second-guess and overthink.

"Write me when you find your courage," Rafael says.

All at once, as if he'd been planning the escape in his head, Rafael swings the door open and retrieves his duffle bag from the truck bed. Carefully, he walks over to a taxi driver stationed a few feet away. The driver is eating, but after speaking to Rafael briefly, he pops open the trunk. Rafael slips into the back seat, without another glance at Neto. The driver takes him far, far away.

Archive of Unknown Universes

All that is left to do is drive. Neto heads to the empty hotel room, where he drinks half a bottle of whiskey, which lets him forget that he is falling asleep alone. When he wakes, he will be hungover, which will be a small mercy. Headaches and nausea are a kind of pain he can understand.

Death did not follow them on this trip, but the grief Rafael shoulders as he boards the plane to Managua is almost as heavy. When a comrade died, or someone was murdered senselessly on the street, there was a body and a funeral. Rafael would stand next to the departed's loved ones, and though his attempts to soothe them were impossibly inadequate, there was proof of the life that'd transpired.

Here, as the plane lifts off, he has nothing physical to hold on to. There is no proof of his and Neto's love. If this is its end, there will be no weeping or vigils or elegies or processions to commemorate it. Rafael will mourn alone, praying that there will be a life worth living on the other side.

2018

The Charles River shape-shifted throughout the year, and no matter the season, Luis loved watching it from above. The walls of his dorm room were concrete blocks painted white, but a massive window redeemed the otherwise lifeless space. In the winter, as sheets of white covered the city, the river crystallized. Veins of water moved below the surface. In the spring, the river thawed, and chunks of ice sailed downstream. He especially loved the view at night when Weeks Bridge lit up and sent a shimmer across the water.

But now, at the start of a sweltering September, the deep blue river flowed freely. Light bounced off its ripples, constellations on its surface. Luis moved the last few pieces of clothing from his suitcase into his drawers before burrowing under his duvet. Staring at the ceiling, everything dissipated: the suitcases, the unpacked boxes, the river, the muggy heat, the sound of his floormates shuffling through their shared hallway. Only his thoughts and the bleached white plaster remained.

Confronted with so many uncomfortable coincidences in the past few months, Luis wondered if perhaps there was a higher plan, a celestial being having a little fun. The first time he saw Ana in Cambridge, the very same day he'd moved into his new dorm room, had felt cruelly planned, though of course it wasn't. The campus wasn't small, but it was small enough for them to cross paths after weeks of pushing her out of his mind. How fortuitous that Ana had bought the Bible the same summer he'd been gifted his uncle's letters by his mother. And how ill-fated that they'd stopped talking before he'd had a chance to bring the two together.

He thought about waiting for another coincidence, one in his favor, that would bring him and Ana together again. A brush in the stacks on a Sunday afternoon or small talk at Café Gato Rojo during a seven-minute passing period. But the desire to know if she had the key to resurrecting Neto was too urgent. He'd promised his mother. I'll do it for Neto, he'd whispered. He texted Ana, for the first time since his relapse, and asked that she meet him at Weeks Bridge at ten. *And could you bring the Bible?* he'd typed.

When the text came in, Luis's name glowed bright on Ana's screen. His texts had been a daily feature for so long, as much a part of her phone as the battery or screen protector, but now, after their quiet weeks apart, it was unsettling to have their text chain revived. The message felt out of place, though not as unwanted as a piece of junk mail if much more difficult to ignore.

When she tried imagining what he might text, if he did again, she drew a blank. The vague request to meet surprised her. Before the breakup, she'd have said there was no one in the world who could read his mind better than her. Now, that confidence had shattered.

Was she obligated to respond? The photographs she'd taken of Neto's letters were open on her laptop. She could tell Luis what she'd discovered. Or she could ignore the text, deleting it from her phone, vanishing it to the cybersphere. She'd toiled to uncover the past. Now that she and Luis had called it quits, she didn't owe him anything. But love does not sizzle out like the flame on a match head. Love is more than the debt one feels for others.

She considered heading to Lamont to see if the Defractor might clarify the situation. The analytical side of her, the part of her that'd gotten her so far, knew she and Luis were done. Heartbreak was a reaction to change, and it'd go away eventually. Or was she making excuses? With enough effort, she could explain away any human connection.

Truthfully, it didn't matter what the device might tell her. The future would be winding and perilous, no matter which fork she followed. Ana would have to live with her choices. She wandered back to her bed, zigzagging the width of her dorm room, as if she were afraid of what awaited her on the duvet cover. Another message had arrived. Luis wanted to see the Bible. Ana began to type.

It was 9:50 p.m. Luis didn't want to be late. His footsteps joined the sleepy sounds of cars rumbling down Memorial Drive and conversations wafting from feet away. The crossing light's red glow masked his face as he waited. The bridge was only a few feet ahead, but because of what would happen there, it felt far, far away. The signal was slow to change.

The usual suspects populated the riverbank. To his left, on the lone bench at the edge of the river, two men sat close together. Luis watched as the flicker of a lit joint danced between their fingers. A hazy cloud of smoke rose above them. The smell tempted him, though he hadn't smoked in almost a year.

Palms pressed against the bridge's railing, Luis pulled himself onto the edge, his back to the water. If I lean too far back, he thought to himself, I'll fall all the way down. The crash of the river around me will be loud in my ears, I'll try not to swallow water, and I'll have to thrash my way to the shore. He gripped the railing's edge, the concrete rough on his fingertips.

A biker zoomed by. A few feet away, a couple giggled. A rogue breeze grazed Luis's cheek. Then he saw her. Ana walked toward him, slowly lifting a hand, either in genuine greeting or as mere acknowledgment. Worried his hands would shake, he didn't wave back, pressing his palms harder against the concrete.

"Don't fall," Ana said. A tote bag hung from her shoulder, the canvas bulging on one side.

Atop the barrier, Luis had to look down to make eye contact with Ana. It was a bit awkward—his body blocking her view of the skyline across the river—but they stayed like this, still, silent, for a while.

"I ran into your mom this summer," Luis said. Cities were always larger than they seemed, and Los Angeles was no exception. He'd seen Felicia at the pupusería on Third and Rampart. He'd said hello, and she responded that she was sorry to hear that he and Ana had broken up, which surprised him.

"She told me," Ana said. She turned, placing her forearms on the ledge. She stared out over the river, saying nothing more. The low murmur of the city, the river, and the few nighttime stragglers distracted Luis, but only for a moment. The longer they went without speaking, the more crushing the silence became. It reminded Luis of that night in Havana. He wondered if he'd made a mistake in asking Ana to meet.

"She told me a lot of things, actually," Ana said, turning back to face Luis. "About her life in El Salvador, and the spots she used to go to when she was young. She asked if I'd seen any of them, and I tried describing what I saw while I was there. She spoke about the war, told me the names of the loved ones she lost. For the first time ever, she told me."

It sounded like the sort of candidness Luis's mother still hadn't offered him. Even when she agreed to let him photocopy the letters, she didn't confess anything new about Neto.

"What are we doing here, Luis?"

Stars are the same everywhere, but looking up and away from Ana, Luis couldn't believe it. There was no way the speckled sky was identical to the one in Havana. The smokers' laughter pierced the pause in the conversation.

"I wanted to see you," Luis began. "The abrupt way we left everything . . . it has me replaying that night in my head."

"You wanted a clean break."

"I'm wrong sometimes."

Ana laughed, not cruelly or sarcastically, but the sound reverberated. It took Luis by surprise.

"This is the we-can-still-try-to-be-friends conversation," she said.

Luis's impulse was to say no, to insist that he knew they were done. They'd tried to be together and they'd failed. Or he'd failed in his attempts to be what she needed. Never

Archive of Unknown Universes

attentive enough, always avoiding difficult conversations. And still, he couldn't bring himself to say yes or no, because truthfully, deep inside, he wasn't sure if he was reaching for friendship or for something more.

"As a friend," Luis said. "Could I see the Bible?"

"Only if you get off the ledge," Ana said. "It's stressing me out. As a friend."

Luis hopped off. He'd left his backpack pressed against the side of the bridge. He bent over to rummage through it, searching for the letters.

"After my abuela's wake, I went to look for the letters I saw in the Defractor," Luis said. "It turns out they're written in code. My mom said it reminded her of the Bible. You bought one in Cuba; I thought that maybe there was a connection. It sounds ridiculous, but I just have this feeling. Call it premonition. Call it delusion."

"Don't get too woo-woo on me."

"That's more your thing," Luis replied, trying to draw a laugh. To cut the tension and to prove he still could. Instead, Ana whispered a secret, clear as the night sky.

"I met someone who knew your uncle."

All his life, Luis treated the war and the country it split open as relics of a faraway past. The nation his mother and grandmother had fled was a haunted, abstract place. Tens of thousands like his uncle had died, a heartbreaking number that was also impossible to wrap his head around. How could one ever measure such a loss? If his uncle's death had shot an arrow through his life, how could he ever understand the weight of the seventy-five thousand lives cut short? The conflict had ended only a few years before Luis was born, but it felt like a war from antiquity, even as the terror of those years gripped Luis's family, forcing their tongues close to the roofs of their mouths. El Salvador was real only in memory.

Until now. History was alive. It had talked to Ana, and she relayed what History had said about Neto. Neto and History were friends, comrades. Secrets slipped between them. At his work, Neto was unmatched. In his politics, shaky. History believed in Neto through it all, even in the harrowing months when his friends and family had searched for a sign of what the government had done to him. Elena and Esperanza knew History, though the three never got along. They blamed History for keeping Neto in the guerrilla effort. History had killed Neto.

And History held on to pieces of Neto's life. There were letters. Love letters written to a man named Rafael.

"When I used the Defractor in Cuba, I was so focused on figuring out why our alternate selves had gone after the Bible," Ana said. "But the other day, after I left San Salvador, I found the printed photograph of that scene folded up in my jeans. It turns out we had both: the letters and the Bible. Those versions knew something we didn't."

Luis's heart raced. Ana had the code to Neto's letters between her palms. Her nails, freshly painted alabaster, pressed against the Bible's cover. And yes, he felt a sinking weight when he realized he couldn't lean in to thank her with a kiss, but he pushed the feeling down.

"I don't know where to start," Luis admitted.

"This'll sound stupid, but as a kid, I loved mysteries," Ana said. "Encyclopedia Brown, Nancy Drew, The 39 Clues."

Archive of Unknown Universes

This was a new detail about Ana's life, unless it'd been displaced in Luis's attempts to move on. They weren't dating anymore, but maybe the confession was worth storing anyway.

It was late, so foot traffic was low, but Luis and Ana huddled toward the edge of the path anyway. In those stories, Ana explained, a combination often referred to a word in a book. Page line, word order in a sentence was the most common code. Ana threw her tote down. The Bible's thin pages fluttered as the book fell open. Luis read a combination out loud, and Ana cross-referenced it. On a scrap of paper, she scrawled the words until they had a phrase.

"'Descendants twelve David wicked order head left ahead,'" Ana said.

Nonsense, gibberish. The cipher uncracked.

"Chapter, verse?" Luis suggested.

"Each set has three numbers: 1:12:4," Ana said. She kept scribbling words down, though it was clear their first guess was wrong. Sweat beaded on her brow. The humidity hadn't waned, even though it was well past sunset.

"Genesis is the first book in the Bible," Luis said. "Try Genesis, twelfth chapter, fourth verse."

Ana read the verse out loud. "'So Abram departed as the Lord spoke unto him; and Lot went with him; and Abram was seventy and five years old when he departed out of Haran.'"

"Write down the first word in the sentence," Luis suggested.

They repeated the process. Thin, hurried lines of pen ink bloomed on the scrap of paper. Ana squeezed as much as she could into the margins.

"So God the and announced after all Jesus when."

A tiredness fell over Luis. They'd been sitting on the bridge for an hour. The stragglers wandering the edge of the Charles had left.

"What if we're looking for meaning where there isn't any?" Luis asked.

"A code is meant to be solved," Ana said.

If they gave up, they'd have to talk about everything else they'd avoided so far.

"230, 530, 601," Ana said. "A ton start in the hundreds, which have to be page numbers."

"Page number, chapter, verse? Try page 430, chapter 9, verse 5."

Again, Ana flipped through the book as Luis called out numbers. Her finger slid down the page, until it stopped at the line she was searching for.

Ana laughed for the first time that night.

"The first word is Raphael," she said. "Tobit 9:5. 'Raphael went with the four servants and two camels . . .'"

Luis leaned in close, trying to see the words as Ana uncovered them. His chin hovered above her shoulder, and their cheeks were closer than they'd been in weeks. How familiar the soft of her skin had been then. How foreign this proximity felt now.

His uncle's words emerged, rendered in her handwriting. Luis whispered them.

"'Rafael, it's past midnight and I can't stop thinking about the night we met . . .'"

Before long, a paragraph unrolled. The process was slow, tedious, but every word they found sent a jolt through Luis.

Archive of Unknown Universes

One letter was done, and Luis read it out loud. His voice was soft. Then, they moved on to the second, then the third. It didn't matter that it was eleven o'clock, then midnight, then one-thirty. On and on, Ana and Luis translated the letters, until they'd gotten through the whole stack. Sound bites of a life reincarnated. Neto, on his own terms, so many years later.

"I have something to show you," Luis said. His phone careened toward Ana, and suddenly there he was: the Nicaraguan from the identification card she'd found inside her mother's passport. His face was bisected by a crack in the screen, but his features were unmistakable. A well-trimmed beard, his deadpan expression, soft eyes.

"Rafael," Luis said.

"Are we selfish people?" Ana said.

"What?"

"For not choosing to be together, even though we could."

Neto and Rafael's love was undeniable, destabilizing in its earnestness, destructive if pushed too far. A relationship of inconvenience. The men had stayed together despite the toll it took. Their love was not a place to hide from their problems, but they'd burrowed into it anyway.

"There's no point in comparing ourselves to them," Luis said.

"When life feels impossible, I need context," Ana said. "A reminder that I'm not alone, that someone else has asked what I'm asking myself. It's why I love history, why I live with one foot in the next room."

"Living for others isn't really living," Luis said.

"That's all an adult relationship is," Ana said. "Choosing someone, and then choosing them again and again."

"For my uncle," Luis said, "love was worth it, despite the danger."

"We haven't risked very much. That's my point."

"Isn't there a chance we will hurt each other trying to fix a broken thing? I run every possibility in my mind, and none of them are easy."

"Love isn't supposed to be easy."

"It shouldn't be difficult."

Ana secretly agreed.

"Neto was so scared," Luis said.

"And he still chose Rafael," Ana said, softly. "I want to live like that. In spite of fear, not because of it."

"I don't want to be just friends," Luis said. "But I don't want us to be together just because the alternative scares me. That'd be selfish."

Ana wanted to disagree, to insist that their bond was salvageable. The past few weeks had been difficult, and her days were interrupted by longing, a true sadness at the Luis-size gap in her life. The time apart, though, proved a previously unimaginable possibility: Untethered, alone, her life would continue. Someone, or something, else would come along to fill the gaps. She couldn't, in good conscience, delay the inevitable.

"We've decided, then," Ana said. No need for more information. They weren't going to work out, not in this time line. Luis nodded.

"That's all life is. One decision, then another."

Archive of Unknown Universes

Silence flowed between them as easily as the river beneath their soles. They'd never erase the ways they'd hurt each other, but their happiness would be scorched into their bodies too, unforgettable, inevitable, the way a first love lingers after burning so hot and reckless.

"I have class in the morning," Ana said. The good night was simple, noncommittal. She walked back to her room before Luis could respond.

This is how their love ends.

The farther Ana gets from the river, the quieter its murmuring becomes, fainter and fainter, but never fully gone, unlike in the depths of winter, where the layer of ice is so impenetrable it silences everything but the wind. From the gate that shields the dorm buildings from the rest of the world, she looks back toward the bridge, searching for Luis's outline in the glow of the streetlamps. Her eyes find nothing but the cars driving down Memorial Drive.

How funny that their love ended in such quiet, in such darkness. They'll run into each other soon, unquestionably, and Ana will be tempted to tell Luis about the photograph of Rafael her mother kept hidden in her room. There are other letters, simmering on her hard drive. When they cross paths again, will Luis ask to see them? The previous version of her—before the summer, the Defractor, the letters—would have given it all away without a second thought.

Ana pulls open the gate and steps into the quad, surrounded on all sides by a carefully manicured lawn. How quiet and dark it is. How small the world has proven to be, despite the shimmering oceans and mountains of concrete, and how free Ana feels within it, ready to grab it between her fingers, pulling it tight, making it hers.

Luis tries falling asleep, but the conversation loops in his head. There'd been a short window where he felt ready to recommit to Ana, to tell her that they should shake the restraint and inhibitions and logic and choose each other. Before the

Archive of Unknown Universes

Defractor, before his uncle's letters, he might have taken the opening, but it is no longer sustainable to live with his eyes glued to the ground, so scared of slipping on loose rocks that he misses the avalanche tumbling down from above.

Still, his stomach turns and his cheeks are hot. He cannot sleep, so he considers walking to Lamont to check out a Defractor. There, he will watch the blockbuster ending he and Ana got in another universe. He imagines it, the sun rising over the sparkling water, Ana and he holding their heads close, whispering welcome to a new day. They'll kiss to the sound of a folksy pop cover and walk away with their pinkies interlocked. Everything he wants—closure, absolution, affection—he will have. He and Ana, together, choosing each other once more.

Sleep never comes, no matter how many different ways he sprawls. Two truths settle into his head, nestled next to each other like a pair of mourning doves: ending the relationship was necessary, and his pain will stick around for many months. The realization does not bring peace, but at least he understands it, a steady logic he can wrap his mind around, even as his heart pounds in his chest.

Finally, he dozes off. The sun rises, illuminating Rafael and Neto's archive.

April 24, 1979

You asked me, the last time we were together, if I remembered how our first meeting went down. It was a game of sorts, one I've never played with anyone else, but one that I imagine is common. That doesn't make it any less special. If anything, I appreciate any reminder that our love can be like that of any ordinary, unexciting couple strolling through the street.

We argued, playfully, of course, about who seduced who. At the end of that conversation, which was short-lived, I said I didn't fully remember it. We weren't going to get anywhere—I said you did, you said I did—so I moved on. But of course I remember every moment of that night.

You sat at that massive, mahogany table in the middle of the room that was otherwise empty. I didn't think much in that moment, which I hope you don't take as an insult. I've never believed in love at first sight. I was more concerned with why the safe house was so empty, especially since Anabel told me that the Sandinistas had a far more sophisticated movement than we did.

When I fled to the kitchen, overwhelmed, you found me. I remember the first words you said to me: Do you want

Archive of Unknown Universes

a cup of coffee? Such a banal question, but even then you delivered it with such care. I know now that extending kindness is as much a part of you as your DNA, but the way you said it—your words like honey—made me notice you. Did I even strike you as a coffee drinker? Or did you look for the easiest excuse to say hello in that voice of yours?

Your pinky finger grazed my hand as you passed me a mug, and I had the sinking feeling that it was intentional. You stalled, in the kitchen, moving your arms so slowly, watching the water boil, asking if I liked Managua. We danced around the question of what we did. You said you did paperwork and left it at that. I told you I was an artist, and even now that sounds idiotic. What kind of revolution needs an artist? But you humored me, and that was the beginning of the fall.

You knew what you were doing, didn't you? In the moment, I wasn't sure they were seduction moves, but thinking back on it, they must have been. You're charming, but not that intensely without a bit of effort. At dinner, my cheeks went red and it was only partially because of the liquor. There were others there, but they seemed to fade away. Even when you talked to them, I could only focus on your lips, though a part of me hoped you didn't notice my attention. If I was wrong, if I was seeing signals where there weren't any, the night might have ended differently. I might have ended up bloodied; dead in a bar fight.

When you suggested another drink at a bar, I was yours. And when we kissed—well, it was a quieter version of whenever I press my lips against yours now. I was nervous, I was taken aback, but it was clear you were someone I'd be intimate with, and not in purely a political sense. So I paused, took mental notes. Mental photographs too. As my love has grown, so have the feelings that shake me when we kiss. If our first was life-shattering for its novelty, the one I long for as I write this letter will surely undo me completely.

I leaned in that night, but after a night of your seduction. That's how it happened. But now I'm curious. Do you remember the night in the same way I do? Or did different moments glimmer for you? Who seduced who? Write me soon. Let me know. Let's play the game just a little bit longer.

Love,
Neto

Archive of Unknown Universes

July 28, 1979

How free I feel, writing this letter without fear that it'll be intercepted in Nicaragua. I'm sure you've written me already, telling me all about the triumph. Waiting for that letter will be no easier than any of the rest. Anabel said that Somoza didn't even put up a fight. He knew that you controlled the rest of the country, and that there was no way for him to win, so he let you march right into Managua with little resistance. Is it true? Did he get on his knees?

I feel selfish saying this, but I hope your revolution doesn't take too long. If it doesn't, you can come live with me here in El Salvador. The idea of moving to Managua tempts me, but leaving Esperanza is tough. Our parents aren't around any longer, and the girl's father is a good-for-nothing sucio. We rely on each other, though we don't always admit that it's a sign of our love.

I may be willing to leave this country, if you're waiting for me on the other side. What I'm saying is that I want to build a life with you. Closer together. If there were fewer letters in our future, I'd be more than happy. It won't be easy, given the circumstances of our love, but if we're reimagining the nations we know, why not shape them to make life easier for men like us?

The postman should be coming around soon, so I better finish up. I pray he brings word from you. When you get this sheet of paper in a few days, put it to your cheek. I'll kiss it before stuffing it in an envelope. That might be silly, but it's all we have.

Ruben Reyes Jr.

November 6, 1979

All day I lay in bed, inconsolable. I picture your face—your stupid, beautiful face. I stay in bed until my stomach hurts. Then I get some coffee or a stale pastry and jump back into bed. The photograph you gave me is on my bedside table. Your stupid beautiful face. And me, just stupid.

I'm sorry for what I said, but I don't regret it. I should have picked my words out more carefully. I didn't walk you through my reasoning. In your eyes, I saw the hurt and personal offense I caused you. My comments were not aimed at you or at the strength of our relationship—they were about how the world views people like us. Men who love men. And it wasn't even that I was reacting to this amorphous mass we call society or our countries. I was speaking with the hurt of two recent conversations fresh on my psyche.

Of course, I should have told you all this earlier. That was my mistake. I sounded so desperate and defeated, but it wasn't your fault. Our relationship keeps me floating—it is the outside world that makes me feel helplessness. And in thinking I could shield you from that peril, I hurt you.

Anabel was the first person I told. She mentioned, off-handedly, that she'd heard that we'd taken off that night in Havana. She asked if we'd gone to a bar or somewhere more salacious. I told her that obviously not, and she asked why it was obvious, and then—I don't know why—I told her. It was stupid. Unnecessary. I was weak to admit it. It's just difficult sometimes to hold this all in, with you as the sole protector of my truth.

Archive of Unknown Universes

Anabel didn't say much, just that she had wondered why I didn't engage with the other guys when they'd talk their shit and jeer at women. That's all she said, before going quiet for a while. I begged her to say anything. She said she couldn't possibly come out and support me. She could keep our secret, offer discretion, but nothing else. I had to stay silent if we didn't want to grapple with what my sexuality means in the context of a revolution. From her tone, it was clear it wouldn't be pleasant. That's not a surprise to you or me, but it still cut when it was verbalized.

When I sat with Esperanza a few days later, I must have still been bearing the weight of that conversation on my face. My sister knew something was off, but I pretended I was unconcerned. I sat on the floor to talk to Elena. She'd brought me a mango that I graciously accepted. Eventually, she went to play in that strip of cobblestone in front of the house.

Esperanza and I sat on the porch, watching her. She asked, bluntly, what was wrong. I said I'd had an argument with a friend. She prodded and asked for details. Eventually, I asked what she made of the fact that she'd never met or heard of any of my girlfriends. She said she figured it was the sort of intimate thing siblings didn't share—like all the details about my niece's good-for-nothing father. And then I told her.

Indignant silence would have been better. Instead, Esperanza said it was good that Mami and Papi weren't around to hear my bayuncadas, my dirty confession. My parents were religious people. They would have thought me sinful. But to hear my own sister say it . . . I left in a hurry, barely kissed Elena goodbye on the cheeks.

I know meeting Esperanza was important to you. I intend to defend you, defend us. I'm just hurt. Her rejection is fresh. The worst-case scenario came true. It shook me, and the insecurity and hurt led to our fight. I should have told you that. I should have said it all. I didn't want to ruin the mood. Our time together is so fleeting. So precious. I didn't want to wreck it. That's what led me to that moment, to say those dreadful things about our future and the slim possibilities we have for building a life together. I still worry about our future, and I think we both should. Limitations are part of our reality. Riddles to solve. Obstacles to surmount.

But I should not have spoken so angrily, so pointedly. You were there—to love me, to hold me—not to bear the brunt of my frustration. I was cruel. I'm sorry.

The truth is, I took Anabel and Esperanza's reactions so badly because I believe them to a degree. My affections for you are real, unavoidable. But I do feel sinful sometimes. I wonder if my attraction is unnatural or wrong.

I didn't choose it, but this life will be rife with problems. It's part of the package. It's what we see on the horizon if we stay together. Hiding isn't sustainable. Living openly is the dream, but won't that mean facing biting looks and words like my own sister delivered? I won't be able to work through this sickness and self-hatred in my soul until I can bask in the sun with you.

This is an apology. I don't mean to make matters worse. I want to see you again, soon. If not for the revolution, then for me. If I don't hear back, I'll assume you've made up your mind and I'll respect the silence. Write back soon. Please, consider writing me back.

Archive of Unknown Universes

November 23, 1977

It's past midnight and I can't stop thinking about the night we met. You introduced yourself as Antonio and I said my name was Domingo. We could have remained there, only known each other by our aliases, content as men with similar goals: liberation for our nations. But that evening after dinner, after drinks, after coffee, with our hands roaming each other's skin, your chest looming over mine, you pulled away from my lips and asked, "What's your name?" And I told you the truth. My real name. And you whispered it into my ear as the rest of my body was on fire.

Is this how you remember it too? Did you say my name to prove that you wanted to know me beyond that night? Or did I beg you, between moans, to say my name? Did I beg: Say my name, Rafael, say my name.

Ruben Reyes Jr.

January 28, 1979

Rafael,

I want you inside me. Is that uncouth? I don't care. I want you inside me.

Archive of Unknown Universes

January 27, 1980

Rafael. Rafael.

If I write your name enough times, it'll bring you to me.

Rafael. Rafael.

November 23, 1979

Rafael,

I have the sense that my last letter was either lost or intercepted. Either way, I'll try reconstructing what I wrote then. Some will be lost, undoubtedly, but that's the nature of time. Memory is an unreliable archive.

I saw a couple of children running around the plaza near the market. They seemed so joyful, unaware that there is a war boiling around them. Despite my optimism, I know a victory will not magically rid the world of its evil. Justice and liberation do not fall over individuals like a country-size blanket. If—when—the revolution succeeds, these children will still have perilous lives, though I hope they will not have to fear an unchecked military the way we do.

And despite my cynicism, the wide smiles and gangly prancing limbs of those children made me think that I want to someday raise a child in this imperfect world. It won't be easy, of course, and I don't even know if it'll be possible in a country like this, even with a political revolution that will overhaul so many other things.

What do you think? Would you want to raise a son with me? We could name him Antonio. Or Domingo. I like Domingo.

Archive of Unknown Universes

October 20, 1978

Cruelty no longer surprises me. The world is full of senseless cruelties. I've spent too many hours trying to decipher them, to make meaning where there is only undeserved pain. All I can do now is point to the cruelties, naming them, making them real. The distance between us is cruel. So are all the things I saw this month that mercilessly remind me of you: fiery red lobsters for sale en la costa, two people clinging onto a dirty motorcycle, the pink-purple sunrise when I'm woken prematurely but cannot drift back to sleep, a pen you gifted me laying on my desk, your latest letter opened like a decaying corpse, Klimt's "The Kiss," the empty valleys between my fingers, the piece of clavicle with its phantom hickeys, a stranger who looks like you but only when I don't look too closely.

January 7, 1980

Longing for you is exhausting. I spend my days hunched over my desk, inking lines and letters under the glow of my lamp. I busy myself as a distraction. But at the end of the day, I find myself reaching for the moment we'll be together for good. I build it up in my mind, piecing the perfect life together. I long for a day without an arrival date. I do it to survive. To prove that love is enough. That distance cannot crush my affections.

But I worry. If I cope by longing for the future I'm imagining, what'll happen if the life we live does not play out the way I've invented it? It won't be your fault that we can't attain the utopia I dream up when missing you. Won't I resent you anyway, when the dream shatters? Will your touch heal any resentment? Will we build something together, different than what I do to cope with the time away from you?

Being away from you diminishes the ugliness and conflict we've already overcome in our relationship. We don't want to talk about the arguments or the weeks we've gone without writing to each other because we regret them. Our impasses have been pushed aside. What if they come flooding in when we're together for good?

The future is a carrot dangling in front of me, but I worry that when we arrive there, it won't be as sweet a reward as I've imagined. Are my anxieties misguided, Rafael? Am I driving myself crazy in this pessimistic spiral for no reason?

Archive of Unknown Universes

January 20, 1980

Raf,

I'm in a panic because I've forgotten how your skin feels against mine. Come see me, soon. Please. Or I'll come to you, somehow. Please.

Ruben Reyes Jr.

IN INFINITE UNIVERSES, THE LETTERS FLOAT ON THE LAYER OF GUN SMOKE THAT BLANKETS THE LANDSCAPE, PIERCED ONLY BY THE TIPS OF PINES HIGH IN THE MOUNTAINS OR THE SOUND OF SCREAMS BY THE SEA.

FOR THE DAYS NETO SPENDS ON THE FLOOR, ONLY THE LETTERS FROM BEFORE EXIST. THERE MAY BE FUTURE LETTERS—DRAFTED, TORN, SMUDGED, STAINED, SEALED, DELIVERED, READ, REREAD—IF NETO UNGLUES HIMSELF AND STUMBLES OUT OF THE DARK DEPTHS OF THE GOVERNMENT'S GUT. BUT IF HE DOESN'T—AND THERE ARE INFINITE UNIVERSES WHERE HE LIES ON THE FLOOR UNTIL HIS LAST MOMENTS—THE SHEETS OF PAPER REPRESENT A HEART-SIZE SLICE OF A LOST LIFE. ALL THAT IS LEFT OF NETO ARE THESE SHEETS OF PAPER, SCRIBBLES OF LOVE, THAT EVERYONE WANTS TO OWN, BECAUSE IT'S THE LAST TRACE OF A BROTHER, AN UNCLE, A LOVER, THE DEAD GUERRILLERO OTHERWISE VANISHED. NO BONES, NO BODY. SOME HEAR THE LETTERS AS THE LAST ECHO OF A LOVE LOST TO A FAILED REVOLUTION, A LOVE LEFT BEHIND. HISTORIANS WANT THE LETTERS FOR PATRIMONY. THE COURTS FOR JUSTICE. THE POLITICIANS, TO DECRY OR DEFEND VIOLENCE. THE ROMANTICS FOR THE MEN'S DEVOTION. THE CYNICS FOR HOW IT ENDS. THE NEWSPAPER FOR THE OBITUARY.

Archive of Unknown Universes

THE NONPROFIT FOR THE ENDLESS LIST OF MISSING PEOPLE.

BUT WAIT, SLOW DOWN. PAUSE, POINT, CLOSE IN AND SEE SOMEONE FIND A FINAL LETTER. IT IS LUIS, OR DOMINGO, OR ANA, OR RAFAEL. ULTIMATELY, THE DISCOVERER CHALKS UP THE DISCOVERY TO EITHER FATE OR COINCIDENCE, DEPENDING ON THE VERSION OF THEMSELF THAT RUNS THEIR FINGERS ALONG THE LETTER'S WEAK CRUMPLED EDGE.

IF THERE IS ANY TRUTH, IT IS THIS:

NETO PERISHES, BUT THERE'S A TRACE OF HIM LEFT IN THE WORLD. THE PAPER IS YELLOWED, AND THERE'S A BROWN RING ON THE CORNER OF ONE OF THE PAGES, A REMNANT FROM AN IRRESPONSIBLE READER WHO PLACED THEIR COLD DRINK ON THE PAPER. NETO'S HANDWRITING IS INSTANTLY RECOGNIZABLE, THOUGH HE NEVER FORMALLY ADDRESSED OR SIGNED THE LETTER. THE INKING IS INCONSISTENT. THE LETTERS CURVE IN LARGER LOOPS IN SOME PORTIONS AND SIT TUCKED CLOSER TOGETHER IN OTHERS. IT'S A SIGN THAT HE WROTE THE LETTER IN CHUNKS, STOPPING AND STARTING AGAIN WHENEVER HE COULD GRASP A FEW MINUTES FOR HIMSELF. HIS SWEAT STAINED THE INK, SO THAT SOME SENTENCES BLUR INTO FUZZY SPOTS. STILL, THE LETTER IS FULLY LEGIBLE. PRECISE. NETO'S HANDIWORK.

Ruben Reyes Jr.

THE LETTER IS A TUNNEL BETWEEN THE PAST AND THE PRESENT. A DEAD MAN REINCARNATES, RISING FROM THE UNMARKED HILLSIDE WHERE HE WAS DUMPED, AND SPEAKS.

Archive of Unknown Universes

They've allowed me a final letter.

Hell. Why pretend things are different than they are? They don't want me to get word out, haven't willing allowed any of the paragraphs I've written for you. This government is not concerned with grace or mercy, only with breaking my soul. One of the guards is mailing this letter for me, though. "Guard" isn't totally right. He's a child. He's young and not wed to the government's cause yet. He's been looped in, and he opposes our liberation attempts, but he does not think us evil or irredeemable. He sees that I am human—Salvadoran like him—and has taken pity on me, agreeing to smuggle out my letter. But only this one.

Rafael, te quiero. Te amo. That's the important part of this letter. It's what you need to know most. I've struggled to admit my affections. Shame has clouded such confessions, but there's no time for guilt or hesitation now, so Rafael, I love you with my entire heart. It's the kind of love that makes my bones ache. Your love is the main reason I'm afraid of leaving this earth. I can convince myself that sacrificing my life for the cause is glorious, valiant. Straightforward, had you not loved me the way you did, cleaving my heart and soul, opening it and joining yours to mine.

I feel feverish. I haven't had much to eat, and I swear that I heard your voice coming down the halls all the way to my cell. I thought they'd gotten you, somehow, and thrown you in a cell not far from mine. But after hours of calling out to you without a response, I realized it must have been another thing I hallucinated here.

Here's how it happened: I was just a few blocks from the safe house when I was grabbed and pulled into a car.

They bound my wrists and blindfolded me before I could react. Blind to the world, it was difficult to figure out how much time passed. I asked questions along the way, but I was met mostly with silence. At one point, I began to yell, and the car's driver shouted at me to shut up. But I wasn't harmed then.

They didn't lay a hand on me until I arrived at the facility. I wish I could tell you where they're keeping me, but I haven't seen the light of day for what I have to assume have been weeks, though we may have slipped into months without my noticing. Time works differently here. When I arrived, I was subjected to my first interrogation. It was gentle and administered by men capable of impersonating pacifists, if you can believe it. They handcuffed me to a steel chair and pulled my blindfold off. They already knew my real name, but at the beginning they addressed me as Domingo. The first question they asked was my real name. They must have said "What's your legal name, Domingo?" a hundred times. I told them I wouldn't say, and I didn't. I believed that, somehow, they'd found me without knowing my full name.

Then they called me Ernesto Guzmán and I knew it'd been a setup. Mind tricks. Things got worse from there. They blindfolded me again and, with my hands still pinned behind my back, pushed me to the ground. They beat me for what must've been hours. They said it was punishment for lying to them, and that I'd be treated better when I decided to tell them the truth. A brawny man had to carry me to my cell from the interrogation room because they'd sprained one of my ankles.

Archive of Unknown Universes

They laid me on the thin pad that I write from now and left me there. They didn't come back for hours, and there was no toilet, so I had no choice but to piss in the corner. It stunk for days, and even now piss spots the floor. I must have scraped myself somewhere along the way as well because in addition to the pain from my ankle, there was a burn from an infection.

After hurting my body, the government puppets tried cracking my mind. Blindfolded, they barraged me with questions every day. Somehow, they knew about Havana. Not about us, but that I'd been there meeting with Cuban officials. I didn't admit that I'd gone, since there's no paper trail. Our transport was under fake names, falsified passports I made myself. But they kept asking and beating me, so I made up a lie. Told them I'd received some letters from friends in Cuba, but not from terrorists or revolutionaries. The admission staved off my torturers for about a day— though I can't be sure that's how much time went by. It felt like a day.

When they returned, they read me names they'd found in the documents they ransacked from Esperanza's home. They read out an alias, and then the legal name it corresponded with. They claimed they'd found it all in my sloppy records, in handwriting they said was mine. They knew Anabel's name, Alejandro's too. Said it was my fault. If something were to happen to them, it'd be my fault. Planting that idea must be a tactic, but guilt has grown deep inside me since then. Will you warn them, Rafael? Will you make sure they stay alive?

God, it feels wrong to write of what's happened to me.

There's so much to say to you, Rafael, about what I wanted for us and about how I failed you. And messages to send: to Esperanza and Elena, who I can only hope made it to Managua. To safety. Perhaps I should apologize to them too. For making them refugees, for putting a larger target on their backs. I gambled with my life but didn't know I was throwing theirs in too. There's so much to say and so little room on these pages.

But I have to etch an outline of what I've been through. If not, they'll say it wasn't true. That I just disappeared, like a cloud of dust settling onto the earth. I didn't just vanish. They're trying to make me vanish, but I refuse to go quietly.

This nation has crushed me, Rafael, and I can barely breathe. My chest feels heavy, and the airflow into my lungs is only slightly stronger than a sigh. If this is what they've done to me, before the conflict has blown into a blazing war, I don't want to imagine what might happen to Esperanza and Elena. To Anabel and Alejandro. To all our comrades in the struggle, and to the innocent men and women lumped in with us simply because they dare ask for their rights. The nation, and its government, might crush them too.

Protect them, Rafael. If they don't make it to Nicaragua, make your way to El Salvador—however you can—and look after them. Take them from this country if need be. Abandon the revolution. Convince them to plan it abroad. I sound like a coward, but I don't care. They've broken me. My fingers ache. I can barely find the energy to pen these words.

Here's what I imagine for us, in a future where I leave this cell. A child, with eyes round and vibrant like gumballs.

Archive of Unknown Universes

A house, here or elsewhere, with enough rooms for friends who stop by to visit. A garden, with herbs and roses poking up from the dirt. A library, where our books sit on the same shelves. A gallery, makeshift on an empty white wall, with the paintings and prints we've collected together. A love, ours, that can breathe and show its face without hiding. A love, real and tender, that isn't afraid of the shadows. A love, where pressures that once felt insurmountable are no bigger than anthills. A love, for you. A love, from you to me. Unknown universes spiraling out endlessly from where our bodies touch.

This room is dark. The floor is hard and smells of iron and mold. The lights flicker to burn my pupils. I remember that I'm alive though part of me wishes I were dead. My pain makes me dizzy. I love you. The straw is slipping out of the scratchy mattress cover. I'm sinking toward the floor. It threatens to open and eat me whole. I love you. I hear a door open but hear no footsteps. My eyelids are heavy, but I keep them open and put ink to paper. I've learned to do this well, to make wonder out of the blank space. Remember me. Remember that I love you. Remember that I loved the world, even when it hurt me. Remember that I loved you, even when I hurt you and you hurt me. Let the war rage on, but don't forget me.

Acknowledgments

I don't know why anyone tries writing a novel. It feels like an impossible task. Without the help of many people, it would have been.

Aemilia Phillips, my agent, has been the best advocate a writer could ask for. Here's to many more books together.

Jessica Vestuto, my editor, believed in this book before it was complete and then made it the best version of itself. Thank you for your faith in me and my writing.

My publisher, Mariner Books, has been an exceptional partner. Thank you to the entire team: Eliza Rosenberry, Tavia Kowalchuk, Jackie Alvarado, Aryana Hendrawan, Andrew DiCecco, Cari Elliott, Karen Richardson, Cecilia Molinari, Jessica Rozler, Mark Robinson, and Dale Rohrbaugh.

María Jesús Contreras is a genius, and the cover she illustrated for this book feels like a true gift. Mil gracias.

This is a book about the destabilizing power of love and breakups. Thank you to my exes.

The historical basis for this novel came from a life-changing research trip to El Salvador in 2018. My deepest gratitude to everyone who opened their doors to me: Jakelyn López, the entire team at the archives at the Museo de la Palabra y la Imagen, Arquimides Cañadas, and all his comrades. I also relied on the scholarship of many thinkers, but especially Leisy

Acknowledgments

Abrego's article "On Silences: Salvadoran Refugees Then and Now" and Arturo Arias's seminal book, *Taking Their Word*. Any inaccuracies or misrepresentations are my own.

Asking someone to read a draft of your novel is mortifying, but I feel so lucky to have received such sharp feedback from writers I admire: Alexia Arthurs, Jamel Brinkley, Indya Finch, hurmat kazmi, and Joan Li.

I finished writing this novel as a fellow at the Yale Center for the Study of Race, Indigeneity, and Transnational Migration. Their financial and academic support was crucial. Thank you, Nicole Edwards, Ryan Huynh, Gabriela Martinez, Stephen Pitti, and Victoria Stone-Cadena.

The Virginia Center for the Creative Arts and the Phillip and Eric Heiner Endowed Fellowship offered me three beautiful weeks to read, write, and watch movies at a time when I desperately needed it. Thank you to the staff, administrators, and residents.

Friends, old and new, have buoyed me through the most difficult parts of this journey. Eternal gratitude to them all. I am lucky to be loved by you.

Thank you to my very first supporters, my family: Dolores, Ruben, Antonio, Rachel, and Kelly. I love you with my whole heart.

And finally, thanks to you, dear reader. Nothing is possible without you.

ABOUT
MARINER BOOKS

MARINER BOOKS traces its beginnings to 1832 when William Ticknor cofounded the Old Corner Bookstore in Boston, from which he would run the legendary firm Ticknor and Fields, publisher of Ralph Waldo Emerson, Harriet Beecher Stowe, Nathaniel Hawthorne, and Henry David Thoreau. Following Ticknor's death, Henry Oscar Houghton acquired Ticknor and Fields and, in 1880, formed Houghton Mifflin, which later merged with venerable Harcourt Publishing to form Houghton Mifflin Harcourt. HarperCollins purchased HMH's trade publishing business in 2021 and reestablished their storied lists and editorial team under the name Mariner Books.

Uniting the legacies of Houghton Mifflin, Harcourt Brace, and Ticknor and Fields, Mariner Books continues one of the great traditions in American bookselling. Our imprints have introduced an incomparable roster of enduring classics, including Hawthorne's *The Scarlet Letter*, Thoreau's *Walden*, Willa Cather's *O Pioneers!*, Virginia Woolf's *To the Lighthouse*, W.E.B. Du Bois's *Black Reconstruction*, J.R.R. Tolkien's *The Lord of the Rings*, Carson McCullers's *The Heart Is a Lonely Hunter*, Ann Petry's *The Narrows*, George Orwell's *Animal Farm* and *Nineteen Eighty-Four*, Rachel Carson's *Silent Spring*, Margaret Walker's *Jubilee*, Italo Calvino's *Invisible Cities*, Alice Walker's *The Color Purple*, Margaret Atwood's *The Handmaid's Tale*, Tim O'Brien's *The Things They Carried*, Philip Roth's *The Plot Against America*, Jhumpa Lahiri's *Interpreter of Maladies*, and many others. Today Mariner Books remains proudly committed to the craft of fine publishing established nearly two centuries ago at the Old Corner Bookstore.